VANISHING ACT

Books by Barbara Block

CHUTES AND ADDERS

TWISTER

IN PLAIN SIGHT

THE SCENT OF MURDER

VANISHING ACT

Published by Kensington Books

VANISHING
ACT

BARBARA BLOCK

KENSINGTON BOOKS

http://www.kensingtonbooks.com

B\0

Although the city of Syracuse is real, as are some of the places and events mentioned in this book, this is a work of fiction. Its geography is imaginary. Indeed, all the characters portrayed in this book are fictional and any resemblance to real people or events is both accidental and unintentional.

KENSINGTON BOOKS are published by

Kensington Publishing Corp.
850 Third Avenue
New York, NY 10022

Library of Congress Card Catalog Number: 98-065136
ISBN 1-57566-326-0

First Printing: September, 1998
10 9 8 7 6 5 4 3 2 1

Printed in the United States of America

For Pearl Katz.
Thanks for treating me as if I
were one of your own. Your kindness
and generosity have meant a great deal
to me over the years.

Chapter 1

"True story," George said, his voice hoarse, the way it always is late at night. "A cop jumps in and rescues someone who's taken a dive into the East River. Three days later he finds out this is the guy who shot his mother in the head."

I burrowed into my comforter. "What's your point?" An attic beam groaned overhead while the wind played with the tiles on the roof. As I closed my eyes, I wondered if that was the beam that needed shoring up. It was after two, and all I wanted to do was sleep.

"My point," George replied, sounding aggrieved that I hadn't gotten it, "is that you never know whether or not you're doing something good or bad until later. You can do something that you think is good at the time but then it leads to a bad result."

"So don't do anything."

"Doing nothing is still doing something." I heard the rustle of sheets and then felt George's breath on my face as he turned his head toward me. "Doing nothing is a physical impossibility. A black hole is still energy. Negative energy. Robin, are you listening to me?"

"More or less." I opened one eye. It was too late for metaphysical discussions. It was too late for any discussions. Especially since I had to open the store in the morning.

George sighed and went back to staring at the ceiling. The headlights from a passing car swept over his profile before illuminating the cracks on the far wall. All planes and angles, his face looked as if it were carved from ebony.

"What the hell am I going to do with a fourteen-year-old boy?" he demanded for what must have been the tenth time that evening.

"The same thing everyone does. Get an ulcer."

He grimaced. "Seriously."

I shrugged and adjusted my pillow. "So tell your sister that Raymond can't come up."

"I can't do that."

"Why not?"

"Because it's family. What am I going to say? 'Cecilia, sorry, but I'm too busy to help you out'?"

"Mine would."

I studied the view out my bedroom window. The wind was whipping the cedars in the yard back and forth. They looked as if they were bowing to someone off in the distance. Tall, skinny, and shallow-rooted, two out of the five had already come down in the storm we'd had in February and were now lying across the hill, anticipating their demotion to the mulch pile when spring came. If I were smart, I'd hire someone to have the remaining three taken down at the same time instead of waiting for them to fall in the next big storm, but I probably won't. I don't like second-guessing fate—even when the outcome is fairly predictable.

George's voice intruded on my thoughts, and I turned back toward him.

"Well, mine doesn't work that way." He looked as if he wished that it did. "Big families don't. It must be nice being an only child."

"Not really," I murmured. I closed my eyes again. Why, I remember thinking, did George always pick the exact moment I was falling asleep to want to talk? His timing was impeccable. I'd been available all evening. I would have been happy to have any number of conversations then. I'd even tried to initiate several. Instead, George had spent the evening watching TV and reading the paper. We might as well be married, for God's sake.

"By the way," George continued, his voice floating out on the darkness, "I almost forgot. Bryan Hayes is going to call you tomorrow morning."

"Who?" I mumbled. The name sounded familiar, but I couldn't place it.

"Hayes. His sister Melissa is the one that went missing around Thanksgiving."

"Right." I'd seen the flyers on the hill but hadn't paid them much mind other than to think, another person gone. There'd been a spate of disappearances in the last couple of years, enough that I'd stopped paying more than perfunctory attention.

"He's in one of my classes. He was asking if I knew anyone that could help him, so I gave him your name."

I sat up. "What does he want me to do?"

But George didn't answer. I glanced over. His eyes were

closed. He was asleep. I, on the other hand, was now wide awake. It figured.

Bryan Hayes called me at the store shortly after ten. By then I'd remembered what I'd read about the story, which wasn't much. We set up a meeting at four-thirty that afternoon at the Yellow Rhino, a campus hangout that was known for its bad beer, greasy chicken wings, and cardboardlike pizza. I arrived on time, but Bryan didn't. Twenty minutes later I was still tapping my fingers on one of the tables and surveying the scene. It could have been the twin of the bar I'd hung out at when I'd been in grad school.

The place had the same smell of old cooking grease, the same dusty green spiky plants—maybe they lived forever and just got moved from place to place by the great bar owner in the sky—the same rickety tables, brown metal chairs, and earnestly talking college students sitting on them. The only thing the room lacked was the bluish haze of smoke hanging in the air. No Smoking signs were prominently tacked up on the wall in several places, which was why I was standing in the doorway digging around in my backpack for my lighter, when a kid tapped me on the shoulder.

"Are you Robin Light?" he asked, his breath coming out in little gasps. A light sheen of sweat covered his forehead. He looked as if he'd been running.

"And you're Bryan Hayes?"

He nodded. I pegged him for mid-twenties. He was about six feet two inches, medium build, with a roundish face, and brown eyes set a shade too close together. He had on hiking boots, khakis, a plaid flannel shirt, an unzipped ski parka, and the inevitable baseball hat. His only sartorial extravagance was a pair of those small, perfectly rounded Japanese titanium eyeglasses that go for four hundred dollars a pop. In short, Bryan Hayes would have looked at home at any college campus in the country.

"Sorry I'm late. I got held up."

I put my lighter away reluctantly and followed him in. He bounded along in front of me, greeting people he knew. Just watching him move made me feel tired.

I snagged a table while Bryan went to get a couple of beers. He came back with four pieces of pizza as well. I took a bite from one. It was as bad as I remembered it being, but Bryan either didn't share my view or didn't care, because he gobbled down two pieces immediately.

"First thing I've had to eat all day," he explained abashedly when he saw me watching him.

I made a polite comment and took a sip of my beer. It was warm and flat and reminded me of the kind everyone drank before beer went upscale.

Bryan reached for the third slice, then stopped, hand hovering. "Do you want this?"

I shook my head. "Go ahead."

"So," Bryan Hayes asked after he was through, "how do you know George?"

"We met through mutual friends." I didn't want to tell him George had been my husband's best friend until he died, for three reasons: One, I didn't like discussing it; two, it wasn't any of his business; and three, the topic didn't make for good social conversation.

Bryan wiped his hands on a napkin. "He's interesting."

"Yes, he is." If Bryan wanted to make small talk for a while, that was okay with me. I watched four girls and one guy at the next table dig into their pockets for change. Pennies, quarters, and dimes materialized into several piles.

"He said he used to be a cop."

"For eight years." Or was it seven? I forget. From where I was sitting, I watched the stream of students coming in swell. The room was becoming packed. The noise level was rising. The place was turning stuffy. I began wishing I weren't wearing a turtleneck sweater.

"So how did he end up in grad school?"

"Why don't you ask him?"

"I did. He said he wanted a change."

I leaned forward. "But somehow you think there's more, right?"

Bryan flushed and adjusted his hat. "It just s-seems unusual," he stammered. "I mean, you don't associate a guy who looks like that with medieval history."

"A guy who looks like what?" I asked innocently, curious to see if Bryan would mention that George was black or that he was enormous or that he not only looked as if he could break someone in two with his hands, but that he would enjoy doing it.

"He could be a linebacker for the Oilers," Bryan replied, skirting the issue. "You just don't expect to find someone like that sitting next to you in a class on manors and land rights."

"True," I allowed. I guess the Ralph Lauren clothes George was wearing weren't as effectively reshaping his image as he hoped.

"I'd hate to get on the wrong side of him," Bryan observed.

"Me too." Actually George was a sweetie pie, much nicer than I was, but why tell Bryan that and spoil the image. I changed the subject to the one we'd come here to discuss. "So tell me about your sister," I said. Even though I remembered the story, I wanted to hear it in Bryan's words.

"Right." Bryan pushed his glasses back up the bridge of his nose with his thumb. "Actually, I think you met her. She was in your store this summer. She wanted a sugar glider, but the guy who works behind the counter said they didn't make good pets."

"They don't." Sugar gliders were the latest in a long line of fad pets. Tiny gliding opossums that come from Indonesia, New Guinea, Australia, and New Zealand, they are small enough to carry around in your pocket.

"He said they have complicated nutritional needs."

"Tim said that?"

Bryan nodded.

"Interesting. I always thought they did fine on fruits, vegetables, a little cheese, and mealworms, myself."

"That's what Melissa fed hers." Bryan took off his hat, adjusted the brim, and put it back on.

"I'm glad to hear it." The kids sitting at the table next to us were arguing about what kind of pizza to get, and I had to raise my voice to make myself heard.

"Melissa sent for it. From a magazine."

"It's amazing what you can get in the mail," I said, thinking back to the viper someone had sent to one of my employees.

Bryan began folding the edge of the white paper plate back and forth. "George said you were pretty good at finding people."

"I've had some successes in the past," I allowed. "Why don't you tell me what happened, and I'll tell you if I think I can help you or not."

"That's the problem. I don't know. One moment Melissa was here, the next moment she wasn't." Bryan's voice quivered for a second, then he regained control. "I dropped her off at the dorm, and when I went to pick her up, she wasn't there.''

''That was how long ago?''

''Forever. Well, it seems like forever. Since right before Thanksgiving.''

''And it's the middle of March now.''

Bryan looked embarrassed. ''I know it's a long time, but the police have been telling me to sit tight, to be patient. But I can't be patient any longer.''

''When did you notify the police?''

''I called the campus police almost immediately. They told me to wait, so I called the city police. They said the same thing, that I had to wait twenty-four hours before I filed a missing person's report.''

''Which you did.''

''Yes. But nothing's happened. I keep calling and they keep telling me they're doing everything they can, but I don't think they are.'' Bryan swallowed. ''I've talked to the dean of the school here, I've talked to the head of security, I've talked to Missy's R.A.'' Bryan's mouth tightened with anger as he remembered the responses he'd gotten. ''Everyone keeps telling me she must have run off with someone and that she'll be back. Well, she hasn't come back.''

''Maybe it's true. Maybe she *has* gone off with someone.''

''If you knew Missy, you wouldn't say that. She's very responsible.''

''You really never know what's going on inside someone's head,'' I observed, remembering the stunt my old college roommate had pulled. She'd been responsible too. Until the Saturday afternoon she'd walked out the door, only to reappear eight months later. Turned out she'd taken off for Mexico with a guy she'd met at the supermarket. He'd said, 'Let's go,' and she'd thought, sure. What the hell. Why not. She hadn't called, she said, because she figured we'd know she was okay. If she hadn't been, someone would have notified us. And anyway, if she'd spoken to anyone, they just would have told her to come home.

Bryan hit the table with the palm of his hand. It wobbled. "Believe me. I know my sister. She'd never walk off like that. She's never even late."

Sharon hadn't been either. "Did she take her wallet?"

Bryan frowned. "Her bag's missing," he conceded. His voice was truculent. "But that doesn't mean anything. She always takes it with her wherever she goes."

"Why?"

"Because she's had money stolen out of it a couple of times when she left it in her room. They never found out who took it either," he said to what was going to be my next question.

"How about her clothes?"

"I don't think anything is missing." Bryan scratched the side of his neck.

"But you're not one hundred percent sure."

"I don't keep an inventory of her wardrobe." Bryan's voice rose. "And even if a few things are gone, that doesn't mean she took off. Something happened to her."

"Maybe. But you have to realize thousands of people disappear in this country every year. Most of them have—for a variety of reasons—just decided to walk away from their lives. Maybe she's one of them."

"Not my sister." Bryan's voice was filled with certainty.

"What makes you so sure?"

"Our mother is dying," he said, the look on his face daring me to utter any of the usual banalities of consolation.

I didn't. I've never been good with that kind of stuff. Instead, I contented myself with observing that appearances to the contrary, maybe Melissa was having trouble dealing with what was happening in her life.

"No." Bryan poked himself in his chest with his finger. "I'm the one who has the trouble going to the hospital, not her." He swallowed, fighting to get himself back under control. "Jesus, all my mom does is ask for her. Every time I go to see her in the hospital, she wants to know if I've found Melissa. She wants to know what happened to her. She's expecting me to find out."

I chose my next words carefully. "Are you sure you want to?"

Bryan leaned forward. "I don't have a choice. I have to find my sister. Whatever state she's in, dead or alive, I have to find her and bring her home."

"Why?"

Bryan studied the stains the pizza had left behind on the white paper plate before answering. I noticed the oil and the tomato sauce had formed a palm-sized, ragged red circle. "Because," he finally informed me in a determined voice, "for once I want to do the right thing."

Chapter

2

The story Bryan Hayes told me sitting there at the table with his legs wound around the chair's metal ones was an old one, one I knew well. His father had died soon after Bryan was born, leaving his mother to raise two kids by herself. She'd gotten a job in a store selling dresses, and when she couldn't meet the bills that way, she'd worked as a waitress two nights a week. To all intents and purposes she was never around, a fact Bryan had hated and felt guilty about hating. He'd resolved the dichotomy by blossoming from a quiet, well-behaved boy into a full-time pain in the ass, playing Cain to Melissa's Abel. There'd been calls from teachers, visits to the principal, fights in school, shoplifting, a stolen car. In short, the usual JD litany.

Although Bryan didn't come right out and say so, it was obvious to me he felt finding his sister was his shot at redemption, his chance to make up for all the grief he'd caused his mother. He'd spent the months since her disappearance hoping Melissa would turn up. But time was running out. His mother was in the hospital, chained to her bed by wires and tubes, begging him to find out what had happened, and he had given his word that he would.

"Maybe it's stupid," he said, giving me a wan smile. "But I don't want to break another promise."

I made a sympathetic noise and waited for him to continue.

Bryan drained the last of his beer and carefully put the glass back down on the table. Then he leaned forward. "I know this kind of stuff is expensive and I don't have a lot of money, but my mom gave me some."

"So she knows you're here?"

Bryan nodded. He took his wallet out of his pocket and handed me a small wad of new-looking bills. "There's four hundred in there. I can give you another four hundred next week."

"Fine." I unzipped my backpack and stuffed the money inside. I'd gotten over feeling guilty about charging for my services a while ago. If Bryan had gone to one of the private investigators listed in the phone book this would have cost him thousands.

"Aren't you going to count it?"

"Should I?"

"No."

"Okay." I left my backpack on the table. "Now that that's out of the way, why don't you show me your sister's picture."

Bryan handed me a copy of the same flyer I'd seen on my walk over to the Yellow Rhino. "Here," he said, smoothing the wrinkles out of the piece of paper with the flat of his hand before handing it to me.

I studied it again. According to the stats at the bottom of the page, Melissa Hayes was nineteen years old, five feet five inches tall, weighed 128 pounds, had hazel eyes and light brown hair, and was last seen wearing jeans, a plaid flannel button-down shirt, a navy jacket with a leather collar, and a pair of sneakers. She had no visible scars or other identifying marks. What the poster didn't say was that she had her brother's smile and the shape of his chin.

As I studied the photograph, I couldn't help thinking that three of the children who had gone missing in the area in the last two years had come to a bad end, but they'd been much younger. The odds of a happier ending for a nineteen-year-old girl were considerably higher. I held on to that thought as I went back to looking at Melissa's picture. In it she was leaning against a tree trunk. A small blue colonial with white shutters figured in the background. Her arms were crossed over her chest. She was wearing jeans and a T-shirt and she'd tied a green shirt over her shoulders. The day must have started off cool and warmed up. Her hair was long and parted on the side. Her smile was bright, her features symmetrical. Like her brother, she could have fit into any college campus in the country.

"May I?" Bryan asked as he reached over and took the flyer from me. He devoured it with his eyes before sighing and handing it back. "She's pretty, isn't she?"

"Very," I replied, noting his use of the present tense. I hoped he was right. I hoped it wasn't just wishful thinking. "When was this taken?"

"Last year."

"She looks happy."

"She was."

I indicated the house in the background. "Is this your home?"

He nodded.

I pointed to the flyer while I tried not to think about how much I wanted a cigarette. "May I keep this?"

"Sure. I have lots more."

"Where'd you put them up?"

"Mostly around campus. You think I should have put them up some other places too?" he asked worriedly.

I reassured him while I smoothed out the paper and laid it on the table. Melissa looked like someone who would be kind to children and animals, and I hoped she would fall in with the ninety-five percent of missing persons who vanish because they wanted to rather than the five percent who are kidnapped and killed.

"Have the police been through her belongings?"

Bryan nodded. "I gave them her address book."

"Do you know if she kept a diary?"

"No. She always she said she was going to start, but she never got around to it. I suppose you want to see her room too?" His voice betrayed the slightest hint of exasperation.

"It would be helpful, unless, of course, you have a problem with that."

"No," he replied quickly. "None at all."

I tapped my fingers on the table while I gathered my thoughts. I was finding it difficult to concentrate in the surrounding din. We should have gone somewhere else. Bryan opened his mouth to say something, thought better of it, closed it again, and took his hat off, ran his fingers through his hair, and put it back on again.

"Do you have something you want to tell me?" I asked as I got my notebook and pen out of my backpack.

Bryan licked his lips.

I opened the notebook. "I can't help you if I don't have all the information."

"Talk to Tommy West." Bryan spit the name out as if it had been a tack.

"Who's that?"

"Melissa's boyfriend."

I felt as if I were playing twenty questions. "Okay. What about him?"

"They were always fighting."

I thought about Murphy. And George. "Lots of couples fight."

"She was getting ready to dump him and he didn't like that. He said he wasn't going to let her go."

"Did you tell this to the police?"

"Of course."

"And?"

"A detective interviewed him. For all the good it did." Bryan's tone was bitter. "Marks . . ."

". . . the detective?"

"Right."

I wrote his name down and underlined it.

". . . said West didn't have anything to do with Missy's disappearance."

I stated the self-evident. "But you disagree. You think he's involved."

Bryan contorted his face into a ferocious frown. "The guy's a scumbag," he told me, stretching out the last word. "I told Missy to stay away from him, but she wouldn't listen. She told me to mind my own business."

"Why is he a scumbag?"

Bryan clenched and unclenched his fists while he talked. "West thinks he owns the world. He thinks he can do whatever the fuck he wants to whoever he wants. His kind always do."

"His kind?"

"Yeah."

"Could you be a little more explicit?"

But Bryan was on a roll and didn't want to stop to answer my question. "I mean on top of everything else, he's got that goddamned snake. Anyone who keeps something like that has to be cracked in the head, right?"

I made a noncommittal noise. I guess George hadn't told him that Noah's Ark, the pet store I ran, specialized in selling reptiles. "What kind of snake?"

"A big one."

Over the past few years owning a pet store, I've learned that when it comes to snakes, people tend to exaggerate measurements. "How big?"

"Big enough. Maybe from there to there," he said, indicating two table lengths and the space between them.

"Twelve feet? Are you sure?"

"Of course I'm not sure. I didn't measure the damn thing."

I put my pen down. "Is it a Burmese? A boa?" I wondered if West had gotten it from our store. I hoped not.

"How the hell should I know?" Bryan's voice began to rise. "He . . ."

"Tommy West?"

"Who the hell else am I talking about? Just lets it crawl around his room at the frat house. You know what I think happened?"

"What?" I asked even though what he thought was obvious.

"I think the snake killed my sister and then Tommy went and buried the body, that's what I think."

"But the police don't?"

"They think she's off on a holiday."

I picked up my pen again and wrote down Tommy West's name followed by a question mark. "Contrary to what you see in the movies, snakes don't usually kill people."

"But it could happen." Bryan's eyes were glittering.

"Yes, it *could* happen. Anything can happen. It's just not very likely that it did. You see, even snakes of that size tend to go after smaller—"

But Bryan wasn't in the mood to listen to a lecture on boids. "Let me tell you," he interrupted. "If it wasn't for my mother, I'd beat what happened to my sister out of him."

"Really?" I regarded him for a moment before I spoke. "The way you're acting, I'm surprised you haven't tried already."

Bryan muttered something I couldn't catch, slumped in his seat, and glared at me while he cracked his knuckles. His cheeks were still bright red, his jaw was clenched. This was a person whose emotions ran close to the surface.

"Well, have you?"

"I just talked to him," he answered sullenly.

"Are you sure that's all you've done?"

Bryan didn't answer. He didn't have to. The look on his face was enough.

"I want you to stay away from him, understand?"

Bryan mumbled something.

"I mean it."

"I heard."

"Good. Because if you don't, I'm going to give you your money back."

"I said, I heard." Bryan's voice was truculent. He'd slumped farther down in his chair and was pulling the zipper on his ski parka up and down. "So I pushed him a little. Big deal. What difference does it make?"

"Let me explain." I leaned forward slightly. "In order to find out what happened to your sister, I need to talk to this guy. He is a primary lead. But, unfortunately, this guy does not have to talk to me. And I can't force him to. The only thing I can do is try and get him to cooperate with me, and he's not going to do that if he's pissed at you. See?"

"Yeah," Bryan muttered. "I see."

"Good. I don't suppose there's anyone else you've been chatting with?"

His no was so low, I had trouble hearing it.

"But you *are* going to talk to him?" Bryan demanded, suddenly alarmed at the possibility I wouldn't.

"Among other people. Yes."

"You don't need to talk to anyone else. Just take a look at the snake. You'll see what I mean."

"Is that right?" I'm not particularly fond of being told what to do, especially when the person telling me doesn't know what the hell he's talking about. I took a deep breath, moved my chair back a little, and watched a couple of girls thread their way through a narrow opening to another table. One of them caught sight of Bryan and waved. He returned the gesture unenthusiastically.

"Yes. It is. Anyway," he added, "I'm the one that's paying."

"That's true. You are. But your money is buying my expertise. Now, this is the last time I'm going to say this. If you don't trust me, don't hire me, but if you want me, you have to let me do things my way. Otherwise you're going to have to get yourself someone else."

"I didn't mean to . . ." Bryan's voice trailed off. He suddenly looked like a little boy caught stealing money out of his mother's purse. "Listen, I'm sorry." He resettled his hat. "It's just hard when—"

I put up a hand to forestall further apologies and asked Bryan for some more particulars on his sister. He started smiling once he began talking about her. According to him, Melissa should have been nominated for sainthood. "A" student. Student council. Honor society. Candy-striper at the hospital. Volunteer at a hospice. To hear Bryan tell it, her only mistake was hooking up with the wrong guy. Well, maybe he was right. A lot of times that's enough. The question was: Was Tommy West the wrong guy?

Half of my mind was listening to Bryan chattering, while the other half was thinking I should call Calli when I got back to the store and see what she could find out about Melissa. She'd bitch, but what else are old friends for. We'd worked together at the *Post Standard* when I'd first come up to Syracuse. Then she'd run off to marry an avocado farmer out in California, acquiring the improbable name of Calli Cornfeld, and I'd quit to write the great American exposé that would win me my Pulitzer.

In retrospect, we'd both been delusional. So here we were again. Older. Single. In debt. Only Calli was a reporter/columnist on the paper and I was running my dead husband's pet store. I gnawed at a fingernail. Calli had always said she was the smarter one. She was right. I was contemplating why I'd kept the store, when I realized Bryan had stopped talking. Then I noticed the red spots on his cheeks were back. I asked him what the matter was. He didn't answer. I don't think he even heard me.

All his attention was focused on something across the room. I noticed his hands were balled up into fists and he'd half risen from his chair.

"Bryan."

He didn't answer.

"Bryan," I repeated, this time more loudly.

He answered me reluctantly, as if he begrudged the energy it took. "That's him," he growled. He didn't shift his gaze. "That's the scumbag I've been telling you about."

Chapter
3

I followed Bryan's gaze, but all I saw was a crowd of milling college students. "Could you be a little more specific?" I asked.

"Over there." With an angry jerk of his hand Bryan indicated the group of guys that had just walked through the door and were now heading toward the bar.

They moved in a tight V formation as they laughed and talked and slapped each other on the back. The crowd gave way before their onslaught, ebbing and flowing around them.

"Which one is Tommy West?"

"The one with the blond hair wearing a Sigma Phi jacket."

I strained to get a good look. There were at least three guys that fit the description. "That doesn't help me much," I observed.

"I'd like to shoot the sonofabitch," Bryan said by way of an answer as he kicked the chair in front of him out of the way. It glanced off the leg of the boy sitting at the next table.

"Hey," he said, turning to Bryan. "What's with you?"

Bryan ignored him and took a step forward. I reached over and grabbed his arm.

"Don't," I said, hoping to prevent the mess he was about to make.

The boy at the other table started to get up too, but the girls sitting on either side of him pulled him back down before he could and started making soothing noises. The kid muttered "schmuck" and turned away.

I don't think Bryan even heard him. His body was coiled. His muscles were twitching in anticipation of the fight to come. Looking at him, I understood the meaning of the phrase "wants him so badly it hurts" for the first time. He shook my hand off—I could have been a fly for all the notice he took of me—and started walking again.

I grabbed his arm for a second time and used all my strength to yank him around. "Your mother," I said. "Remember her?"

Bryan furrowed his brow. "What about her?"

"You just told me you want to do right by her."

"I do."

"If you start a fight with this guy West, you could end up in jail."

"So what? It'd be worth it," Bryan snarled, doing a bad imitation of a grade-B movie gangster, but the snarl lacked conviction.

"She needs you here. Don't do something you're going to regret."

"I didn't mean . . ." Bryan swallowed. I could feel the tension flowing out of the muscles in his arm.

"I know." I grabbed our jackets and hustled him outside.

As the Rhino's doors banged shut behind me, I realized that I still didn't know what Tommy West looked like, but there would be time for that later.

"Thanks," Bryan mumbled. I handed him his parka. He kept his eyes fixed on the ground as he shrugged it on. "I have this problem with my temper."

I put on my jacket. "No kidding." Talk about stating the obvious.

"I'm working on it with my therapist."

"You ask me, you should work a little harder."

He grimaced. "But you *are* going to take the case?"

I nodded. Bryan might be a little rocky, but money was money and at this point I could sure use every little bit. "How about showing me Melissa's room?"

"Now?"

"You have a better time?"

He shook his head.

We drove over to Bryan's house in my Checker cab. Another legacy from my husband, the only one I was thankful for, my New York City yellow Checker taxicab had close to two hundred thousand miles on it, but the thing still ran and I intended to keep it going for as long as I could.

Bryan spent the five minutes it took to reach his house talking about how overwhelmed he felt, a feeling, given his position, I could empathize with. The Hayes house was located in the Outer Comstock area, about five blocks from a small vest-pocket park, in a neighborhood populated mostly by students, teaching assistants, high school teachers, and the occasional assistant professor.

I pointed to the maple in the front yard as I parked in

the driveway. "Is that the tree in the picture Melissa was leaning against?"

"We used to have a swing in it when we were little," Bryan noted, getting out of the cab. He fished around in his jacket pocket for his keys as we walked over the snow-covered front lawn and up the three icy steps to the front porch. After a couple of seconds of fumbling with the key in the lock— "damn thing always sticks," he groused—we went inside.

Bryan pointed to the stairs. I wiped my feet on the floor mat. "Missy's room is up there."

I peeked into the living room as I followed him. The beige carpeting needed to be vacuumed, one end of the brown tweed sofa was covered with what must have been a two-week accumulation of newspapers, and the top of the television supported a line of soda cans.

"I'm going to clean everything up today," Bryan said, motioning me along.

Something told me he'd been saying that for weeks.

Melissa's room was at the head of the stairs.

Bryan stepped inside and gestured for me to follow. "All her stuff from the dorm is still here. I just left it. I didn't know what to do."

I looked around. The room surprised me. It was the room of an eight-year-old girl, an eight-year-old girl from twenty years ago. The wallpaper was a floral, with faint green and white stripes in the background, while the foreground was dominated by bunches of white and yellow pansies. The bedspread on Melissa's four-poster was white chenille. Her furniture was antique white. Stuffed animals and dolls decorated her shelves and the top of her dresser.

"She didn't want to change anything," Bryan informed me as I took another step inside. "My mom offered, but she said she liked it like this."

"She seems conservative."

"She is." Bryan pointed to the duffel-sized laundry bags lying on their sides on the beige carpeting and the four cartons next to them. "That's her stuff from the dorm."

"Do you mind if I look?"

"Be my guest."

The cartons turned out to be full of books, toiletries, cleaning supplies, and the other ephemera of dorm living. I dug around a little and came up with a beer stein, a small stuffed bear, and a key chain with a .45 shell attached to it.

"What's this?" I asked, holding up the key chain.

Bryan laughed. "All that stuff are the prizes Missy won at the state fair last year."

I put everything back and straightened up. "What's in the duffel bags?"

"Bed sheets. Towels. Pillowcases. Dirty laundry. I hung her clean clothes in the closet." He crossed the room and opened the closet door. "See."

Melissa's closet was crammed with slacks, jeans, shirts, jackets, and dresses, all of which seemed to have come from the J. Crew catalogue or the Gap.

"I can see why you can't tell if something is missing or not," I said, studying the jumble inside.

"You should see her drawers," Bryan said, and he opened one for me to prove his point. "How many T-shirts does one person need?"

"Evidently, a lot," I said, rummaging through the dresser.

"The police couldn't find anything," Bryan said.

"Maybe I can do better."

After an hour, though, I was forced to conclude that I couldn't.

Chapter
4

It was a little after seven in the evening when I left Bryan Hayes and headed over to the store. It was dark. Smoke streamed out of house chimneys, cars had their lights on, and the people that were out walking hurried along. I wished spring would come, I reflected as I waited for a light to turn green on State Street. I could deal with December, January, and February, but March in Syracuse seemed interminable. Winter's charms, such as they were, had worn thin.

All I wanted was sunlight and the tender greens of May, but spring wouldn't come till the end of April—if we were lucky. As far as I was concerned, March and April were the bleakest months of the year, the time, if you could afford it, to go south. Unfortunately, I couldn't do that even if I could afford to, which I couldn't. Stores are jealous mistresses—take too much time off, and they might not be around when you get back.

I thought about bleak again when I pulled up in front of

my store. It certainly was a good word for the window display, although boring was probably a better one. Window dressing had never been my forte. Fortunately, this wasn't Bloomingdale's and I wasn't selling clothes. Most of our clientele came because they needed crickets or birdseed, not because they'd been window-shopping and something had caught their eye. The store wasn't in the kind of area that promoted leisurely strolling anyway, unless, of course, you enjoyed looking at run-down houses and convenience stores.

At one point I'd been thinking of taking out a loan and setting up in one of the malls, but after going over the figures with my accountant, I'd decided it wasn't worth it. The overhead was too high. Most of the shops in the mall were chains—and with good reason. It took deep pockets to keep one going, and I didn't have those.

Besides, the items that usually attracted people—large boids and parrots—were precisely the ones I wasn't about to put on display. The stress was bad for them, and they were too easy to steal. All you had to do was smash a window, grab, and go. Three pet stores in the area had been robbed recently. The thieves had gotten away with thousands of dollars worth of birds that they would probably resell down in New York City, a loss I couldn't afford. So maybe boring wasn't so bad after all.

Noah's Ark had started off on the ground floor of an old house that had received a variance for commerical use. I'd liked that space better, even though it had been harder to maintain, but when it had burned down, I'd moved us to your standard small-size commerical space, consisting of a front room with a storeroom, small office, and bathroom in back. I'd packed as much product as I could—we had shelves running to the ceiling—into the store without making it look cluttered. We continued to specialize in reptiles and miscellaneous exotics such as hissing cockroaches and tarantulas. What we didn't sell were puppies and kittens, except for the ones dumped at our front door by irresponsible jerks.

Tim looked up from the leashes he was sorting through as I came in. The smell of cedar shavings permeated the air.

"Ah," he said. "The great detective returns." He was a slight guy in his early thirties. In the last few years he'd gone through some sort of midlife crisis and shaved his head, pierced his ears and his nose, and taken to dressing in black. Maybe he thought we were really in SoHo. He'd worked with my husband when he'd opened the store and stayed on when Murphy had died and I'd taken it over. He was good with snakes. I always thought he knew as much, maybe even more, than the herp curator at the zoo, and, given his appearance, was also surprisingly good with little old ladies and kids.

"That's me. Sherlock Holmes in drag."

"You've had about ten phone calls from Tino."

I cursed under my breath. I'd forgotten all about him. I was working on getting an indigo and a red-tailed Haitian boa for the guy. I'd found a couple of babies down in Florida, but it was too cold to fly them up since the cargo areas in planes aren't heated, and so far I hadn't come up with anything from the local breeders I'd phoned. I had three more people to call though. I'd hoped one of them could help me out. If not, there'd be something at the herp show down in Philly—with one hundred dealers there always was.

Tim gave me a baleful glance. "I've got more than enough to do here without acting as your secretary." The gurgling of the fish tanks punctuated his sentence.

I apologized. Tim disapproved of what had become a

regular part-time gig for me because it took me away from the store. My cases had me spending a lot of time becoming acquainted with stupid people who not only did stupid things but occasionally did them in the store.

On the other hand, once in a while my cases did bring in some extra off-the-books cash, which we could definitely use. Unfortunately, it wasn't often enough, because my clientele usually do not tend to be the rich and well connected. I'd fallen into the work when I'd become a murder suspect and had to clear myself. Then several people had asked me to help them out. I'd said yes because I have trouble saying no, and after a couple of go-rounds I'd become hooked on the action. Sometimes I even think about selling the store and opening up an office. Robin Light. Private detective. I could work off someone else's license. I don't know. I can't decide. But until I do, I still have a business to run, which was why I asked what else had happened since I'd been gone.

Tim shrugged. "Aside from the phone never stopping ringing, not much. We sold some feeders since you've been gone. A couple of mollies, a bag of that all-natural dog food. That's about it."

Business had been sluggish since after Christmas and, if previous years were any indication, it would remain that way until the spring, when sales would start picking up again.

"Oh." Tim slapped the counter. A guinea pig, momentarily distracted by the noise, glanced up and then went back to its food. "You'll enjoy this one. Some lady wanted to know if we sold Gaboon vipers. She wanted to give her boyfriend a surprise birthday present."

"That would be quite a surprise. Did you explain about them?"

"I think she knew."

"Nice lady." Depending on the size of the person, a bite from a Gaboon could be fatal, a fact that reminded me of the conversation I'd just had with Bryan Hayes. "Speaking of which, do you remember if we sold a boa or a Burmese to a kid called Tommy West?" I inquired as I went behind the counter to stow my backpack. Zsa Zsa, my cocker spaniel, looked up from her bed by the back wall and yawned. I swear that animal sleeps at least eighteen hours a day. Maybe I should cut back on her beer ration.

Tim twirled the stud in his ear around while he thought. "Sorry," he said after a minute. "The name doesn't ring a bell. Why?"

Zsa Zsa got up, stretched, and came over for a pet. I scratched behind her ears. She gave my hand a hello lick, then went in the back to get some water. I straightened up and put the flyer Bryan had given me on the counter.

"What about her? Does she look familiar?"

Tim glanced down. "That's the case you're working on? I remember reading something in the paper, but I can't remember what." He frowned. "After a while all these missing-person cases sound alike. Another couple and I'm going to begin believing what those alien abduction guys are saying."

I nodded. "According to her brother, she was in our store last year wanting to buy a sugar glider. You told her they make bad pets."

"Well they do. Sorry, I don't remember her. I guess she didn't make much of an impression."

"He thinks she was killed by her boyfriend's snake." I told Tim the story.

He snorted. "When in doubt, blame the reptile."

"Well, it is a possibility. Remember down in New York,"

I said, referring to an incident that had recently taken place in the Bronx.

"The guy didn't feed the snake. He was a moron."

"Now he's a dead moron."

"It was a nine-foot retic."

I wondered what kind of boid Tommy West had and how often he fed it.

The bell on the front door rang. A customer walked in.

"I don't know," Tim said as he watched him approach. "If I had to trust a reptile or a person, my money would go with the reptile. At least they're predictable."

I was inclined to agree.

Chapter
5

George changed lanes without looking, cutting off the Blazer behind us. The guy in the Blazer pulled up next to us, rolled down his window, and screamed, "Why don't you learn how to drive, asshole?"

George muttered an obscenity and we shot forward, two cars in a choreographed dance. A moment later George slowed back down. "Aren't you going to say anything?" he demanded while he checked the rearview mirror. The Blazer was nowhere in sight. It had turned off.

"Like what?" I wanted to say a lot—I mean, it's hard to get into an accident when there are three cars on the road— but George was looking for a fight and I was damned if I was going to oblige.

He glanced at me suspiciously, waiting for me to continue. When I didn't, he began fiddling with the radio. A moment later he turned it off. "Twenty-five stations and nothing on any of them," he complained.

I remained quiet. We were in George's car driving toward the bus terminal on Erie Boulevard. The Greyhound Raymond was on was due to arrive in ten minutes. I don't think I'd ever seen George so distracted or nervous. He'd been calmer when I'd found him stuffed in a trunk after he'd been shot and left for dead. But then, that was probably easier to handle than the thought of playing daddy to his prodigal nephew. After all, one was over quickly, the other could linger on and on. Not, of course, that he had to do this. He could have said no. But we'd already had that discussion—twice. I got a cigarette out of my backpack.

"Not in the car," George said.

I was good. I kept my resolution. I didn't say anything. I just put it away.

"I thought you were quitting," George continued.

"Did I say that?" No. This was going to be fun, I decided. Especially after all the toughlove lectures George had given me about Manuel. I was going to enjoy seeing how he was going to handle his very own JD. "When are you going to register Raymond in school?"

"Tomorrow," George snapped, switching lanes and topics at the same time. I guess anything was better than talking about his nephew. "So what did you think about Bryan?"

"I thought he was a little bit edgy."

"Edgy? Not when I've been around him."

"How well do you know him?"

"Not well at all. We've just had a few beers together after class. Why?"

I told George about what had happened at the Yellow Rhino.

"Hey. You don't think you can handle him, don't take him on."

"I didn't say I couldn't handle him." Despite my resolution, I could hear the testiness in my voice.

"Sorry." George began rifling through his CDs. Finally he found the one he wanted and put it on. The sound of Miles Davis filled the car.

"You think you can find his sister?"

"I don't know." I drummed my fingers on the door. "A fair amount of time has elapsed."

Usually the longer someone's been gone, the harder it is to track them down.

George turned off Erie Boulevard into the bus terminal's parking lot. "I don't think the police exactly went out of their way to look for her."

"That's what Bryan said. You know a guy called Marks?" I asked as the Taurus jounced over the potholes. I'd driven down better roads in the jungle in the Yucatán.

"Is he the primary?"

I nodded.

"I know him. I'll call him up. See if I can grease the wheels a little." George cursed as we hit an especially deep rut.

"What's he like?"

"He's okay," George replied. "He's just been on the job too long." He stopped the car a little ways from the terminal. The parking lines that had been painted on the tarmac had long since washed away, and the few cars parked on the lot were splayed out like teeth in a bum's mouth.

George checked the time on his watch. "Do you have any ideas yet about where Bryan's sister got herself off to?"

"None. I went through her room this afternoon."

"And?"

"And she has a lot of clothes."

"What else did you find?"

"Nothing. Dirty laundry. Hair dryer. State fair souvenirs. That sort of thing. Evidently Marks took Melissa's address book with him." I nibbled on my fingernail. "I called Calli and asked her to nose around the newsroom and see if there are any rumors floating around. I guess tomorrow I'll go out and start talking to people and see if I can turn anything up."

George turned off the car and took the key out of the ignition. "Want any help?"

"Thanks, but I think you're going to be busy enough as it is. How long is Raymond here for anyway?"

George sighed and tapped the Taurus's key against his top teeth. "Cecilia wants him to stay until September." He dropped the car keys into his jacket pocket. "She says he's not going to school. He's just roaming the streets. Even when she takes him over, he waits till she's gone and sneaks out of the building. She thinks a change of scene will be good for him. You know, get him away from his friends, that kind of thing."

"Has he been up here before?"

"No."

I remembered when I first arrived. "He's going to go into shock."

"I know. I wouldn't care if I didn't have so much work to do."

I raised an eyebrow. George had lived alone too long to do well with anything that interrupted his schedule. He was as hidebound in his ways as a turtle.

"Well, I wouldn't," George protested as he glanced at his watch again. "The bus should be here soon." He got out of the car, slamming the door shut, and began striding across the lot. I had to hurry to keep up. "I'll have to cook his dinner and check his homework instead of going to the library,'' he said in an aggrieved voice.

''Not to mention no more nights at my house.''

''Why the hell not?'' Even though the light in the parking lot was dim, I could see a vein throbbing under George's right eye.

''You're going to leave a thirteen—''

''Fourteen—''

''Pardon me, a fourteen-year-old boy alone all night? Especially one who gets into trouble?''

George muttered something I couldn't hear and viciously kicked at a soda bottle lying on the sidewalk. Then he pushed the terminal door open and went inside. I followed.

''What the hell am I supposed to do?'' he demanded.

''Get dressed and go home.''

''That's ridiculous. Next I suppose you'll tell me I should sneak back in my house?''

I shrugged. ''Hey, don't take this out on me. You didn't have to say yes.''

''So you keep telling me.'' He rubbed his ear. ''My sister's other kids are fine. They're not running around on the streets. They're going to school. Doing what they're supposed to. Raymond's always been a pain in the ass. What's his problem anyway?''

''I'd say you're going to get to find out.''

''Just what I want,'' George muttered as he glanced around. ''I'd forgotten how bad this place was.''

''Well, buses aren't the transportational choice of the rich and famous.'' Or even the middle class, for that matter. If they were, the place would have looked a lot different.

The air in the station smelled of sweat, alcohol, and disinfectant. The fluorescent light George and I were standing under flickered on and off. The walls and floor were different shades of grayish-brown. Video games and vending machines took up the wall nearest to us. Wanted posters were pasted up beside the cashier's window. Lines of straight-back chairs were bolted into the middle of the floor. Ten people were slouched down in them, piles of bags at their feet. The place was quiet except for the canned laughter coming from one of the small televisions three kids were clustered around and the squeals from two small boys who were chasing each other while their mother, gray with fatigue, watched helplessly.

George rocked back and forth on the soles of his feet impatiently. A minute later the loudspeaker crackled into life.

"At least the bus is on time," he noted.

I nodded. We watched the doors across the way open and disgorge a stream of people into the terminal. They were mostly old men and women and young women with small children.

George craned his neck to look. Then he pointed. "There he is."

I followed his finger. Raymond was wearing a ski hat pulled down over his ears, an open triple-fat goosedown jacket, an immense purple sweatshirt, and pants that I was willing to bet came down below his ass. He had a boom box in one hand and a duffel bag in the other. He could have been a poster boy for ghetto couture. There wasn't one cliché he'd managed to avoid.

"God," George muttered, appalled. As Raymond sauntered toward us, George unconsciously straightened his tie and touched the collar buttons of his light blue oxford shirt as if reassuring himself. "He didn't look like that at Thanksgiving."

I began feeling sorrier for George. He was definitely going

to have his hands full. By now Raymond was about six feet away. George plastered a big smile on his face. "So, how was the trip?" he asked.

Raymond gave a sullen shrug.

George tried again. "Where are your other bags?"

"Out there." Raymond jerked his head to indicate the direction he'd just come from. Then he looked me up and down. It was a long, insolent look. "Who's the white bitch?" he asked his uncle.

I could hear the intake of George's breath.

"It's okay." I put my hand on his arm to restrain him. "I can handle this." I smiled at the kid. He looked like fourteen going on twenty. "Cute." Raymond didn't say anything. He just stood there, grinning and staring at me. "Just so you know," I continued, "I understand that you don't want to be here. I understand that you figure if you're obnoxious enough, maybe your uncle will put you on the next bus out of here. But that's not going to happen." I took a step toward him. "And don't call me bitch again. I don't like it."

Raymond kept grinning.

Suddenly I wanted to smack him and wipe that grin off his face. I had a feeling George did too, but I couldn't tell what he was thinking. His face had become all angles and planes, the way it did when he was upset.

I wondered when the first blow-up was going to come, because I didn't want to be around when it happened.

Chapter
6

Marks shifted around in his seat and wiped the barbecue sauce off his hands with a paper napkin, wadded it up, and added it to the growing pile of red, grease-stained paper beside him. It was a little after one the following afternoon, and Marks and I were sitting in a booth in Tippy's, a barbecue and beer joint that wished it were on a North Carolina back road instead of Syracuse's North Side. The decor leaned to driftwood, fishing nets, old license plates, stolen traffic signs, Christmas lights, and anything else the owners had on hand. It was a down-and-dirty place frequented by truckers, bikers, and other assorted carnivores. The only vegetable Tippy's listed on the menu was potatoes, and those came deep fried.

I'd lucked out and gotten Marks on the phone around ten that morning, a pleasant surprise, since I'd been expecting to play telephone tag with him for the next couple of days.

"I just got off the phone with Sampson," Marks had told me, his voice sounding as if he'd smoked a couple of packs a day for the last thiry years. "He said you'd be calling."

I blessed George.

"I was wondering if I could buy you lunch?"

"Maybe. You own Noah's Ark, right?"

"Right."

"My stepson's been in your store."

"Really?" I said, snuggling the phone against my ear with my shoulder as I broke open a roll of quarters and put them in the drawer.

"He was looking at a three-foot Burmese."

"That's an expensive investment," I'd observed. "About four hundred dollars if you add in the aquarium, heat rock, and lights."

"That's what the guy behind the counter told him. It's for his birthday."

"Birthdays should be special." Pickles, the store cat, had jumped up on the counter and begun meowing for her mid-morning snack. I fed the cat a couple of treats. She grabbed them out of my hand and retreated. She'd been under ten pounds when I found her—now she weighed almost twenty. "Maybe we could help each other out," I'd suggested as I watched my cat eat.

There'd been a short pause on the other end of the line, then Marks asked if I knew Tippy's.

"Who doesn't?"

"Meet me there at one. I can give you twenty minutes. Thirty tops."

I gave Pickles one more treat and closed the box. "How will I know you?"

"I'll be the fat, balding guy sitting in the front, eating barbecue."

As it turned out, that described half of the men there. The other half might have been bald too, but they were wearing baseball caps, so I couldn't tell.

I was standing in the doorway looking around and brushing snowflakes off my jacket, inhaling the wonderful odors of frying potatoes and roasting meat, when a guy sitting in a booth halfway down the room raised his hand and waved me over. His scalp gleamed like a freshly waxed floor. His skin was pink and flushed. When he looked at me, I saw that his most prominent facial feature were his earlobes. They were long and fleshy and totally out of character with the roundness of the rest of his face. In the Orient that feature would have have made him a man of good fortune; here it just made him a customer for cosmetic surgery.

"So you're Robin Light," he said, looking up.

I nodded, took off my jacket, and slid into the banquette across from him.

"You look better than the guys downtown said you would," Marks observed, his eyes lingering on my breasts a fraction longer than necessary.

"That's a relief." I could just imagine what the guys downtown had said.

"Yeah. I bet you were worried." He gave a mirthless laugh. "How's old George doing?"

"Well enough."

"He sounded good. Maybe I should quit my job and go back to school too."

"Why not?"

"Because I got too many expenses, that's why." He pointed to his sandwich. "My wife is trying to get me to cut down on red meat. She feeds me fish and pasta. I hate fish and pasta."

"She's probably doing it for your own good."

"That's what she tells me, but personally, I think she's doing it to make my life miserable. I mean, what's the point if you can't eat what you want? Skim milk in your coffee?" He shuddered. "And now she's got something worse. Rice milk. Whoever invented that should be shot." He absent-mindedly pulled on his earlobe. "This is what I get for marrying again. Now, my first wife, she served me meat loaf and mashed potatoes when I came home for dinner. I'm lucky if Lucy fixes me anything at all. She's too busy driving her kid out to the rink for hockey practice." He broke off as the waitress came over to take my order.

"How old is your stepson?" I asked after she left.

"Fifteen." Marks speared six or seven french fries. "I don't know why he wants a snake, but he does. I mean, it's not like that thing is going to greet you when you come through the door."

"And his mother says it's okay? She doesn't mind?"

Marks reached for the ketchup bottle. "Mind? She thinks it's a great idea. 'So educational,' " he said, mimicking her voice. "My first wife wouldn't have had a thing like that in the house." He doused his french fries and put the bottle down. "Sometimes you don't know when you're well off."

I made a sympathetic noise as the waitress came back with my order, and I changed the subject. I really didn't want to hear about Marks's marital mistakes. "Why don't you bring your son in," I suggested after I'd taken a bite of my barbe-cue sandwich. "I'm sure we can fix him up with something he'd like at a price you'll like."

Marks smiled and picked up his sandwich.

"Saturday afternoon would be a good time." Tim wouldn't be working then. Which would save me from explaining why I was about to make a sale that the store wasn't going to make money on.

"Who hired you?" Marks asked.

"Her brother."

Marks didn't say anything, which was interesting.

"He seems sincere." I had to raise my voice to be heard over a woman wailing about the man she'd lost. Someone had put money in the jukebox.

"I'm sure he does."

"And a little intense."

"Yeah. He's that all right." Marks folded up his napkin. "He was pulled in on a second-degree assault a couple of years back. Did he tell you that?"

I shook my head. "No. He didn't." But thinking back to the way he'd acted when he'd seen Tommy West at the Yellow Rhino, I wasn't surprised. "What happened?"

"The usual crap. A bar brawl."

"That's not a big deal."

"Except in this case he was waving a gun around." Marks inspected a french fry before popping it in his mouth. "Also right after his sister disappeared, Hayes started threatening her boyfriend. The kid's family had their attorney get an order of protection taken out on him."

"Did he use a gun there too?"

"Naw. Threatened him with a bat. Sometimes they can do more damage than a bullet." Marks took a gulp of soda. "Of course, the punk denies the whole thing."

"He told me he just pushed him a little."

"Not exactly."

"Is there anything else about him I should know?"

Marks hesitated for a moment. Then he said, "Oh, what the hell," and went on. "Not that this necessarily means anything, but when he was fifteen he got sent away for a while."

From what Bryan had told me, I'd half expected as much.

"As in juvie?" The singing stopped as suddenly as it had begun.

"As in one of these private places that rich kids go when their parents can't handle them anymore. If he'd been poor, he'd have had a PINS taken out on him."

What Bryan had told me about his father dying and his mother having to go out to work flashed through my mind. "Where did the money come from? I thought the family was supposed to be poor."

Marks shook his head. "You got me. I'm just telling you what I read in the report." He took another bite of his sandwich.

I did the same while I considered what Marks had just said. It was interesting, but only from the point of view of Bryan's veracity. "Are you saying that Bryan is involved in his sister's disappearance?"

"No, I'm not saying that."

"Then what are you saying?"

"Nothing. I just thought you'd like to know that I wouldn't consider him to be what you would call a reliable informant." Marks started in on his french fries again.

"Thanks." I had come to that decision myself. The men sitting in front of us got up. Their bodies filled the aisle. I watched them ambling to the cashier as I spoke. "You think that Bryan Hayes's scenario of Tommy West's snake killing his sister is bullshit?"

Marks snorted. "Have you seen the snake?"

I shook my head.

"It's true it's long, but it's real skinny. Maybe the thing could choke a kid to death, but it sure couldn't do an adult."

I took a sip of my soda and another bite of my sandwich. I chewed slowly. I'd forgotten how good the food here tasted.

"What do *you* think happened to Melissa Hayes?" I asked after I'd swallowed.

Marks shook his head. "You got me. Maybe she just couldn't stand things anymore and she took off."

"What makes you say that?"

"Some of her clothes were missing. A couple of pairs of jeans. A couple of T-shirts."

"How do you know?"

"Her roommate went over her stuff."

"She must know her clothes pretty well," I said, thinking of Melissa Hayes's jam-packed closet.

"She said they shared. Also the Hayes girl's pocketbook was gone."

I repeated what Bryan had said to me about Melissa always taking it with her.

"He told me that too."

"But you don't believe him?"

Marks shrugged. "It's possible."

"What did her roommate say?"

"She said she didn't know about any theft."

"Did you check and see if one had been reported?"

"This isn't Weedsport," Marks replied, a defensive edge in his voice. "I'm responsible for hundreds of cases."

I took that as a no. "I'm sure you are."

"Damn straight." Mollified, Marks settled back down and took a sip of his coffee. "At the time, I didn't know she was going to fall off the face of the earth."

I thought back to the conversation I'd had with Calli that morning at breakfast as I put some ketchup on my fries.

"Sorry, but I didn't find out much," Calli had said after she'd ordered an egg-white omelet and dry wheat toast from the waitress at Denny's. "I spoke to the guy who worked on the Melissa Hayes thing. He told me everything he knows is in here." She'd pushed the manila envelope next to her coffee cup across the table.

I couldn't help noticing that she'd gotten fake nails, which was in line with the other changes she'd been making. Since coming back to Syracuse, Calli had lost twenty-five pounds, cut her hair, changed her makeup, and gotten contact lenses.

As I opened the envelope I thought that every time I saw Calli she looked younger. I took the articles out and quickly scanned them.

"You're right," I'd said. "There isn't much here."

"Evidently there wasn't much to write about."

There were three articles. For all practical purposes, they said the same thing. Melissa Hayes disappeared on blah, blah, blah. If you have any information, please contact the police at blah, blah, blah. "I'm surprised more of a fuss wasn't made."

Calli had taken a sip of coffee. "I put it down to compassion fatigue."

"Compassion fatigue?" I'd said.

"Yeah. What is it? Four or five kids have vanished over the past two years. No one wants to read about it anymore. It's too depressing."

"Great."

"That's just the way it is," Calli had said before asking me whether or not I thought she should get a cat.

I'd read the articles again before my lunch with Marks, hoping I'd missed something the first time around, but unfortunately I hadn't.

Now I was hoping I'd get more information from Marks. I leaned forward slightly and listened intently as he continued talking.

"Since she disappeared right before Thanksgiving, at first

I figured she'd decided to take an early holiday. Maybe she decided to skip out on her finals. Maybe she'd met someone.''

"She had a boyfriend.''

Marks looked amused at my naivete. "So?''

"Right.'' Dumb comment. I ate a few french fries. "Were any charges logged on her credit cards?'' I asked after I'd eaten a few.

"No, but Melissa took three hundred dollars out of her bank account the day before she left. And yes,'' Marks said, anticipating my next question, "the teller remembers her doing it.''

Another thing Bryan hadn't mentioned. I wondered if he knew, but then I realized he had to have. The police would have told him. "Three hundred dollars isn't a lot these days.''

"True,'' Marks conceded. "But it's enough to take you out of here if that's what you want. She could be in New York City. In Florida. Who the hell knows?''

"Did you check the bus terminal?''

"And the train depot and the airport and the cab companies. Nothing.''

I ate a few more fries. They were crisp and salty and had their skins on, and I could have just eaten a plateful of them and been happy. "What about the sugar glider?''

"The sugar what?''

"The pet she just bought. She'd gone to a certain amount of trouble to get it, and then she abandons it at the dorm. Her brother said she'd never do that. That she always took it everywhere she went.''

Marks shrugged. "Bryan told me that too, but, hey, maybe she got tired of it. Look at all the dogs running around Westcott at the end of every semester. Kids get them and then let them go because their parents won't let them take them home and then we get the calls from the neighbors complaining about them tipping over the garbage cans.'' When I didn't say anything, Marks leaned forward slightly. ''Listen, we followed procedure. We went through her phone book. We talked to the people we were supposed to talk to and checked the places we were supposed to check. We didn't come up with anything. Not even a hint of anything.''

''So Melissa just disappeared? One moment she's in the dorm, the next minute she's gone. Her mother is dying and she decides to do what? Go on a vacation somewhere?''

''It's happened before.'' Marks took another bite of his sandwich. ''I told Bryan and his mother to just sit tight and wait, that she'd probably show up.''

''You don't seem very concerned about this.''

''I am concerned.'' Marks put his sandwich down and wiped his hands on a new napkin. ''But college kids disappear all the time.''

''Maybe for a weekend, maybe even for a week or two, but not for four months.''

Marks pushed his plate away and sat back. ''Look, you wanted me to tell you what I know. I'm telling you.''

''It's not much.''

''Listen, I've done everything I could do,'' Marks said.

I took a sip of my soda and lit a cigarette. At least no one would tell me not to smoke here.

Marks looked at my Camel wistfully. ''That's another thing my wife made me give up.''

I moved the pack toward him. ''You want one?''

''No . . . I . . .'' But his hand was already in motion. ''Oh, what the hell. One can't hurt, right?''

''Right.'' I gave him my lighter.

"My wife's gonna skin me alive," he said as he lit up and drew the smoke deep into his lungs. "But it's worth it."

"Definitely." We sat in silence for a moment, linked by the pleasure, surrounded by a haze of smoke. "Do you have any suggestions, any place you think I should start?"

Marks tapped his ash into his coffee cup. "One of her friends said she was depressed. Her roommate, a girl called Jill Evans, died last year. End of the year. Right before finals. It was in the papers."

I put down my cigarette and sprinkled more salt on my potatoes. "What happened?" I had a vague recollection of what Marks was talking about, nothing more.

Marks shook his head, his expression that of a man who had seen the world and found it wanting. "She fell out of a window and cracked her head open."

I raised an eyebrow. "Fell?"

"She was drinking too much. It happens." Marks shook his head again. "Must be a hell of a thing for her family. Send your kid off to college, pay all that money, and she comes home in a box. She and Melissa were real tight. According to her roomie, Melissa never got over the death." He took a puff of his cigarette and flicked the ash into his water glass. "Some of the guys said those two had something going. You know," he went on when I didn't say anything. "Some kind of lesbo thing."

"Jill and Melissa or Melissa and her roommate."

"Jill and Melissa."

"Why would they say that?"

"Just a feeling."

"There had to be a reason for the feeling."

Marks gave me a blank look. "Maybe they were jealous. You know, they couldn't get into their pants." He began tapping his fingers on the pitted Formica tabletop. Then he looked at his watch. I glanced at the clock on the wall. We'd been there for almost thirty minutes. My time was up.

"Is there anything else you can tell me, anything at all?"

Marks stubbed his cigarette out on his plate and reached for his jacket. "You want my opinion?"

"Yes."

"Don't knock your brains out on this one."

"Why not?"

Marks stood up. "I've worked cases like this before. Either these people show up on their own or someone finds them five years from now when they start building their house."

He turned and walked out the door. I got the bill.

Not bad, I thought when I looked at it. At least he and Calli were cheap dates.

Chapter
7

It was now a little after two in the afternoon. I'd told Tim I'd come right back to the store after my meeting with Marks, but I'd driven over to Schaefer, the dorm where Melissa had been living when she disappeared, instead. Talking to Marks had heightened my desire to see the place from which Melissa had vanished. I hoped it would help me put what I had been told and what I was going to be told into context.

I'd passed Schaefer a fair number of times on my way to this or that place over the years, but I'd never paid close attention to the building. I'd never had any reason to. Now I did. The dorm was perched up above the campus, across the street from Tyler Park. The building was a nondescript three-story, modern rectangular structure, commonplace to the point of invisiblity. You could walk by it a hundred times and not be able to recall its details if asked. In the fall, when Melissa had disappeared, the lawn surrounding it would have been littered with Frisbee-tossing students. Now the space was empty, the remaining couple of inches of snow cross-hatched by footprints.

I found a parking place about twenty feet down from the entrance, maneuvered the cab in, lit a cigarette, and sat and thought. Had Melissa walked out of the dorm, down the two steps that led to the walkway, and then into the park? Tyler was fairly safe in the daytime, but maybe she was unlucky and met up with someone who wasn't very nice. Or had she gotten into someone's car and driven off? I tapped the ash from my cigarette out the window. Then there was the question, what was she doing outside anyway?

According to Bryan, he'd met his sister for lunch, then dropped her off at the entrance to Schaefer at two in the afternoon. She was going to do some work, then he was going to pick her up at four and they were going to go to the hospital to visit their mother, only Melissa wasn't in her room when he got there, though the door was ajar. Her books were lying open on her desk. A pen and notebook were nearby, one page half filled with notes on the psych text she'd been reading.

Bryan said it looked as if she'd just gone down the hall to get something, so Bryan had sat down and waited. Only Melissa hadn't returned. Around four-thirty Bryan had gotten restless and started walking around the floor, banging on doors. Everyone who answered had either been napping or studying. No one had seen his sister or heard anything unusual. Her roommate had come back from a late class around five, as had Melissa's suitemates. They hadn't seen her either. The bottom line was that somewhere between two and four on a sunny September afternoon Melissa Hayes had vanished into thin air.

That everything was just as she left it; that no one had

seen or heard anything suggested what? That Melissa had run out for a second to give or get something from someone she knew and that that someone had forced her into a car and driven away? No. Forcing her into the car would have created a scene. Somebody would have noticed that. Melissa had gone willingly with whomever she had met, expecting to be back in a minute or so at most, but that wasn't what happened. She'd left with a friend or an acquaintance and hadn't returned. I stubbed out my cigarette, tossed the butt out the window, and grabbed my backpack. It was time to go inside.

Except for two girls and a boy chatting by the soda machine, the lobby was deserted. The security guards that the university spokesman had announced they were posting in every dorm the week after Melissa Hayes disappeared weren't there. Maybe they were on a coffee break. I took another step inside and looked around. The place reminded me of the dorm I'd lived in when I'd gone to college. Large windows looking out on the park. Cream-colored walls with scuff-marked baseboards. Metal-framed blue and tan Naugahyde chairs and sofas grouped in strategic locales. Three vending machines. A large bulletin board by the entrance full of notices for dorm meetings, campus events, and people seeking rides. Someone had written 'Remember, quiet time means quiet' on a piece of pink paper in red Magic Marker and tacked it on the wall facing the stairwell. Someone else had written 'Get a life' under it. A third person had scrawled 'Get drunk' under that.

The two girls and boy fell silent when I approached them.

"I've been hired by Bryan Hayes to help find his sister, Melissa," I explained. "I'd like to ask you a few questions."

The boy scowled. "Listen," he told me. "We've been

through this already. We didn't know her. We told the police, we told the campus cops, and now I'm telling you.''

''So you're not going to help me?''

''We can't help you.'' The boy sounded annoyed.

''Can you at least tell me who her friends were?''

He put his hands on his hips. ''How can I tell you who her friends were if I didn't know her?''

It struck me that none of them sounded particularly upset, and I told them so.

''Of course we're upset,'' the girl who was wearing tortoiseshell-framed glasses said. ''But Melissa disappeared four months ago.'' She made the four months sound like four centuries. I guess when you're raised on sound bites, your time sense gets messed up.

After a few more tries along those lines I gave up and started toward the stairs. Hopefully, I'd find someone who was a little chattier on Melissa's floor, but not many students were around, and the ones who were didn't have much to say. According to them, Melissa was a girl who kept to herself. Well, maybe she was or maybe they didn't want to talk to me. I couldn't decide which, but I handed out my cards in case anyone remembered anything later on.

The room Melissa had lived in, Room 203, was down the corridor and to the left. My eyes caught the names on the door as I stopped in front of it. Beth Wright and Stephanie Glass. It looked as if the university didn't expect Melissa to come back either. From where I was standing I could see white curtains, a row of teddy bears sitting on the heat register, a desk, a chair full of clothes, and two made-up beds. A boy with a military haircut was lying on his side on the one closest to the window, reading.

''I'm looking for Beth Wright,'' I said after I knocked.

The boy sat up and swung his legs over the bed. "She's not here."

"So I see." I smelled pizza and some sort of floral perfume as I took a step inside the room. I could tell from the way the kid looked at me, he didn't like me in there. "Maybe you can help me," I asked before he could say anything.

"Possibly." He studied me, his expression guarded, waiting to see what was coming next.

"Did you know Melissa Hayes?"

"Why do you want to know?"

"Her brother hired me to find her. I'd like to ask you a few questions if I may."

The boy put a bookmark in his book, closed it, and stood up. Despite the T-shirt, jeans, and two pierced ears, his bearing was military. "It's a little late for that, isn't it?"

"I hope not."

"You really think you can locate her?"

"If I didn't, I wouldn't have taken the job." I pointed to the sugar glider's cage. "I'm surprised that he's still here."

The boy's face softened slightly. "Well, Melissa's brother didn't want him, and since her mother is sick, Beth didn't know what else to do."

"And her new roommate doesn't care?"

"No, ma'am. She likes him."

I went over to the sugar glider's cage and peered in. The little animal was curled up in its sleeping box. All I saw was a tiny ball of silvery gray fur.

"He's noctural," the boy explained.

"I know." I straightened up. "Do you mind my asking who you are?"

"No, ma'am." He came to attention. "I'm Chris Furst, a friend of Beth's." A soldier on the parade ground. The only thing missing was the salute.

"Are you a student here?"

"Yes, ma'am."

Getting this kid to talk was definitely going to be a trick and a half. "Did you know Melissa?"

He nodded.

"Did you know her well?"

The sound of rap music from down the hall seeped into the room while Chris thought. He obviously wasn't someone given to unconsidered statements. "As well as anyone, I expect," he finally said. "She pretty much kept to herself."

"I've gathered as much. What do you think happened to her?"

"At first I thought she just took some extra vacation time, but obviously that didn't turn out to be the case."

"Was anything bothering her?"

Chris ran a hand over the top of his brush cut. "Such as what?"

"I don't know, that's why I'm asking you." When Chris didn't answer, I added, "I'm never going to find her if I don't get some help."

"It probably doesn't matter much now anyway."

"Does that mean you think she's dead?"

"Maybe she just doesn't want to be found."

"Why do you think that?"

"I don't know."

"Are you sure?" I caught his gaze and held it. After moment he looked away.

What he said next, he said begrudgingly, measuring out each word. "She was upset."

I waited. A phone began ringing. After eight rings it stopped and another one started.

"Beth told me she used to cry in her sleep a lot. Beth told her she should go talk to a counselor at the health center. She kept saying she would, but I don't think she ever did."

"Do you have any idea why she was crying?"

Chris looked embarrassed. "Well, her mother is . . . you know." Death as the unmentionable.

I nodded to show I did. "But is there anything specific that happened? Anything traumatic?"

"Not that I know about."

I pointed to the bed I was standing near. "Is this where Melissa slept?"

"Yes." Irrelevant observation. Chris had long eyelashes. "Her brother came and got all of her things. Except for this." He walked over to the far desk, grabbed a book, and handed it to me.

I read the title. *Moral Responsibility: Why We Are Our Brother's Keeper.*

"Beth keeps on meaning to give it to Bryan. Will you?"

"Sure." I casually thumbed through it.

"It was one of her philosophy texts."

On the front page someone had written:

> We are our sister's keepers
> Keepers of ourselves.
> Keepers of the flame
> Fanning the embers of tenderness.

I showed the poem to Chris. "Is that Melissa's hand-writing?"

"I guess so. I'm not really sure."

"Did Melissa write poetry?"

"She never showed any to me if she did."

The book's pages came together with a dull thud when I closed them. Writing bad poetry was the prerogative of college students. I'd done my share when I'd gone to school. For a few seconds I wondered if Chris wrote any too, but then I got back to the matter at hand. "I take it you know Bryan Hayes?"

"I've seen him around."

"What's your opinion of him?"

Chris looked straight ahead. "I don't have one, ma'am." He was back in parade-ground mode, obviously his refuge against questions he didn't want to answer.

"Why is that?"

"We haven't spent much time together."

"You don't like him, do you?"

"I don't know him."

"But you must have formed an opinion."

"No, ma'am."

He obviously had, but I let the lie go by. "Did you hear Bryan tried to beat up Melissa's boyfriend?"

Chris nodded.

"Do you know what happened?"

"I heard he charged into the frat house with a bat, but the guys got him before he could do any damage."

"Do you know why he attacked him?"

Chris blinked. Lots of women I knew would kill for lashes like that. "He blames him for his sister's disappearance."

"But you don't, right?" I asked, interpreting the look on his face.

"That's right, ma'am, I don't," replied Chris. He was looking at everything in the room except me.

I stifled a sigh. Talking to this kid was like walking in

molasses. Slow and irritating. I wondered if he was trying to hide something, or was he just naturally cautious. "How about calling me Robin?" I suggested, trying to lighten the conversation.

"Yes, ma'am." He laughed and apologized.

"You know, when I went to college, all the guys I knew wanted to stay out of the army."

"That's what my dad says."

"How long have you been in ROTC?"

Chris looked genuinely surprised. "How'd you know?"

"Innate genius."

"This is my third year," he told me as I studied the view from the window. You could see the park. The trees and grass were covered with a thin dusting of white powder.

"Pretty, isn't it?" I observed.

"Very." The line of his mouth softened.

"Do you ski?"

"I used to. I don't have the time anymore." His tone was wistful.

"Did Melissa?"

"No. She just jogged."

"I understand she was upset about her roommate's death."

"Jill's?"

I nodded.

Chris pulled his shoulders back ever so slightly. "We all took that pretty hard, ma'am."

"I bet." At least he was willing to talk about her. Interesting. I thought about what Marks had said during lunch. "Did they have a special connection?"

Chris blinked. "As in how?"

"I heard they might be lovers."

"Forget it. That's the stupidest thing I've heard. Who told you that?' ''

I waved my hand in the air. "It doesn't matter." I changed the subject. "Who were Melissa's friends?"

Chris answered that question immediately. "After Jill died, Beth was about it. Except that once in a while she'd hang out with Holland and Brandy. Her suitemates," he explained.

I wrote down their names.

"And then, of course, there's Tommy."

"You sound as if you know him."

"I do."

"What kind of person is he?"

Chris shrugged. "A regular guy."

"Meaning?"

"You know." He hesitated while searching for the right word. "Normal."

Well, you couldn't get more specific than that. "As opposed to Bryan?"

"I didn't say that," Chris objected.

"That's true. I did." I walked over to the heat register and absentmindedly picked up a teddy bear. It had the dilapidated look of a much-loved stuffed animal. "Whose are these?" I asked.

Chris smiled and folded his arms over his chest. "Beth's. She collects them." He pointed to the three in the corner. "I gave her those."

"Nice." I put down the bear I was holding. "Maybe you can tell me something?" Chris cocked his head, waiting for my question. "I hear that Tommy and Melissa fought all the time, that she was going to leave him, and that he wasn't real happy about that."

Chris laughed derisively. "I don't know where you're getting your information from, but it's not true.'' It was the first time I'd heard real emotion in his voice. He was about to add something else, when there was a knock on the door. A moment later a guy stuck his head in.

''Can I speak to you?'' he asked Chris.

Chris excused himself and stepped out into the hall.

I went back to looking out the window, imagining myself watching Melissa leave the dorm four months ago, willing myself to see what had happened to her, but the only thing I saw was a man dressed in a bright red and blue jogging suit, yellow lab in tow, laboring up the path that twisted through Tyler. Two spots of color in a black and white photo. Which wasn't much help. So much for visualization. When the jogger rounded the bend, I turned and headed toward the sugar glider's cage, thinking I'd get another glimpse of him. Maybe we should carry them in the store after all. On the way, I walked past a desk piled high with books. A piece of paper lay on top. I glanced at it.

"Chris," I read. *"Went to library. Usual spot. Meet me there when you're hungry. Love, Beth."*

''I wouldn't have let you in if I'd have known you'd go snooping around Beth's things.''

I jerked my head up. Chris was standing in the doorway, watching me. His arms were crossed over his chest. His eyes were narrowed.

''Too bad.'' I grabbed his jacket off the chair and threw it at him. ''Now, let's go.''

Chapter
8

It took me twenty minutes to find a parking space near the library—even the illegal spaces were taken—and in the end I capitulated and did the unspeakable, parked in a lot. The building made me wish for the one it had replaced. Even if the old one hadn't been efficient, the wood, the stained glass, the slight musty smell of old paper, had made me feel as if I were home. Walking inside here made me feel as if I were entering the corporate world, but then, that was what universities were these days—big business.

We got in the elevator and Chris pressed the button for the third floor. When we got off, he led me through the maze of cubicles to where Beth Wright was sitting.

"That's her," he said as we approached, pointing to the left and indicating the girl with short blond hair sitting at a table piled high with books.

Beth Wright was fine-featured, small-boned, and very pretty in a classic, understated way. Her only flaw, a nose that was ever so slightly pushed over to one side, served to underline the regularity of her other features. The color on her cheeks rose, making her even prettier, when she saw Chris coming toward her. They held hands as he explained why I wanted to speak to her. She leaned against him as he talked, and when he left, her eyes followed his progress out the door.

Watching them brought on an attack of nostalgia. I don't think I will ever have that intensity of feeling for someone again. Then, while I was wondering if I wanted to, Beth rose and beckoned for me to follow her. She was even shorter and smaller than she appeared sitting down. She must have been five two and ninety-eight pounds at the most.

She stopped in the hallway and turned and faced me. Her expression was worried. She began fingering the cardigan she was wearing. "I've already spoken to the police," she said. "I don't think there's anything I can tell you that I haven't told them."

"Sometimes if you retell something you remember a small detail or two you might have forgotten before, something that's more important than you realize," I told her, hoping that that would indeed be the case.

She frowned. "There are no details. That's the problem. I have nothing to tell anyone."

"Don't be too sure."

"But I am." Her voice rose slightly. "I'm sorry you had to waste your time coming, but I really have nothing to say."

"That's what Chris said."

"He's right."

She reminds me of a sparrow, I thought as I told her to let me be the judge of what was important and what wasn't. "Unless, of course, you don't want to help," I added.

"Oh, I do, I do," Beth cried. "It's not that." She fingered

one of her buttons. "I just hate talking about it, that's all. It's so upsetting, thinking that someone can just disappear." Her eyes misted over. "And I feel guilty. I mean, I thought she'd be back. I thought she just needed to get away from things for a while."

Watching her, I understood why Chris hadn't wanted to bring me here. He wasn't hiding anything. He'd known this conversation was going to upset her. He'd been trying to protect her.

Beth straightened her shoulders and tried for a smile. "I'm such a dunce, I don't know how Chris puts up with me."

"I don't think he minds."

"I know." She grinned. "Isn't he great?"

I agreed that he was, and guided the conversation back to Melissa. This time Beth was willing to answer my questions. I asked her to start by telling me what had happened that day. Once Beth began talking, she kept on going. Despite what she said, it was obvious to me she was eager to share her thoughts.

"Well," she began, "Melissa left the room before I did because she had a nine o'clock and I had a ten o'clock class."

"What class?"

"Clinical psych. She said she was going to get some breakfast and she grabbed her backpack and walked out the door." The corners of Beth's mouth twitched and were still. "That was the last time I saw her."

"Did you return to the dorm at any point during the day?"

Beth shook her head. "I had classes all day. After I was done, I went to the library, then I hung out with some friends at the Rhino. I didn't get back to my room till after five. Bryan was waiting for me when I walked in. He was really upset.'' Beth nervously unbuttoned and then rebuttoned the bottom two buttons on her cardigan. ''He got even more upset when I told him I didn't know where Melissa was. After my suitemates came in and told him they hadn't seen her either, he flipped out and called the police. They told him to wait until the next day and see if she came back. He went nuts.'' Beth bit her lip.

''I tried to calm him down. I tried to tell him Missy was just off doing whatever, but he wouldn't listen. He kept on pacing back and forth like a lunatic. It was making me crazy. Finally I suggested we go look for her. I figured it would give Bryan something to do. Give him an avenue to express his emotions.''

I looked at her quizzically.

She laughed ruefully. ''I guess I've been taking too many psych courses. Anyway, we went all over the dorm that night. We called everyone we could think of. We even walked through Tyler Park. The only people we found were a man walking his dog and a group of high school kids drinking beer.'' She tucked a stray lock of hair behind her ear. ''I was sure Missy would turn up. But it looks as if Bryan was right after all.''

''What made you so certain?''

''Because there was no reason she shouldn't.''

I leaned against the wall. ''Had she done this type of thing before, gone off without telling anyone?''

''No, but she was under a lot of pressure. I thought maybe she just needed a little time to think.''

''You're talking about her mother, right?''

''Yeah. That and—'' Beth put her hand to her mouth.

''And what?'' I prompted her, my pulse quickening the way a hunter's does when he spots his prey.

Beth looked away. The two spots of color were back on her cheekbones. "I don't know if I sh-should tell you," she stammered.

"Is it that bad?"

"No," Beth said indignantly.

"Then why not tell me?"

"She didn't want anyone to know."

"Given the circumstances, don't you think the time for confidences is past?"

"I suppose you're right." Beth let out the breath she'd been holding. She drew herself up. "She and Tommy were planning on getting married."

I thought about Bryan's reaction in the Yellow Rhino when he'd spotted Tommy and raised an eyebrow. "I can see why she'd want to keep it a secret."

Beth nodded.

"Who else knew about this?"

"No one as far as I know. I don't think she would have even have told me if I hadn't been in the room when she came in. She was so excited, she just couldn't stop herself from talking." Beth fingered the bottom of her cardigan. "I just figured maybe she'd had second thoughts and had gone away to think things through."

"I could see why you didn't want to say anything to Bryan."

"He was bad enough as it was. I didn't want to make anything worse. I didn't want to cause trouble for Tommy. Poor guy."

"Poor guy?"

"He's just one of those people who always has things happening to them. If it isn't one thing, it's another."

I could relate. "So," I said, going back to what we were

talking about, "you didn't tell the police because you were afraid they would tell Bryan."

Beth looked as if she wanted to cry. "I thought she'd be back."

"I would have thought so too." I patted her shoulder.

She gave me a timorous smile and turned slightly to let a crowd of students go by her.

"I puzzled about something though."

"What?" she asked.

"Bryan told me she and Tommy fought all the time. That she was getting ready to leave him, but he didn't want her to go."

"I think that was just wishful thinking on Bryan's part."

"So they didn't fight?"

"No. They were always going at it." More students were coming in now. "They argued a lot, but Melissa enjoyed it. She liked dramatic relationships. Big fights. Reconcilations. One moment they were screaming on the phone at each other, the next they were cooing. Sometimes when they fought she'd scratch Tommy. She though it proved how much she loved him." Beth's expression left no doubt what she thought about such behavior.

I clicked my tongue against the roof of my mouth. Beth's statement certainly didn't square with Bryan's description of his sister or with the picture I'd formed of Melissa by looking at her room. "And what did Tommy do?"

"Nothing. He never lifted a finger to her. Personally, I think that kind of thing gets real old, real fast, but, hey, that's just me." Beth fingered the buttons on her sweater again. It was beige and blended in with her white T-shirt and navy pants. "I always thought her relationship with Tommy kept her from thinking about other things."

"How do you mean?"

"All that drama takes your mind off things."

"And Melissa had a lot on her mind."

"Well, her best friend had died and her mother was in the hospital, dying. What do you think?"

"I think that's a lot for anyone to deal with."

Beth readjusted the collar of her sweater. "She was doing okay. At least I thought she was. But with her it was hard to tell sometimes."

"I thought she talked to you."

"She talked to me as much as she talked to anyone—which isn't saying a whole lot." Beth put her finger to her lips. "Maybe you should go speak to Professor Fell."

"Who's he?"

"Melissa's psych professor. She really liked him. If she confided in anyone, it would have been him."

Chapter
9

I got Fell's extension from the university operator and called him on my cell phone when I got to my cab, but he
wasn't in his office, so I left a message on his machine and
drove back over to Schaefer. Maybe Missy's suitemates were
in their rooms. As I maneuvered around the groups of students that insisted on stopping to talk in the middle of the
street, I lit a cigarette and thought about what I'd learned
so far. Four salient facts had emerged. Melissa was planning
on eloping. Her brother hated her boyfriend. Her best
friend had recently taken a header out the window and her
mother lay dying in the hospital.

I'd say the girl's stress level was over a thousand. Given
the circumstances, I could certainly see Missy taking that
three hundred dollars and leaving town for a while. But
Marks had said they'd checked the airport, and the bus and
train stations, without turning up anything. Of course Missy
could always have decided to hitch a ride and been unlucky

enough to have been picked up by the wrong person. If that was true, what I was doing was pointless, but that was a thought I couldn't entertain. At least, not yet.

I sighed and flicked my cigarette out the window as I pulled up in front of Schaefer. When I was younger I thought that hope was the most important thing to have. Now I'm beginning to think that closure is. I parked in front of a fire hydrant and ran upstairs, but I could have saved myself the trouble, because Holland Adams and Brandy Weinstein still weren't in. I wrote a note on the back of one of my business cards telling them I'd be back, wedged it in the crack above the door lock, and drove to the store. The first thing I saw when I stepped inside was George.

He was leaning against the counter. His weight was on his right foot, while his left one was going up and down so fast, I wouldn't have been surprised if it wore a hole in the floor. I could feel the tension radiating from him from across the room. Less than twenty-four hours with Raymond, and he was wound as tight as the string on a top.

"Having a bad day?" I asked as I closed the door.

"Bad day doesn't begin to describe it," George replied. He rubbed his forehead with his hand. "This whole day has been a total waste. I haven't gotten one thing done. Not one." His tone was incredulous. For a control freak, this was truly a fate worse than death.

I glanced past George to Tim, who was standing a little ways off, out of George's line of sight. He looked relieved I was there. George had probably been regaling Tim with tales of Raymond's wrongdoings while he was waiting for me to return.

"I'm going to start writing out the signs for tomorrow's sale," Tim told me, making his escape into the back room as quickly as possible.

Obviously, he didn't want to hear the story that was coming again. Something told me I didn't want to either.

"Aren't you going to ask me why?" George demanded before I could think of a way to get out of it.

"Of course." I bent down to pet Zsa Zsa. Not that it would have mattered if I hadn't. George was so fired up, he'd be talking even if we were in the middle of a hurricane. I automatically pulled a small mat of hair off Zsa Zsa's front leg. She whined and licked my hand.

"Just getting Raymond ready to go to school this morning took me two hours." George's voice rose in righteous wrath. "We were screaming at each other in the driveway. I finally had to pick him up and throw him in the car. I can't imagine what my neighbors thought. I wouldn't have blamed them if one of them had called it in."

"If they have kids, they understand," I assured him after I straightened up.

"None of their kids act like Raymond. I can tell you that. Then," George continued, unwilling even to entertain the notion of the meager solace I was offering him, "just as I'm finally settling down in front of my computer and beginning to work on my paper—I've got my coffee to one side of me, my notes to the other"—he moved his hand to show me where everything had been—"and I'm calmed down from the morning—the nurse at Wellington High calls to tell me Raymond is sick and I should come and pick him up. Naturally I race down there. He's clutching his side. I think he has appendicitis."

I took off my jacket and threw it behind the counter. "Let me guess. Nothing was wrong with him."

"I should have had you go get him," George replied, the bitterness in his voice unmistakable. "On the way to the doctor's he miraculously starts feeling better."

"What did you do?"

George's scowl could have peeled the paint off the wall. "What do you think I did? I took him back and marched him right into the principal's office." George chewed on the inside of his cheek. "Now he has Saturday school."

Zsa Zsa stood up on her hind legs and clawed at my legs to get my attention. I rubbed her chest before replying. "Naturally, he thanked you for your kindness and attention."

George slammed the counter with the palm of his hand. Zsa Zsa, startled by the noise, ran off. "That kid has to learn, and he's going to—one way or another—that, I can promise."

"Learn what?"

"Why?" George demanded, glaring at me. "What would you have done?"

"Probably given him a break, taken him out to Friendly's, bought him a sundae."

George stared at me as if I'd lost my mind. "As a reward for cutting school? Maybe when he fails out, I'll buy him a mountain bike."

I ignored the sarcasm. "No. As a way to get to know him." I knew I sounded self-righteous and smarmy, but I couldn't help myself. The words came out anyway.

"I think you're dead wrong."

I shrugged. No surprise there. "Fine."

"That's the kind of muzzy-headed . . ."

"Liberal?" I supplied as I watched Tim come back out and start rooting around under the other side of counter for something.

"Yes," George said, taking up where he'd left off. "Muzzy-headed liberal thinking I would have to put up with when I—"

"Ladies. Gentlemen," Tim interrupted, straightening up. He was holding a packet of Magic Markers. "Enough."

I brushed my hair out of my eyes. "Okay with me."

"Me too," George said even though I could tell he was itching to continue the conversation.

"One last thing," I couldn't resist adding. I was beginning to understand how children can make relationships worse, not better.

"That would be a miracle," George muttered.

I ignored the jibe. "I think you should get Raymond a pet, something he can take care of, something that will help—"

"I wouldn't even get him a goldfish right now," George snapped. "I wouldn't get him a cricket. That kid wants something, he's going to have to earn it. You know," George added, "contrary to what you believe, animals are not the solution for every problem."

"I never said they were."

We spent the next half hour arguing.

"Maybe things will calm down in a week or so," Tim commented after George had left. He was making dinner for Raymond courtesy of Taco Bell.

"Actually," I said as I glanced through the day's mail, "I think they're going to get worse."

Tim made a popping sound with his mouth. "Why is that?"

"Because Raymond really wants to go home. I think he figures if he acts bad enough, George will put him back on the bus."

"Will he?"

"*I* probably would, but George is such a stubborn—"

"Determined."

"Same thing."

Tim absentmindedly twirled the diamond stud in his ear. "I'm glad the kid isn't my problem."

"I wish he weren't mine."

"He's not."

What Tim said was true. Up to a point. George and I weren't married—his family was his problem, not mine—but his problem was beginning to spill over into our relationship, which made it my problem too.

"Keep out of it," Tim advised.

"I'm going to try." I went into the back room to feed Zsa Zsa. Unfortunately, I didn't see how I was going to be able to.

I was trying out a sample of a brand of low-cal dog food I'd just gotten in, but I guess it wasn't very appetizing, because Zsa Zsa took one sniff, growled, and walked away. I was telling her she couldn't live on beer, pretzels, and Big Macs, when the phone rang. It was Mary Margaret Hayes, Bryan's mother. Her voice was low and I had to strain to hear. Her son had just told her he'd hired me, she said. That being the case, could I come over to Crouse tonight and talk?

I lied and told her I'd be happy to, even though I was tired and had been looking forward to going home after work, watching TV, taking a bath, and going to sleep. I spent the rest of the afternoon and early evening cleaning out the bird room, arguing with a sales rep about why I wasn't going to carry an all-natural kibble that retailed for thirty dollars a twenty-pound bag, recapturing two skinks that had escaped from their aquarium, and explaining to a man why a ten-foot ball python was not a good snake to start out with. By seven-thirty I'd managed to finish most of what I had to do, so I packed it in and Zsa Zsa and I headed for the hospital.

"Leaving?" Tim asked, looking up from the book he was reading as I got my backpack from behind the counter.

"Yes."

Tim grunted and turned a page.

"Is it good?"

"Very," he replied, not bothering to look up.

As I headed toward the door, it occurred to me I didn't read anything but the newspaper anymore and that it was an activity I sorely missed. Then I realized that somewhere along the way I wasn't doing a lot of things I enjoyed anymore and that maybe it was time I got back to them.

Now, if I could just remember what they were.

Chapter
10

Three Catholic lay sisters came out of Mary Margaret Hayes's room as I entered. The woman I took to be her was propped up in the hospital bed closest to the window, watching TV, when I walked in. She was alone in the room, a shrunken, skeletal figure of a woman who could have been anywhere between fifty and seventy, having been stripped clean of whatever individuality she'd possessed by the cancer that was eating her alive.

She was clutching a large crucifix with both hands. The skin on them looked thin as tissue and was covered with large bruises caused by the various needles and injections to which she'd been subjected. Her grayish-blond hair was sparse. Pink patches of scalp shone through. But I could see Bryan's and Melissa's features stamped in her profile, from the slight tilt of their noses to the determined jut of their chins. I was about to knock on the door and ask if I could come in, when Mrs. Hayes turned her head and saw me.

She frowned. "Who are you?" she demanded in a suspicious voice.

"Robin Light." As I took another step in, I noticed the statue of Jesus standing on the night table next to her. This woman definitely had all of her bases covered, I recall thinking. "Remember you called and asked me to come over."

"Of course I remember. Because I'm dying doesn't mean I'm an idiot," she rapped out in a voice as sharp as vinegar. She pointed to a chair. "Sit down. Bryan's already left for the night. Robin Light." She repeated my name, turning it over in her mouth while she scrutinized me. "What kind of a name is that?"

Something made me say "What do you mean?" even though I knew exactly what Mrs. Hayes meant.

When I was younger, my grandmother had asked my friends that question whenever I brought a new one home. It had embarrassed me then. It seemed that along with sipping tea through a lump of sugar, that question had marked my grandmother as the immigrant she was. I'd jump in before my friend could reply, and make a joke out of the question. Eventually, though, she'd ask me again after my friend had left and I'd always answer, just as I was going to do now.

"And Bryan told me you were very smart." Mrs. Hayes sighed in exasperation. "Are you Catholic? Protestant?"

I was going to say Buddhist, but her look made me feel guilty and I told the truth. "No. I'm Jewish," I replied as I pulled the chair she'd pointed to next to her bedside and sat down. "Is that going to be a problem?"

She snorted. "Of course not. I've always liked the Jews.

It's those Pentacostals I can't stomach. Anyway, I'm not one to point the finger. I didn't come back to my faith till later in life. Are you religious?''

"Not really." Not at all, I would have answered if I were being strictly truthful. When was the last time I'd been to synagogue? I couldn't remember. Was it ten, fifteen years ago? There are lapsed Catholics. I wondered if there are lapsed Jews as well.

"Well, it's a good thing to have a spiritual life, an important thing." Mrs. Hayes gestured to the empty bed across the way, all made up and waiting for its next customer. "I've gone through five roommates now." She leaned forward and touched my wrist. Her touch was as light as dust.

"They come and go. The last one, poor dear, didn't have anyone to visit her. Her family had been killed in the camps and she could never bring herself to get involved with anyone else. They finally had to send her to a nursing home even though she didn't want to go. Luckily God's not going to let that happen to me. I wouldn't like that at all." Her eyes strayed to the TV and back to me. *Friends* was on. "I don't think they expected me to live as long as I have, but He's not going to take me to Him until I know what happened to my girl." She pointed with a trembling finger to the statue of Christ. "Jesus will see to that."

Well, it was nice to know He was on the case.

"My Bryan spoke to you, right? He told you what happened?''

I nodded.

"He's trying, and that's important. Could you?" She pointed toward the water pitcher on the nightstand. I poured her a cup and helped her drink. "I'm glad he's in school. It's a good thing. A good thing." A spasm of pain twisted her face. She closed her eyes and clutched her cross, her fingers grown white from the pressure of her grasp. When she released it a moment later, her upper lip was beaded with sweat.

I leaned over. "Can I get you something?"

The shake of her head was almost imperceptible. A moment later she opened her eyes and continued as if nothing had happened. "I need to know," she said, her voice a fierce whisper, willing me by force of her desire to understand. "I need to know whether Melissa is alive or dead. It's all right if she's passed on," she continued, dropping her voice even lower, "then we'll just meet on the other side." Suddenly I was surprised by a pang of jealousy. It must be wonderful to have that kind of faith, I thought while Mrs. Hayes paused for a few seconds to gather her strength before continuing. "I want this all straightened out before I go. I've never left anything a mess in my life, and I don't intend to start now."

I nodded again.

"Is that all you can do?" Mrs. Hayes snapped, glaring at me. "Shake your head up and down? You must have questions. Don't you have anything to ask me? Anything at all?"

"Of course I do." If Mrs. Hayes was like this when she was at death's door, I didn't even want to imagine what she was like when she'd been on her feet. Bryan and Melissa must have had a tough time of it growing up, I decided. I asked her if she had any ideas about what had happened to her daughter.

Mrs. Hayes studied the lights out the window for a minute before answering. "I'll tell you what I told the police. I don't know what happened to Melissa. The only thing I do know is that something was bothering her before she disappeared. We were close, Melissa and I." Mrs. Hayes turned back and looked at me. "I know you may find that hard to believe."

She brushed away my assurances that I didn't. "But I could feel something was bothering her."

"Did you ask her what it was?"

"Naturally. Several times. But she wouldn't say—I don't think she wanted to worry me—she said it wasn't a big deal, that I shouldn't worry, she'd take care of it herself. She liked doing that, you know—taking charge, fixing things—that's one of the reasons she and her brother were always fighting."

"Because she tried to fix him?"

Mrs. Hayes gave a sad little smile of remembrance. "He used to call her bossy, but he would have been a trial for Mary herself when he was little."

"So you don't have a hint of what was bothering your daughter?"

"I know whatever it was happened at school."

"How do you know that?"

"Because she'd changed when she came home after the end of her freshman year. She seemed . . . distracted . . . as if she were wondering what to do about something."

"She wasn't depressed?"

"Thoughtful might be a better word. She was very quiet, quieter than usual, but not in a sad type of way."

"Could the way she was acting have had anything to do with her roommate's death?"

"No, I don't think so. We talked about that." Mrs. Hayes swallowed. "This was something else."

Score one for Beth. "Her boyfriend?"

"My Bryan seems to think so."

"But you don't?"

"Melissa was a level-headed, sensible girl. She knew better than to put herself in a position where anything bad could happen to her. She was planning on going on and getting her Ph.D. in education. She really didn't have time for men.''

I made a noncommittal comment. I didn't have the heart to tell her that according to Beth, her daughter was anything but sensible when it came to men, that she'd been planning on getting married very soon. As I listened to Mrs. Hayes speak, I couldn't help wondering what else she didn't know.

She picked her next words carefully. ''Bryan feels very strongly about his sister. He's someone who feels things deeply, sometimes too deeply.'' Her voice trailed off.

I didn't say anything, preferring to sit quietly and listen to the comings and goings in the hospital corridor instead. Mrs. Hayes would come around to what she wanted to tell me in her own time.

''Bryan's offered to pay you, hasn't he?'' she asked suddenly. ''I told him to.''

''Yes.''

''Is it enough?'' Her tone was worried.

''It's fine,'' I assured her.

''Good.'' Her eyes focused on the TV again. ''If you need more, you be sure and tell me.''

I told her I would.

She licked her lips. They were cracked and red. ''I shouldn't have taken that second job,'' she informed me. ''I should have stayed at home.''

''From what I heard, you didn't have a choice.''

''I should have had more faith in the Lord.'' Mrs. Hayes's voice had dropped lower, and I was having trouble hearing her over the clatter of the cart being pushed down the hallway. She turned toward me and reached for my hands. ''I want you to promise me something.''

''If I can,'' I said cautiously, thinking Mrs. Hayes was going to ask me to promise I'd find out what happened to her daughter in the next week or so, which at the rate I was going looked like an impossibility; but that wasn't what she wanted at all.

Mrs. Hayes studied my face for a minute before going on. I began to grow uncomfortable under the intensity of her scrutiny. "Swear to me," she finally said, "that no matter what happens, you'll protect my son."

The window curtains were billowing back and forth, rising and falling in time with the air from the heat register. I watched them as I thought about the implications of what Mrs. Hayes had just said. I wanted to say the right thing, I wanted to say something tactful. Instead, I heard myself blurting out, "You think Bryan had something to do with his sister's disappearance, don't you?"

Mrs. Hayes scowled at me and withdrew her hands from mine. I'd been judged and found wanting. For a moment I was sure she was going to order me out of her room, but she clasped her crucifix instead. "That's a terrible, terrible thing to tell me," she replied, anger and sorrow warring in her voice.

"I'm sorry," I said, apologizing even though I knew with absolute conviction that I was right. I leaned forward slightly. "I don't understand."

"Precisely."

I waited for elucidation.

"I don't think that," Mrs. Hayes explained. She grabbed my hand again and rubbed its top with her fingers. "You believe me, don't you?"

I didn't, but I said I did. I wasn't going to tell a dying woman I thought she was lying to herself.

"I'm afraid the police might though," Mrs. Hayes went on. Her scowl was gone, replaced by a worried frown.

"Why would they do that?" I asked, curious to hear what

she was going to say. I'd heard Marks's comments. Now I wanted to hear hers.

She released my hand and once more touched the crucifix lying on her chest. She ran a finger absentmindedly along the edge of the cross before replying. "Because of all the trouble Bryan got in when he was younger. That's why I sent him away, you know," Mrs. Hayes continued when I didn't say anything. "I didn't want to, I just felt I had no other choice. I just couldn't stand the phone calls from school anymore or finding his friends lounging around on the sofa. Every time I opened a cabinet door I'd find beer bottles someone had hidden. And his behavior was beginning to affect Melissa. She didn't say anything, she never would, but I knew it really bothered her, even though she begged me not to send him away, to let him stay in the house." Mrs. Hayes stopped speaking and glanced out the window again into the darkness outside. "Things would have been different if his father had lived. Boys need their fathers." Mrs. Hayes turned her eyes to the television.

I watched with her and waited for her to start talking.

A moment later she took up her narrative. "I'm glad I sent him to that school. It was so hard, but it was the best thing I've ever done. God only knows what would have happened if I hadn't. But he's better now. Much better. And he and Melissa have become very close, but you know how the police are, dear." She favored me with a look. "They're paid to see the bad side of things, and they see so much of it that they don't believe people really do change."

"Change is difficult. People tend to backslide," I observed noncommittally, wondering if she'd tell me about Bryan's arrest. "Does your son still have a gun?" I asked when she didn't.

She sat up straighter. Her eyes blazed. Anger gave her energy. "Who told you that?" she demanded.

"A detective," I replied, feeling bad that I'd brought up the subject.

"It was his friend's gun. He was holding it for him. Did this detective tell you that?"

"No."

"That proves my point." Her voice was triumphant.

"The guy must have been a good friend of your son's."

Mrs. Hayes pursed her lips. "Bryan's problem is that he's too trusting. He'd be willing to give a stranger the shirt off his back. He's always been like that, ever since he was a baby."

"That can lead to problems."

"I know." She started to cough.

I gave her some water. After she was done drinking, she sank back in her pillow, her meager store of energy spent. "So you'll take care of things for me?" Mrs. Hayes said. Her skin was so pale, she seemed to blend in with the sheets.

I told her I'd do as much as I could.

Given the circumstances, what else could I say?

She smiled and nodded her head approvingly. "Good. I'm going to ask the sisters to light a candle for you." I thanked her, but there must have been something in the tone of my voice I didn't realize, because she said, "You don't believe in that sort of thing, do you, dear? You think it's silly."

"It's not that," I stammered.

"You should believe," she told me. "It helps a lot. I don't think I could go on if I didn't." Her eyelids fluttered, then closed. It was time for me to go.

I knew what Mrs. Hayes was saying was true. Believing does help a lot, and I envied people who were able to.

Unfortunately, I'd never been one of them. I guess that's why I didn't go to synagogue anymore.

I checked my watch as I walked out into the corridor. It was a little after eight-thirty. I could have gone home, but I decided to try to catch up with Melissa's suitemates and boyfriend instead. Maybe they could provide with me with a little more information.

Chapter
11

The frat Tommy West belonged to was housed in a big white faux-antebellum plantation job that would have looked at home on the *Gone With the Wind* set, but had actually been built by one of the city's rich merchants when the Erie Canal was in use and the cities along its banks thrived. But not anymore. Rome. Utica. Syracuse. All were on a long downward slide.

I stepped inside and shouted out a hello. It was easy to imagine a white-gloved butler gliding through the high-ceilinged hallway with its wainscoting and decorative molding to inform the lady of the house that I had arrived. A sweatpants-clad, pimple-faced kid showed up instead.

"I'll get Charmer Boy," he volunteered when I told him whom I wanted to speak to.

"Charmer Boy?"

"You know. Snakes." He took off, leaving me standing there, studying the parquet floor, which was cluttered with sneakers, sporting equipment, and boots, and inhaling the orders of take-out Chinese food and pizza.

Someone was playing rap music in one of the rooms upstairs, and I amused myself by trying to make out the lyrics over the force of the bass. Six guys were sprawled out in the living room, watching a movie. I nodded to them and they nodded back indifferently. A minute later Tommy West appeared from a door to the left. He was tucking his denim shirt into his jeans with one hand. In the other he was holding a glass of milk and a couple of Oreo cookies. Of medium height, he had tousled curly dirty-blond hair, a squarish face, pale blue eyes, a small nose and mouth, and a chin that receded slightly.

He frowned when he saw me. "Do I know you?" he asked, approaching me warily.

"I doubt it." I held out the business card that says inquiries conducted.

He put the milk and cookies on the table along the wall and took the card. "I don't understand," he said after he read it, though his expression said he did.

"I'm trying to find Melissa Hayes. I've heard you were her boyfriend."

"Yes."

"That's why I'd like to talk to you."

He wet his lips with his tongue. "I've already spoken to the police. And campus security. A couple of times."

"I was hoping you'd speak to me as well."

Tommy scratched his ear indecisively. "She's been gone for a while. You really think you can find her?"

Then his eyes narrowed as a new idea occurred to him. "Who hired you?" he asked suspiciously.

"Her brother," I replied, making the decision not to lie. It turned out to be the wrong one. "But—"

"That asshole," he spluttered, anger sweeping his tentative manner aside.

"Listen—"

"No. You listen." He pointed to the door. The blue in his eyes had darkened. "You can just turn around and go right back out again."

"No." I folded my arms across my chest. What was the worst that could happen? He'd threaten to call the cops and I'd leave. I watched the muscles on the sides of Tommy's jaws tighten. "I can understand why you feel that way."

"Can you?" Tommy jabbed the air with a finger, using the gesture to punctuate the end of each sentence. "Can you really? My father had to go to court and get an order of protection taken out on that jerk."

"He told me."

Tommy's voice was loud enough to have attracted the attention of his television-watching fraternity brothers. They had drifted over and now stood around in a half circle, their interest piqued, waiting with anticipation to see what was coming next.

Tommy moved closer to me. I could smell the chocolate from the Oreos he'd been eating on his breath. "Did he also tell you that he threatened me with a bat?"

"Marks told me," I replied, thinking as I did that this was the second time in two days that I'd heard Bryan and a weapon mentioned in the same sentence.

"He burst in here and started right for me. That guy is crazy. You tell him, he comes near me again and me and my friends will hurt him real bad."

The perks of living in a fraternity. "I don't think that'll be necessary."

"So you say," he sneered. He was now about six inches away from me.

I held my ground. "Yes, I do."

Tommy stopped. I think he'd expected me to flinch and move back. When I didn't, he didn't know what to do. I looked up at him. "Don't you want to know what happened to Melissa? Don't you care?"

"Of course I do," he exclaimed.

"Then why don't you help me find her?"

"You want to find her, talk to her brother."

"I have, and now I want to talk to you."

"My father told me not to talk to anyone else."

"You always do everything your father asks you to?"

Tommy flushed. A murmur went up from the guys standing around us. "It's not that," he stuttered, deflated.

"Then, what is it?"

He ground his heel into a floorboard and glared at me helplessly.

I glared back. "Bryan said you didn't care. I guess he was right."

Tommy swallowed. I watched the conflicting emotions march across his face. I could understand why his father had told him not to talk to anyone. He seemed like the overly emotional type, reactive, vulnerable to whatever came along, easy to bully. In that way he and Bryan were a lot alike. They acted first and thought about the consequences later. Maybe that's why Melissa had been attracted to Tommy in the first place. Because he reminded her of her brother.

"He's always hated me, right from the day we met," Tommy stated, intruding on my train of thought.

"Actually, I think it's your Burmese he hates."

Tommy's frown dissolved into a mischievous grin, transforming his face into one that looked boyishly charming. He chuckled. "Yeah, he's scared of her all right."

I couldn't help smiling as well. I knew the guilty pleasure of handing someone a snake and watching them jump back.

"But Missy loved Burma. She used to say she thought she was the perfect combination of beauty and strength."

"They are that," I agreed as I watched the guys around us turn and drift back into the other room. Since there wasn't going to be a fight, there was no point in staying.

"Can I see her?" I asked after they'd gone.

Tommy beamed. Who said the way to man's heart was through his stomach?

"I've had her since she was six months old," he told me as I followed him up the large winding staircase that I was sure, in its younger days, had heard the crinkle of taffeta as young women swept down the steps in their ball gowns.

"What's she eating?"

"A mouse once a week. I was feeding her twice a week, but I read that wasn't good."

"No, it's not." Overfeeding is as bad for snakes as it is for people. "She shedding okay?"

"Fine. You sound like you know about this stuff. Do you have one?"

"In a manner of speaking. I own Noah's Ark." By now we'd reached the landing. I glanced around. The long, wide hallway meandered off to the left. A worn red print carpet covered the floor. The yellowish-white walls looked as if they could use a coat of paint.

Tommy smacked his forehead with the palm of his hand as he walked. "God, I feel like an idiot. I hear you got some great stuff in there."

I smiled. "We try."

"Could you get me an emerald boa?"

"I could order one for you, but they run somewhere between four and five hundred dollars."

He paused in front of a door. "That much?"

I nodded.

He pushed it open.

"Think about a corn snake. They're attractive and they're easy keepers."

"How much do they go for?" Tommy asked.

"Anywhere between eighty and one twenty-five," I informed him as we stepped inside his room.

It looked like your standard college-student disaster area. Clothes, all that Tommy possessed from the look of it, were piled on a chair next to a state-of-the-art stereo system. A couple of garbage bags full of empty beer cans stood along the far wall. Tommy's lacrosse equipment lay on the floor nearby, as did his scuba gear, weight-lifting belt, and golf clubs. Books and papers covered every inch of the desk's surface. A couple of Syracuse lacrosse posters sat next to pictures of bands I'd never heard of. The room smelled of sweaty socks and stale beer.

"Sorry for the mess. I guess I should dig it out. Melissa used to help me clean up. But since she's gone . . ." Tommy shrugged his shoulders and closed the door behind us. "I never seem to get around to it."

It's amazing. Twenty years of women's lib and nothing has changed, I thought as I negotiated the distance to Burma's cage. Getting to it involved an obstacle course of shoes, socks, and empty pizza boxes. "Nice setup," I observed. If the room was a mess, Burma's cage was pristine.

Tommy nodded. "I make sure to keep it that way. You want to see her?"

"Sure."

I watched him as he unfastened the metal clips and took the top off. Burma uncoiled herself and glided upward. Tommy reached in and grabbed her. His grasp was gentle but firm. He seemed at home with her. He stroked her for a minute before handing the boid to me.

She lay quietly in my hands. "Nice coloring." She was seven feet at the most, thin by Burmese standards. Marks was right about this one. Bryan was full of it. She didn't have the power to strangle a girl of Melissa's size. "Is she always this docile?"

Tommy grinned, took her back, and put her around his neck. "She's a real sweetie. She wouldn't hurt anyone."

"Except a mouse." I looked for a place to sit and finally settled on an upside-down plastic milk crate. "When did you last see Melissa?" I asked.

Tommy smiled nervously. "How big do corn snakes get anyway?"

"Big enough." It looked as if Tommy was having a change of heart. "Talking to me can't hurt," I urged.

He stroked Burma. "I don't know."

"I won't tell your father if you don't."

He hesitated again. I wondered if his father was really that protective, if Tommy was really that obedient, or if he knew something he didn't want to tell me and was using his father as an excuse.

I repeated the question I'd asked downstairs. "Don't you want to know what happened to your girlfriend?"

"Of course I do." Given the circumstances, what else could the kid say? "It's not that." Tommy licked his lips. I tried to catch his eye, but he kept looking away from me.

"Maybe you don't want to talk to me because you have something to hide."

His eyes darkened again. "That's ridiculous," he snapped.

I shrugged. "Sorry. I just figured from the way you're acting . . ."

"You're wrong." Tommy kicked the pizza box by his foot for emphasis. Burma arched her back and hissed in alarm.

"Then tell me when you last saw Melissa," I said to Tommy as he calmed Burma down.

"Fine." The boid relaxed her spine. "I saw Missy two days before she disappeared, but I spoke to her on the phone the evening before. Everything was okay."

"What did you two talk about?"

"The usual stuff. The paper she had to write. How she was behind in psych. You know, like that. She was going to come over here after she got back from seeing her mom at the hospital." He furrowed his brow.

I pushed a lock of my hair off my face and tucked it behind my ear. "What did you do when she didn't show up?"

He fidgeted. "Actually I wasn't here," he admitted sheepishly.

Chapter
12

I raised an eyebrow.

Tommy explained. "I'd gone from class straight to the mall. When I realized what time it was, I called the house and told John O. to tell Missy I'd be a little late. I told him to tell her to ring me on my beeper when she got to my room, but she never called."

I ran my thumb over my lip. "Did you tell Marks this?"

"Of course."

"You didn't come back to wait?"

Tommy looked defensive. "It's only ten minutes from Carousel to here. It wasn't like we had a date. She was going to drop by. I figured something else had come up."

"Like what?"

"I don't know. Maybe she'd gotten involved in a discussion with her brother and she didn't want to tell him she was meeting me. Maybe she was at the library and had lost track of time. Maybe she was hanging with Beth and her suitemates. It could have been anything.''

My calf muscles were beginning to cramp. This didn't sound like someone who was planning to elope, I thought as I stretched out my legs and massaged them. "What were you doing at the mall?"

"I was buying my mom a birthday present."

"What did you get her?"

"A scarf from People's Pottery. A hand-printed silk job. With big flowers. It's real nice."

"I assume you can prove this?"

"The police have my credit card slips."

"Did you buy anything else?"

"Socks, a new pair of sneakers, some sweats, a couple of CDs.'' He named some groups I hadn't heard of. "Then I had a bite to eat and caught a movie."

"So you got back here . . ."

"A little after ten."

"When did you realize Melissa was gone?"

"Not until Beth and Bryan came by to check. He just went off, man." Tommy shook his head at the memory. "Me and John O. had to throw him out of the house. He kept yelling that it was all my fault. Truth is, I think he had a guilty conscience."

"How so?"

Tommy hunched forward. "They were always fighting."

"I heard you and Melissa did too."

"But our fights didn't mean anything," Tommy protested. "The fights she got into with Bryan did."

"What were they about?"

"Me, among other things."

"Why does Bryan dislike you so much?"

Tommy twisted his mouth into a wry smile. "I think he'd

dislike any guy who got too close to his sister. He thinks she's too good for everyone. He didn't even want her to live in the dorms. He wanted her to stay home and take care of the house.''

''But she didn't want to?''

''Of course not. She loved him, but she wanted her own life. The guy's a nutter.''

I moved my leg back and forth. The cramp began to go away. ''Maybe he doesn't like you because he found out you were planning on marrying his sister and he thought she should finish school.''

The color on Tommy West's face rose again. It made his eyes look bluer. ''Who told you that?''

''Her roommate.''

''I told Missy not to tell anyone.''

''She was excited.''

Somewhere nearby someone had turned a stereo on. The sound of the Grateful Dead flooded the room.

Tommy frowned and bowed his head. Burma began crawling up his neck, past his ear, and onto the top of his head. ''That's not exactly true.''

''You mean you're not.''

Tommy raised his head. ''We were going to, but . . .''

''But what?''

He pulled Burma off his head and put her back around his neck. ''My father found out. He said he wouldn't pay for college if I did. I told Melissa we could wait till after I graduated, but she didn't want to do that.''

''Why?''

''She said if we loved each other, nothing else should matter. We had this fight over the phone.'' He closed his eyes and opened them again, as if he were blanking out the scene. ''I thought we'd made up. But with her, sometimes you can't tell. When she didn't show up, I figured she was still pissed at me.''

He frowned and looked out the window. I followed his gaze. A boy and girl were kissing in front of the fraternity house. Tommy bit his lip. The girl walked to her car, got in, and drove away. The boy went inside. Tommy brought his attention back to me.

''Did she do that kind of thing a lot?''

''You mean not show up?''

I nodded.

''Yeah.'' I heard the clump of shoes as someone walked down the hall outside.

''I understand that's not all she did when she got upset.''

Tommy tensed his shoulders and pulled his arms into his sides. ''That's Beth talking, isn't it?''

''I don't think it matters.''

He scrunched his neck down and chewed on the inside of his lip. ''Okay,'' he finally blurted out. ''She used to get a little overemotional about stuff. So what? It wasn't a big deal.''

''It must be hard not to hit someone when they're scratching you,'' I noted.

''Forget it,'' he cried.

''Forget what?''

''What you're thinking. I would never hurt her.''

''I didn't say you did.''

''But you implied it.''

I apologized. ''What do you think happened to her?''

''You got me.'' Tommy pulled on his earlobe. ''At first I thought she was doing this disappearing act to get me upset, to try and teach me a lesson. You know, one of those he'll-be-sorry-when-I'm-gone routines. I thought she'd be back in a couple of days. I told Bryan to cool it, but he was too whacked to hear what I was saying.''

''And when she didn't return?''

He cracked his knuckles. ''I don't know. I don't know what to think anymore.'' He lapsed into silence. I watched as he got up and put Burma back in her cage.

''Was anything else bothering her?''

''Her mother.''

''Besides that.''

''Like I said, she was fighting with her brother a lot.''

''About what?''

''Mostly me. Listen to this!'' Tommy said indignantly. ''He wanted her to go to the psychologist at the health center. He said her going out with me was indicative of a deep-seated depression.''

''Was she depressed?'' I asked as he refastened the latches that held the top on the cage.

Tommy turned around and faced me. ''She was stressed.''

''Her roommate said she used to cry in her sleep.''

''Really?'' Tommy raised an eyebrow, indicating his surprise. ''I never heard her do that.''

''Maybe she never did it with you. Do you mind?'' I asked, pointing to the pack of cigarettes I'd just taken out of my backpack. Tommy shook his head and I lit one, drawing the smoke deep into my lungs. He passed me a shot glass to use as an ashtray.

''She always acted fine when she was with me.''

''Her mother told me something had happened that was bothering her. I figured maybe it was her roommate's death.''

Tommy began folding a piece of paper into little pieces. ''Sure it bothered it. That kind of thing gets you where you live, but I think she was over it—at least as much as anyone is ever over something like that. You should talk to Beth.''

''I did. She said I should talk to her psych professor.''

''Fell?'' Tommy scrunched up his face.

''What does that mean?''

''Nothing. I just don't like the guy.''

''Why's that?''

Tommy didn't answer. He looked as if he were thinking about something else. I repeated my question.

''Sorry.'' He ran his hand through his hair. ''I guess because Missy was always running off to ask him for advice,'' he replied, picking his words carefully.

''Jealous?''

''It's not that.'' Tommy smiled ruefully. ''Or maybe it is. I just thought we would have talked more if he wasn't there. I was always hearing about how he said this or he said that. It got annoying after a while.''

''I bet.'' I took another puff and tapped the ash into my glass. ''Is that why you and Missy fought?''

''Among other reasons. All right. We did argue a lot. That's true. But we always made up.'' Tommy swallowed. He picked up his lacrosse stick and started twisting it from side to side. ''She really . . . I don't know . . . We couldn't stay together without fighting . . . just stupid stuff . . . we got on each other's nerves a lot . . . but whenever we were apart, I couldn't stop thinking about her. I still can't. We could have worked something out. I know we could have. I really miss her.'' He blinked several times. His eyes misted over.

When I left ten minutes later, Tommy had Tony Bennett on the stereo and a bottle of Jim Beam in his hand. I hoped he'd done his homework, because from the look on his face, he wasn't going to be doing much of anything else that night.

As I was going down the stairs, a man was coming in the front door. He looked familiar, but I couldn't place him. Stocky, with a strongly featured face, and dark, commanding eyes, he strode into the TV room.

"Is my son around?" he asked in a loud, booming voice.

"Yes, Mr. West," someone answered. "I think he's upstairs."

I made it my business to be out the door before Tommy's father went up the stairs.

Now I began to see why Tommy hadn't wanted to talk to me.

His father looked like somebody I wouldn't have wanted to argue with at Tommy's age either.

Chapter
13

Zsa Zsa wagged her tail as I let her out of the cab. We took a brief walk and I gave her a couple of big lamb and rice dog biscuits once we got back in. Her scent filled the car, and while other people might not like the combination of dog and night air, I found it soothing. Then I drove over to Schaefer. I wanted to talk to Missy's suitemates, Holland Adams and Brandy Weinstein, and I figured they were probably back at the dorm by then. I wouldn't have gone if Zsa Zsa had complained, but since she had curled up on her sheepskin blanket and gone back to sleep the moment we returned to my cab, I figured I might as well get the interview over with. Driving down the street, I found myself thinking about the conversation I'd just had with Tommy West.

The kid had seemed sincere about missing Melissa. Of course, that didn't mean he didn't have something to do with her disappearance. Lots of people kill someone and feel guilty afterward. As I lit a cigarette and waited for the car in front of me to turn, I conjured up another possibility. What if one of the fights Tommy had told me about had gotten out of hand? What if Melissa had done something like call him a gutless wonder for not marrying him? What if she'd raked her nails across his face? Slapped him? Maybe this time Tommy hadn't played the patient, understanding lover.

Maybe this time he lost his temper and belted her. Maybe he hit her harder than he meant to. Much harder. And Melissa had fallen back, hit her head, and died. A freak accident. But possible. Then Tommy panicked and hid the body.

Which was where my hypothetical construct broke down. I could get around the fact that according to Marks, Tommy's alibi checked out. What I couldn't get around was that while I could see Tommy killing Melissa and hiding her body, I couldn't see him sitting on something like that for four months. That required a degree of cold-bloodedness I didn't see the kid as having. I thought about it some more as I watched the smoke ring I'd just blown dissolve in the air.

For a change, luck was running my way, because I found Holland Adams and Brandy Weinstein in their room. They were sitting cross-legged on one of the beds, splitting a pizza. I knocked on the half-open door and walked into their room. The smell made my mouth water. Up until then I hadn't realized how hungry I was.

"You're that Light person," the girl who turned out to be Brandy told me, glancing in my direction.

"We got the card you left," Holland chimed in, raising her voice over the sound of the movie they were watching.

Both girls looked the same. They had shoulder-length streaked blond hair, tan complexions, long, silver fingernails, and regular features. Each was wearing jeans and a cropped, curve-hugging sweater, only Brandy's was blue and Holland's was green. They had been, I was willing to wager, in the in group in high school.

"Beth said you'd be back," Brandy told me before she took a bite of her slice and swallowed. "You want some?" she asked, indicating the box on the bed.

I'd like to think her offer wasn't prompted by the fact I'd been staring at the pizza the way Zsa Zsa stares at a bottle of beer. I took the proffered piece and leaned against the dresser while I ate. It tasted really good. I tried not to gobble it down.

Holland clicked off the video. "We really didn't know Missy that well," she told me, laying the remote on the pillow. "So I don't think we can help you."

"She called us the Barbies," Brandy volunteered, starting on another piece.

"The Barbies?" I almost choked on the food in my mouth.

Holland tossed her head to get her hair out of her eyes. "She was trying to be nasty, even though she said she wasn't, but Barbie is still my favorite doll. I took it as a compliment."

"If you ask me," Brandy said, licking a spot of tomato sauce off her finger, "I think she was jealous. I mean, Tommy's such a wimp."

"They fought all the time."

"She fought with everyone," Brandy observed.

"That's not what her brother says," I interjected.

"Maybe because he was the one she fought with the most." Holland put her arms above her head and stretched the way my cat did after a particularily satisfying nap. "She'd gotten on this feminist, personal-responsibility kick. I tried to tell her to lighten up. Intensity is *so* unattractive, but she just got pissy.''

''Everything was always such a big deal to her,'' Brandy said. She turned to her roommate. ''Remember when she found out I'd gone to the movies with Tommy?'' She rolled her eyes. ''The way she carried on, you would have thought I was giving him a blow job in the middle of the quad.''

''She was jealous?''

''Duh.''

Holland reached for another slice. ''Even though she said she wasn't.''

''She'd never talk to you,'' Brandy said. ''You never knew what she was thinking about. And then she'd get mad. Excuse me.'' Brandy's face quivered with indignation. ''But if you're studying and I'm watching TV, how do I know if it's too loud? Don't storm in here like some Nazi and complain. Personally, I think she needed something chemical. I even offered to give her some of my Prozac. You'd think I was offering her smack the way she carried on. I hope nothing bad happened to her, but it is *so* much nicer not having her around.''

Holland nodded. ''Absolutely.''

I thought about the three hundred dollars Missy had taken from her bank account. ''Did she do drugs? Gamble?''

Brandy guffawed. ''Are you kidding? Little Miss Perfect? Don't be ridiculous. She didn't even take a drink.''

The rest of the conversation proceeded along the same lines, and after a while it was obvious I'd heard everything they had to say, at which point I said good night and left. It had gotten colder out since I'd been inside the dorm, or perhaps it just felt that way because the wind had picked up again, bringing with it the smell of snow. I glanced at the sky. It had gone gray with clouds. A storm was moving in. God, I hoped it wouldn't be a bad one. It was time to put away the shovels for the season, not that the weather would necessarily agree with me. Last year we'd gotten socked with over a foot of the white stuff on Mother's Day. The crocuses and snowdrops had died, frozen in their thin tombs of ice.

I got in my car, petted Zsa Zsa for a minute, then pulled out into the road. I should have gone straight home. I was exhausted, I had bills to pay and a pile of laundry to do, but I found myself driving to George's house instead. We hadn't parted on the best of terms, and I wanted to touch base with him. Once he opened the door, though, I was sorry I'd come.

"Oh, it's you," he said when he saw me, disappointment written on his face and in his voice.

"Excuse me." I turned to go. Doing the wash would be more satisfying than this.

He reached over and put his hand on my shoulder. "Sorry. I was just hoping you were Raymond."

"Where is he?"

George took a deep breath. "That's the question of the hour. I wish I knew. Come on. I'll get you and Zsa Zsa a beer."

I waited until George had poured a little of my Sam Adams into a saucer for Zsa Zsa and handed the rest to me to ask what had happened.

"Raymond and I had a fight after dinner, and he ran off."

"He's been gone about what? Two hours?"

"Three." George grabbed a bottle of Saranac for himself and headed into the living room. I followed closely behind.

"What did you fight about?"

"I wanted him to turn his box down. He told me to fuck

myself, I told him I was taking his box away, and he ran out the door instead.''

''You couldn't catch him?''

George's laugh was dry and humorless. ''Of course I could have. I didn't try. I was afraid I'd hurt him if I touched the little shit. Anyway, I figured he'd come back in twenty minutes or so.''

''But he hasn't.''

''No indeedy. He has not.''

''Have you gone out looking for him?''

''What do you think?'' George ran his thumb over his bottom lip. ''About an hour ago I called downtown and checked the hospitals. Wherever he is, he isn't in those places.'' As George lowered himself onto the gray leather sofa, I couldn't help reflecting this was not the sort of furniture that went well with teenagers. ''He'll probably come home when he's ready,'' George said, but his voice lacked assurance.

I sat down beside him. ''Maybe he just got lost.''

''Maybe. Or maybe he decided to hitchhike home.''

''You think he'd do something like that?''

''He said he was, before he hightailed it out the door.''

''Six ninety is a long way from here.''

''Maybe he got a lift from someone,'' George snapped. His body was so tight, you could have put it in an orchestra and played it.

I knew George was thinking about the things that can happen when fourteen-year-old boys get into cars with strangers. I wanted to tell him not to worry, but I couldn't, because it wasn't true, and George, being an ex-cop, knew it. Instead, I put my Sam Adams down on the glass coffee table in front of me and went to massage George's shoulders, but he stopped me with a gesture of his hand. He was doing what he always did when he got upset—withdraw—leaving me on the other side of the moat. It was one of the qualities I liked least about him, maybe because it reminded me of Murphy.

"I knew this wasn't going to work out. I knew it," he muttered as I picked up my beer again. "That kid belongs in a military school, not here with me in Syracuse. Hell, he belongs in one of those Shock camps." George's left leg began to vibrate as he jiggled his foot up and down in time with his anxiety. "What am I going to tell my sister if she calls?"

"Maybe he'll turn up before then."

"God, I hope so. If I were a praying man, I'd be on my knees."

Zsa Zsa came out from the kitchen, jumped up on my lap, and turned over on her back. I absentmindedly rubbed her belly. A minute later she jumped back on the floor.

George took a long pull on his beer. "This," he observed, "is why I'm glad I never had kids."

"If he were your kid, he'd act differently."

"Yeah. Right." George reached for the remote.

I didn't say anything. What was the point? For the next fifteen minutes George stared straight ahead at the screen and channel-surfed. I drank another beer, threw pretzels to Zsa Zsa, and leafed through George's copy of the *Atlantic Monthly* while I grew more and more impatient. Finally I couldn't stand it anymore. I stood up.

George glanced at me. "Where are you going?"

"Home. There's no point in staying here."

"You think I should be out looking for him, don't you?"

"It beats doing what you're doing now."

George wavered for a minute, then hit the power button

on the remote control. "You're right." He levered himself off the sofa. "Let's go."

Five minutes later George, Zsa Zsa, and I were walking across the lawn to George's Taurus. The thin crust of ice on the snow crunched under our feet. It was a cold night to be wandering around outside, especially if you weren't properly dressed, I reflected as we got into the Taurus. We drove over to Westcott Street.

Located a little over a mile from George's house, Westcott Street had three pizza shops and a convenience store that didn't make a fetish of checking IDs when it came to selling beer, which made it the most obvious place to start our search. The area, which was three blocks long and five blocks deep, was in a perpetual identity crises, occupied as it was by college students, poor blacks, and an enclave of sixties radicals who had never made it through to another era.

Unfortunately tonight the street looked deserted. Just two cars were parked in the lot in front of Fast Break. Which didn't surprise me. It was late, it was midweek, and the weather was lousy. Everyone was home. Except, of course, for Raymond. And Melissa.

George went around some broken glass and pulled into a parking place next to the bus stop. He turned off the ignition and slipped his car key into his pocket. "Let's do it," he said to me. "You check Charlie's. I'm going to go down to Little John's Place. We'll meet back here in five minutes."

"You want me to grab Raymond if I see him?"

"Not unless he makes a run for it."

As I headed toward Charlie's, I wondered if I'd actually be able to hold on to the kid. He might be just fourteen, but he was a big fourteen and he didn't like me very much—which also wasn't going to help. But it turned out to be a non-issue. Raymond wasn't in Charlie's. Nobody had seen him either, although I realized as I described him that he could have been any one of the dozen kids who go in and out of the pizza place each day. A picture would have helped. Unfortunately, I didn't have one.

I got the same result at Al's. Raymond wasn't there and no one remembered seeing anyone like him come in in the last three hours or so.

I arrived at the car a fraction of a second before George did.

"He was at Little John's about an hour ago," he informed me as he jumped into the Taurus. "He hooked up with a couple of kids, but Darius doesn't know their names. He thinks they live around here though."

We cruised the neighborhood for ten minutes. No one was out. Nothing was moving. We checked out Barry Park next. Within walking distance, the two-block square was another place kids liked to hang out. They played hoops or sat and smoked on the park benches, passing a filched beer back and forth. But tonight the ball fields and the playground stood silent. Even the cats that prowled the fields by night were inside.

We moved on. I scanned the streets as George drove.

"Maybe you should let Raymond go home," I said as we went up Beech.

"No."

I stole a look at George. His mouth was set in a grim line.

"This isn't working out very well."

George didn't answer.

"I really think you should put the kid on the bus."

George took his eyes off the road and glared at me. "First of all his name is Raymond, not the kid. Second of all, this isn't your business. You don't know anything about this."

"I just think—"

"I'm not interested in what you think," he snapped.

That did it. I told him to stop the car.

"Fine." George slammed on the brake. By then we were on Dell. "You want to get out, be my guest."

I was about to open the door, when I spotted two kids midway up the block. They were standing in the street alongside a car. The door was open.

"They're breaking in," George said, our argument temporarily forgotten as the kids, startled by the noise from the Taurus, froze.

A second later they'd recovered enough to sprint onto the sidewalk, across a lawn, and disappear into an alleyway. They were followed a few seconds later by a third kid getting out of the car. He took off too.

George pointed at the retreating figure. "That's Raymond."

"How can you tell?" The kids were all the same size. They were all wearing the same clothing.

"Because I can."

George went after him.

I followed.

Chapter
14

It's hard to chase someone by foot in Syracuse in March, especially at night. During that time temperatures traditionally rise above freezing during the day and fall after sundown, which makes for large patches of thick ice over sidewalks, steps, and paths. The fact that George was wearing leather-soled boots and his nephew, in addition to being lighter and more agile, had on hightops didn't help either. I'd gotten halfway down the street, when George came trotting toward me. He was hard-faced and empty-handed.

"Why didn't you follow in the car?" he growled, heading back toward the Taurus.

"Maybe because you have the keys."

He got in the car without answering and slammed the door shut. If I'd been wearing my ski parka instead of a leather jacket, I would have walked the mile back to my cab.

We circled the area for the next half hour locked in tension-filled silence, but the kids were gone. They were crouched down in the backseat of an open car or they'd slipped through an unlatched basement window and were hiding in someone's house. Judging from the look of fury on George's face, I couldn't help thinking it was just as well he couldn't find them. I found myself sitting toward the door. I was glad to get out of the Taurus when we got back to his house.

"You know, sometimes you really are a schmuck," I told him as he marched up the path toward his house.

He kept on marching.

Zsa Zsa and I got in the cab and went home.

It had not been a good evening.

Calli took a sip of her latte and pushed an envelope containing the articles I'd asked her to get on Jill Evans across the table with the tip of her finger. "What would you do if I were still in California?"

"Pay the fee."

Calli laughed. I suddenly realized how much I'd missed not talking to her.

"You didn't have to bring them. I would have picked them up."

"I know. But this gave me an excuse to see you and have some coffee."

We were sitting in the café at Barnes & Noble.

Calli looked around. "I know we're not supposed to like the big chains, I know they're driving out the little book-stores, but it's still nice to have a place like this in Syracuse. It gives me the illusion of being au courant."

"Sorry you've come back?"

She ripped open another packet of sugar and poured it

into her coffee. "Well, this isn't exactly the center of the universe. Especially if you're single."

"Too true." I put the envelope in my backpack. I wanted to read the articles in a quiet place, where I could concentrate.

"Of course, you have George. If I had somebody, maybe I wouldn't feel this way."

"I wouldn't be too sure." I told her what had happened earlier. I'd found out from Tim how a beat cop had knocked on George's door at one in the morning with Raymond in hand. "He picked him up on East Genesee. George could have called and told me."

"You did call him a putz."

"Schmuck."

"Big difference."

I ate a piece of my cheesecake. The one I used to make was better, but this one would do. "So I called him to ask him why he hadn't called me, and you know what he said?"

Calli shook his head.

"He said he didn't think I'd be interested." I grimaced and ate another piece of cake. "I wish he'd put that kid back on the bus to New York."

"And admit that he can't whip his nephew into shape? Don't be ridiculous. What's he doing with him?"

"He has him under house arrest."

"Should be fun for you," Calli observed.

"The man is an asshole."

Calli took another sip of her latte and scraped the last crumbs of icing from her chocolate cake from the plate with her fork. "They all are, but at least yours is good in bed," she said, licking the fork.

"I'm not sure that's enough."

"You used to say it was with Murphy."

I finished off my cake. "I'm changing my mind. Talking would be nice too."

"You must be getting older."

"That's probably it." I changed the topic to Jill Evans.

As I read the articles in the store later that afternoon, I thought about what Calli had told me. What she'd said was that for all practical purposes all the information on Evans was contained in the newspaper articles. Sometimes that wasn't the case, sometimes rumors swirled around the newsroom that never found their way into print, but evidently, as with Melissa Hayes, that wasn't so here.

I stretched, settled back in my chair, lit another cigarette, and considered what I'd read. According to the first article, a short item on the front page of the *Post Standard,* on the night of May 5, Jill Evans had fallen out of a third-floor window at 1800 Cumberland. According to the chief medical examiner at the Onondaga County medical examiner's office, she'd died instantly from "multiple blunt-force injuries." The university vice president of public relations had expressed his sorrow to the girl's parents, said that foul play was not suspected, and taken the opportunity to state that more information would be released as soon as possible.

The second article appeared the next day and ran for four paragraphs. It stated that toxicology reports from the coroner's officer were pending, and though the university and the police department would not confirm or deny anything, the paper quoted a number of students who had seen Jill Evans engaging in what was called "heavy drinking" earlier that evening at the party she'd been attending. She'd evidently been doing Jell-O shots. No one seemed to know why she'd wandered up to the bedroom on the third floor, although she'd said something about feeling the need to lie down.

The article went on to state no one at the party had seen her fall or even been aware that she had because the music had been so loud, it had blocked the sound. Her body had been discovered by a neighbor who had seen something lying on the ground in the back of the house. Curious, he'd gone to investigate and found Jill Evans, at which point he'd run into his house and called 911. The last paragraph of the article was an exercise in damage control from the university's vice president of public relations to the effect that underage drinking was illegal and obviously forbidden to any of the school's students and that appropriate measures would be taken if warranted. What those measures were and what would warrant them were not spelled out.

The third article confirmed that Jill Evans had indeed been drinking and that her blood alcohol level was "quite high." It also featured a bouquet of quotes from dormmates about what a nice girl Jill Evans had been; but then, when people are dead, they always are. You rarely read about someone saying "That guy was an absolute shit. The world's a better place without him." I became more interested when I noticed one of the people quoted was Melissa Hayes. "Jill was my best friend and now she's gone," she'd said. "It was a stupid way to die. I should have done more."

Done more of what? I wondered. Melissa had obviously felt guilty, but did she have a reason to, or was she feeling that general guilt that survivors get. Had that guilt gnawed at her till she couldn't take it anymore? Despite what her mother had said, she was at an age when the death of a friend would hit her especially hard. I stubbed my cigarette out. I'd been smoking way too much lately, and pulled the last two articles out from underneath Pickles, who'd just vaulted onto the desk from the floor. She'd meowed a protest which I ignored. The cat shared a genius with most animals of her ilk for lying on whatever I was trying to read at the time.

Both of these articles were short. One was a general article dealing with the problems of drinking on college campuses. It discussed the possible reasons for the increase in binge drinking over the last ten years in schools across the country, detailed fraternity drinking games, and ended with statistics on the concomitant rise in alcohol-related deaths.

The last article, published two weeks after Jill Evans's death, featured a quote by the now-familiar vice president of public relations to the effect that disciplinary action was being contemplated against any underage students who had been drinking with Jill at the time of her death. The vice president was also careful to point out the house the party had taken place in had been rented by non-students and was therefore not under their aegis, which was a fancy way of saying this whole mess wasn't their responsibility.

And that had been that. I put the copies of the articles in the folder I'd started for Melissa Hayes. On the surface, Calli was right. The story was clear cut. Jill Evans had gone to a party. She'd gotten very drunk. She'd leaned out a window, lost her balance, and toppled out. Sad, stupid, but no suggestion of foul play. As a previous article had pointed out, similiar incidents happened on college campuses all across the country every year. Pickles meowed for attention. I petted her, and she began to purr. A moment later she turned around and bit me. This, I decided, as I sucked the edge of my hand, was why I liked dogs better. At least with them you know where you stand. I was in the middle of trying to shoo Pickles off my desk—she didn't want to move—when the phone rang. A voice identifying itself as Mr. West asked to speak to Robin Light.

Mr. West, hunh? Tommy must have decided to tell his

dad about our conversation. Why else would he be calling? From what Tommy had said, something told me this wasn't going to be a friendly chat.

"I'm Robin Light," I said into the receiver.

"Do you have any children, Ms. Light?"

"No, I don't."

"Well, as I know you know, I have one and he's the most important thing in the world to me."

"I can appreciate that," I replied cautiously.

"I'm sure you can." Mr. West's voice had a rough quality to it. "That's why I'm calling."

I waited to see what was coming next.

"Tommy told me you paid him a visit the other day."

"That's true," I allowed.

"It upset him a great deal."

I started to apologize, but Mr. West cut me off. "I'm sure you didn't mean to do that."

"I didn't."

"And I can appreciate why you wanted to talk to him—this thing with Melissa is terrible—but I have to ask you to stay away from my son."

I reached for my lighter and started flicking it. The flame spurted up, sputtered, and died. I tried again. Nothing. I put the lighter down. The damn thing was out of fluid. "Melissa's mother is terminally ill. She doesn't have much longer to live."

"I'm aware of that."

"Then how can you, as a parent, not understand how important it is to her to find out what happened to her daughter before she dies?"

"Believe me, I do. My heart goes out to her, and if I thought my son could help her, I wouldn't hesitate to have him do whatever was necessary to bring that end about."

"Maybe he can."

"I'm afraid that isn't the case. I promise you that he's already told the police everything he knows, which, unfortunately, isn't much."

"He left out one thing."

"What's that?" I could hear the note of caution in Mr. West's voice.

I leaned back in my chair till it was balanced on its hind legs and contemplated the water stain on the opposite wall. Suspense is good for the soul.

"I'm afraid I don't have time to play games, Ms. Light," Mr. West responded after a few more seconds had passed. "If you have something to say, say it."

"I was going to. Your son didn't tell the police he and Melissa were planning on getting married."

There was a long pause on the other end of the line. Then I heard a sigh. "You see, this is the kind of thing I'm talking about. People like you take statements and then make them out to be something they're not."

I ignored the "people like you." Instead, I said, "I think it's indicative that Tommy hasn't told everything he knows."

"It isn't indicative of anything," Mr. West snapped. "I was the one who told him not to mention it to the police."

I brought my chair back down. Pickles stretched and nudged my hand with her head. She wanted me to pet her again. I kept my hand where it was. She meowed. I'm such a sucker, I thought as I caved in and stroked underneath her chin. She began purring again.

"And why was that, Mr. West?" I asked. "That seems like an odd thing to do."

"I did it precisely because of what is happening now between you and me."

"Which is?"

"You're making more of this than it warrants."

"Maybe so. But I heard Melissa was very upset."

There was a short pause on the other end of the line, then West said, "Unfortunately, from what my son told me, Melissa was the kind of girl who became emotional about a lot of things. She had an extremely unrealistic view of the world."

"How so?"

"She believed everything she learned in parochial school."

I wound the phone cord around one of my fingers. "Obviously you think that's bad."

"I don't think it equips people to deal with life as they will find it. Now, if there's nothing else . . ."

"I have one more question I'd like to ask."

"Yes?"

"Well, I'm just wondering: What else did you tell Tommy not to say anything about?"

"Do you know who I am, Ms. Light?" he asked. An icy edge had crept into his tone.

"You're Mr. West, Tommy West's father."

"That's right. My first name is Michael."

I let out a low whistle.

Chapter

15

When I told Tim whom I'd been on the phone with, he stopped putting new bedding in the dwarf Russian hamsters' cage and straightened up. Little shreds of pine bark clung to his black T-shirt. "Michael West?" he asked, brushing them off.

I nodded as I watched the five hamsters, upset that their carefully amassed food store had disappeared, scurry around.

"*The* Michael West?"

"That's what I just said."

"You're kidding."

"Do I look as if I am?"

"How could you not have known?"

"Hey, West is a common name. No one told me," I said, thinking of Marks. That son of a bitch. After the bargain I'd given him on the snake for his stepson. He'd owed me that much, at least.

"But you saw him," Tim protested, dusting himself off.

"Only for a minute." No wonder the guy had looked familiar. "Anyway, his picture isn't in the paper that much. And it's not exactly as if I travel in that social circle." Zsa Zsa danced around my feet, and I absentmindedly held out a treat to her. "No wonder Mr. West didn't want his son to get married," I observed as she grabbed it out of my hand and ran away to eat it.

"How much is West worth?"

I clicked my tongue against the roof of my mouth. I wasn't good remembering numbers. "A lot." The guy was a builder who'd made his fortune by taking inner-city housing, rehabing it, and convincing middle-class people to move in. He'd started out as a framer working for a contractor down in Miami and ended up a multimillionaire. In the last couple of years he'd been profiled in several magazines as an example of what businesses can do to save American cities. Recently, he'd taken up politics. A major player in the Republican party, he was rumored to be up for an important party position.

"What did West say to you?" Tim asked.

"Basically, in so many words, he told me to stay away from his son."

"What did you say?"

"Not much."

Tim gently tugged on the diamond stud in his right earlobe. "One of my friends did some electrical work for someone who worked for his company down in Georgia. He said he had ties to the mob."

One of the parrots started to shriek. "That doesn't mean anything. If you work in that business, you work with the mob or you don't work at all."

"Kip said he heard West's a real bastard."

"No surprise there. You don't get to where he is by being a nice guy."

"Yeah. The assholes are running the world."

"They always have."

Tim snorted. "What are you going to do?" he asked.

I nibbled on the edge of a torn cuticle. "That depends on where the questions I'm asking lead. I'm not going to go out of my way to talk to Tommy again, but I won't not talk to him either, if I feel it's warranted."

"Do you think his kid is involved?"

I weighed the alternatives. "Given the way Mr. West is acting, it's possible. His son certainly could have a motive for wanting Melissa out of his life. On the other hand, maybe Mr. West is telling the truth. Maybe the guy's just trying to shield his kid. Maybe he's an overprotective father." A dull ache of pain made me look at my finger. Somehow I'd managed to rip the cuticle off. I cursed silently. The damn thing was going to hurt for a week now. The way my luck was going, it would probably get infected. "If I had a kid, I'd probably do the same thing myself."

"I wouldn't," Tim said, starting in on the hamster cage again. "I don't think you do people favors by protecting them. If they don't suffer the consequences of their actions, they're never going to learn."

I thought about some of the things I'd done and gotten away with when I was younger. "I'm not sure that's true."

Tim and I wasted ten minutes debating the issue before we went back to work. The rest of the day was uneventful. I set up two appointments regarding Melissa at the university, after which I caught up on my orders, paid my bills, and inventoried the freezer in the back room. I wanted to make sure everything I was supposed to do was done, because I was planning on spending a large amount of time tomorrow out of the store working on the Hayes case and I didn't want to give Tim anything to complain about.

When I'd spoken to the head of university security the previous day, I'd gotten the strong impression he wasn't exactly eager to talk to me, but he'd agreed to the meeting because he couldn't afford not to, which was why I was trudging up what had looked like endless sets of stairs from the street below, at nine o'clock in the morning, fighting against gusts of wind that were making my eyes tear and my skin feel numb. Given the conversation Mr. Morrell and I had had, I wasn't expecting much, but I had to go through the motions. And anyway, you never know what you're going to get out of someone till you talk to them face-to-face.

Morrell's office turned out to be located on the ground floor of a tired-looking building that was crying out for a good sprucing up. The trim could have used a couple of coats of paint and the bricks needed pointing. Tucked away on a far corner of the campus, like a poor relation no one wants to acknowledge, it had taken me a while to find. The view as I labored up the steps to the campus was less than inspiring.

From where I was standing, if you looked down from the hill, you could see the 690 overpass, a parking lot, and a housing development known informally as the Bricks. A poor, mostly African American area, it would have been called a ghetto in a more plain-speaking time, before euphemisms became the order of the day.

I was wondering why so many universities are built on hills looking down at the poor below, when I reached Morrell's office. I crushed the cigarette I'd been smoking out with my heel, deposited the butt in the sand-filled ashtray nearby, and went inside. When I told the secretary, a Betsy Seyffert according to the nameplate on her desk, who I was, she gestured to the open door on my left and told me to go in.

Morrell pointedly glanced up from the papers he was reading to the clock on the wall as I entered. "You're late," he observed, sounding pleased at having the opportunity to catch me in a mistake.

"I had trouble finding your office," I replied, sitting down in the black armchair in front of his desk.

"That's funny. I would have thought that you of all people, seeing how you're a detective and all"—here he turned the corners of his mouth up slightly—"would have been able to figure out where it was."

Ah. A guy with a sense of humor. I let the crack go and studied the man who'd made it. Morrell's hands were lightly resting on the edge of the desk. They were big, but then, so was Mr. C. Morrell. He was in his fifties, his bearing radiating the remnants of the military man I was sure he'd been. Deeply tan, his long, narrow face was cross-hatched with the type of thin, deep lines the sun etches in your skin after a lifetime spent out in her.

Handsome, with regular features, he had pale blue eyes and neatly clipped gray hair. His clothes, white shirt, striped regimental tie, and gray jacket reinforced his conservative, "man-in-charge" image. I wondered if his appearance had played a part in the getting of this job. He was someone the handlers could trot out before parents. *See,* his looks said. *Your son or daughter will be safe with me.* It was the feel-good approach to security.

Which is what most of it was about everywhere anyway. The majority of measures at airports, offices, and schools was packaging designed to make people think "things are being done to ensure that everything is under control."

Whereas the truth is, if you want to do something bad enough, you can. All it takes is a modicum of thought. And a little bit of luck.

Security requires loss of freedom, an increase in inconvenience.

Even then the measures might not work.

Short of putting a homing device on Melissa Hayes, could anyone have prevented what had happened to her?

Especially since the odds were she was a willing participant in whatever had occurred. At least in the beginning.

Morrell made a minuscule adjustment to his tie and said, "Explain to me again why I should tell you anything about Melissa Hayes's disapppearance."

"I thought we went over that on the phone."

"Refresh my memory."

I suppressed my rush of irritation and let a couple of beats go by before answering. If he wanted to play Lord of the Manor, so be it. "I see the question as: why shouldn't you?"

"Legally, I'm not required to give you any information."

I leaned forward slightly. "That's what you told me yesterday on the phone."

"That's right, I did." Morrell brushed his tie tack with the tip of his finger. "That being the case, I'm curious. Why did you insist on coming here?"

"Why did you agree to see me?" I countered. If the guy wanted to rehash the conversation, that was fine with me.

He acknowledged my comment with a wintry smile.

"You know," I continued, "what happened to Melissa Hayes is every parent's worst nightmare. You send your kid off to college, a college, I might add, that has taken all possible measures to ensure your child's safety."

Morrell's expression didn't soften, but he gave a slight nod to indicate acceptance of the compliment.

"And she walks out the door of her dorm and disappears in the middle of the afternoon without a trace and no one sees anything."

Morrell formed a steeple with the tips of his fingers. "That is correct. No one did. But that said, what's your point? Why should I cooperate with you?" he asked. "I don't think the university wants any more publicity over this. We would prefer to put this painful episode behind us."

"I can imagine." I reached over and idly ran a finger along the edge of Morrell's desk. He frowned. I deliberately repeated the gesture, then, point made, leaned back. "In fact, I empathize. Unfortunately, things being the way they are these days, that seems the best way to ensure adverse coverage. You know what media people are like. Always twisting things. Making something out of nothing."

The corners of Morrell's mouth twitched. Maybe they were the only facial muscles he could use. He brought the tips of his fingers up to the bottom of his lip. His expression stayed the same. Unreadable. "That's right. How could I have forgotten. You used to work for the local newspaper, didn't you?"

I nodded. "Refusing to talk to me makes the university look ungenerous at the very least. At the most, it makes you guys look as if you're stonewalling, when the reality is that you're not. From what I heard, your staff did everything you could to help find her."

"True. We did."

"And if you throw in the fact that I'm working for Melissa's mother and she has only a few months left to live . . ." I trailed off, leaving thoughts of bad PR dancing in Morrell's head.

"I see," he said.

"I thought you might."

The sounds of footsteps from the hallway outside filtered into the room. Morrell's phone rang. He didn't look at it. A moment later the noise stopped. His secretary must have picked up. He brought his hands back down and rested them on the edge of the desk again. "All right. What is it, exactly, that you'd like to know?"

"Your ideas about what happened to Melissa. Who your staff talked to. What they noticed. What they did after the disappearance. That kind of thing."

Morrell didn't answer immediately. Instead, he picked up a pencil and twirled it between the fingers of his right hand while he mulled my request over. After a few seconds he put the pencil down and gestured to the door leading to the outer office. "Would you mind waiting outside," he said. "I need to make a phone call."

"No problem." My guess was that he was calling the head of public relations for final clearance on whether he should talk to me or not.

While I was waiting, I approached the secretary.

Secretaries, I've found, usually know more than anyone else in the place. Sometimes, especially if they don't like their bosses, they can be invaluable fonts of information. A case that was true here, I was willing to wager, judging from the expression of distaste on Betsy Seyffert's face after she got off the intercom with Morrell.

I judged her to be in her late thirties. Her face was thin, her profile Roman, her hair ash blond. Her makeup was immaculate, her blouse white silk. She looked as out of place in this office as a calla lily would among a bouquet of daisies.

"Been at this job long?" I asked.

"Long enough," she replied as she went back to scanning papers on her desk. Her movements were quick and precise.

"I used to work at NYU. As a secretary in the poli sci department. I left after a year."

"Well, I'm leaving here in two weeks. I'm going down to New York City. I have a sister who lives in Queens. She's going to get me a job with an advertising firm."

"Sounds good."

She gave me a confiding smile. "Believe me, it'll be better than this. At least I'll meet some interesting people."

I leaned against the side of her desk. "Your boss seems as if he'd be a tough man to work for."

She rolled her eyes by way of an answer. "His only saving grace is that he's out of the office a lot. Like today, after his meeting with you, he's gone for the rest of the day."

I laughed. I liked this woman. I was thinking about how sometimes you just connect with someone, when her intercom buzzed. She pressed a button. It was Morrell telling her to tell me to go back inside.

"You are summoned," she intoned, capitalizing each word with her voice.

When I entered, Morrell was glancing through a folder I assumed to contain the Melissa Hayes case. "There isn't much to tell," he said as I sat down.

"That's all right. I'll take whatever you can give me." I got my pad and pen out of my backpack and prepared to take notes.

"We received a call at four-thirty on Friday, November twenty-second from her brother, Bryan Hayes. A member of our security team responded, and after ascertaining what the problem was, advised Mr. Hayes to wait until twenty-four hours had passed before recontacting us." Morrell looked up from the paper he'd been reading from. "That's standard policy everywhere when the subjects are above sixteen," he explained, emphasizing the word *everywhere*.

I told him I was aware of that.

Morrell ignored me and kept talking. "In ninety-eight percent of the cases, we find students reported missing turn up within twelve hours. Usually, they've taken a road trip with their friends and failed to inform their family of their plans or they've become intoxicated and passed out somewhere."

"Interesting," I murmured even though he wasn't telling me anything I didn't already know. I doodled an M on my pad. "What did you say the name was of the guard that caught the call?"

"I didn't."

"Could you give it to me?"

"The gentleman has moved on. Anyway, it's against university policy." The way Morrell pronounced the words *university policy*, you would have thought he was talking about the National Security Act.

"Why is that?"

"Experience has shown us that it's more efficient to funnel our communications through one person. That way we avoid miscommunications and misunderstandings."

"Very commendable." What was even more commendable was that I managed to make the comment with a straight face.

"We like to think so."

"Is that the royal we?"

A tic of annoyance traveled across Morrell's face. "People I've spoken to told me you had quite a mouth on you."

"What people?" I asked, though I really didn't care. Not being well liked has a certain freeing power.

"Would you like me to continue or not?"

"By all means." I went back to taking notes. I could always get the guard's name if I needed it. "Fine. I can live with that. What happened next?"

"The brother contacted our offices again twenty-four hours later. When we ascertained that Melissa Hayes was indeed missing—"

I interrupted. "How did you do that?"

"We spoke to her roommate, her boyfriend, her suitemates, interviewed students in the dormitory, talked with her teachers, as well as conducted a visual examination of the grounds."

Morrell gave me the information in a flat tone of voice. As he scanned the report in front of him and precised it for me, I was thinking about how much I would have loved to have seen the file, but that, I knew, was out of the question. Unless, of course, I paid a visit to the office when he wasn't there. Lots of times, people in security aren't as tight about that kind of stuff as one would think.

Morrell lifted his eyes from the paper and looked at me again. "Once we had concluded our search and come up empty-handed, we immediately got in touch with the Syracuse Police Department and turned the matter over to them. From that point on we have rendered every available assistance asked."

"I'm sure you have."

"Unfortunately the gravity of the situation was obscured by the fact that Miss Hayes disappeared right before Thanksgiving break. I fear we all assumed she'd decided to take her holiday early."

"With her mother in the hospital?" I asked incredulously.

"She was having trouble with her academics as well."

I stopped doodling. "No one told me that."

Morrell gave me a tight little smile. "Maybe they didn't know. Maybe she was too embarrassed to tell them. Over the years, I've found that good students don't take failure well. That and her mother's illness. Her friend's death . . ." Morrell's voice drifted off. "Frankly, given the circumstances, I'm surprised she elected to return in September. She should have taken the semester off. I don't know why she didn't."

Here was something Morrell and I could both agree on. "Anything else I should know?" I asked.

Morrell shook his head.

"Unoffically, what do you think happened to her?"

He spread his fingers out on the desk's surface. "Given the circumstances, your guess is as good as mine."

"You must have some idea," I insisted.

He studied the onyx pen holder on his desk while considering his answer. "In this job, I've found that college students don't seem to be very good at processing stress. They tend to overreact to life's setbacks."

I translated to English. "Are you saying you think Melissa killed herself?"

Morrell picked up his pen and put it back down. "I don't think we can rule out the possibility."

Chapter
16

"Suicide," Fell said reflectively, combing his mustache with his fingers. "I can't say the thought hasn't crossed my mind."

He had to raise his voice to be heard over the construction noises. I looked out the window. A building was going up not more than fifty feet away from Fell's office.

"They started building in November." He got up and closed the window a little harder than necessary. "It's making me crazy. When I leave the window open, it's so noisy I can't think, and when I keep it closed, it gets so hot I feel as if I'm in a sauna."

"What's it going to be?"

"A new computer center. God forbid they should put any money into the humanities and the social sciences." He raised his eyebrows in disgust. "Look at this place." He waved his hand around to indicate his office. "Could it possibly be any smaller?"

"Not really."

The room was cramped and narrow, the height almost double the width of the room. It reminded me of an elevator shaft. If you could have magically tipped the room on its side, it would have been spacious, but as it was, there was barely enough space for a desk and two chairs. Add a love seat, bookshelves overflowing with textbooks and professional journals, and an aggressively large ficus, and the effect was claustrophobic in the extreme.

"But that's the university for you." Fell took a chocolate chip cookie out of a Tupperware container. "They've got plenty of money. They're just not putting it in the right place. If it doesn't have an immediate payoff, they're not interested. The humanities have become the stepchildren of higher education." He stopped and laughed. "God, listen to me. My wife said I'm becoming a certifiable old fogy. I think she's right." He took a bite of his cookie. "Here. Have one." He pushed the container across the desk. "I made them from scratch. Good, aren't they?" he asked after I'd eaten one.

"Very." I brushed a crumb off my notebook.

Fell reached for another, leaned back in his chair, and rested his hands on his belly. With his slight double chin, unkempt mustache, and his plaid shirt, he had a homey, rumpled appearance, and I could see where Melissa would have felt secure confiding in him.

I shifted around in the chair in front of his desk, trying to get comfortable, but it was no use. The seat was lumpy and there were small cracks running along its arms. It reminded me of the chair in my office that I'd taken to piling old newspapers on. No wonder Fell was annoyed by the new building going up. Not only was the noise a constant irritant, but here they were, spending millions of dollars, and he couldn't even get a new chair for his office.

Fell took off his glasses and rubbed the bridge of his nose before putting them back on. Black-rimmed, with Coke-bottle lenses, they were the glasses of someone who either couldn't afford or didn't care about buying better. "Melissa disappearing like this almost makes me glad I didn't have children." His voice was reflective.

"Me too."

He smiled wryly. "Well, now that we're agreed on that, how I can help you? We have a half hour before my next class."

"I understand from her roommate Beth that Melissa liked you a lot."

"And I liked her. She was a pleasure to work with. Melissa was a rare commodity these days—a good student. She had a genuine interest in psychology. She was thinking about becoming an industrial psychologist," he added. "It was a good choice, a bankable one in today's market. Most of my students want to go into clinical work. But that field is dead."

"HMOs."

"Exactly." There was a loud boom. Fell winced at the noise. "The building was supposed to be finished a month ago, but what's the good of complaining. No one around here listens anyway. If you don't bring in contracts, they're not interested." He went back to talking about Melissa. "She was thinking about doing an internship, and I was trying to help her set one up."

"It was good of you to give up your time like that," I observed.

"Not really." Fell smiled warmly. "I know other professors don't feel this way, but I love teaching. I love the students. To me, they're the best part of my job. In fact, they're the only reason I'm still here. I look upon them as the children I never had.''

''That's nice,'' I said. And I meant it. Most of the professors I'm acquainted with see teaching as, at best, a necessary evil, and at worst an activity to be avoided at all costs. ''What I'm hoping is that during the time you and Melissa spent together, she also talked to you about more personal matters.''

''You're asking if she confided in me?''

''*Hoping* would be a more accurate word.''

Fell nibbled on a corner of his mustache. ''And you want what from me? Exactly.''

I pushed a lock of hair out of my eyes and tucked it back behind my ear. One of these days I was going to get it cut short. ''Some insight into Melissa's state of mind. Was she depressed? Anxious? Was she fighting with her boyfriend? How did she feel about her brother? Her roommate. That kind of thing.''

''I see.'' Fell slowly chewed another cookie while he considered my questions.

I resisted the temptation to fan myself with my notepad while I waited for his answer. Fell was right. This room did heat up fast.

''The funny thing,'' he finally said after he'd finished eating, ''is that we really didn't talk much about Melissa's personal life. She was someone who kept herself to herself. She wasn't self-revelatory in any sense of the word.''

''Her roommate said that if Melissa had talked to anyone, she would have talked to you.''

Fell shook his head slightly. ''How sad. Some of my other students discuss personal matters with me, but Melissa never really did.'' He absentmindedly slid his gold wedding band up and down his finger. ''I made myself available. I even, although I don't usually do this kind of thing, since I'm not in private practice anymore, tried to initiate a conversation with her on more than one occasion.''

I began to hope I was finally going to get some information. ''Why did you do that?''

''I had a feeling something was bothering her, especially in the last few months, something other than her mother's ill health. But when I approached the subject, she became very defensive, so, naturally, I eased off. I was hoping that in time we'd be able to talk.'' Fell began chewing on the tips of his mustache again. ''In retrospect, what I should have done was called Roberts at the health center.''

''Would you characterize her as depressed? Stressed?''

Fell sighed and swiveled his chair an eighth of a turn to the right, and then did an eighth of a turn to the left. ''She was anxious. Although she could have been depressed and been compensating. Lots of times people do that. They can be in the depths of despair and give no indication of that at all. That's one of the things that makes depression so tricky. Did her roommate say she was?''

''As a matter of fact, she did.''

''What a pity,'' said Fell.

''Then I guess you also didn't know that at one point she'd been planning on getting married.''

Fell looked incredulous. ''To Tommy?''

''You know him?''

''He was in one of my classes. I just never thought . . . I'd never have put those two . . .''

''It didn't go through because the boy's father objected.''

''It seems as if I really didn't know Melissa at all,'' he observed sadly.

''I'm getting the feeling no one did.'' From where I was sitting, it looked as if Melissa Hayes was one of those people who told different people parts of the truth but didn't tell one person the whole truth.

Fell pressed his lips together. "I'm sorry I couldn't have been of more help."

"Maybe you still can."

"I don't see how."

"You said earlier that you thought something was bothering Melissa."

Fell nodded.

"But you have no idea what it was?"

He hesitated for a fraction of a second before replying. "Not really."

I looked him in the eye. "Are you sure?"

He looked away. "Yes."

"You don't even want to hazard a guess?"

"I don't think I do."

"Why is that?"

"Because I don't like making statements I can't back up."

"I'm not asking you to back things up, I'm just asking for your opinion."

"Believe me, I understand." Fell began twisting a few strands of his mustache between his fingers. "But what you have to understand is that I can't say certain things. Especially when I have no proof. Especially when I just have a gut feeling to go on. I'm talking about libel here."

I sat back. "You know Melissa's mother is dying."

"I'm aware of that."

"And that she desperately wants to find out what happened to her daughter."

Fell didn't say anything.

"Only she can't get out of her hospital bed."

He looked down and began fiddling with the knobs on his desk drawer.

"Look," I continued. "This is all going to be off the record. As you can see, I haven't been writing anything down."

"I noticed."

"I'm at a dead end. I need some help. Anything you can tell me, anything at all, would be a great plus. Please."

"I'm sorry, but I can't."

I sat forward. "Mrs. Hayes probably has less than a month to live. Are you going to deprive a woman of a dying wish?"

"That's not fair," Fell protested. "That's a terrible thing to say."

"But true."

"The reason I'm not telling you is to protect her," Fell shot back.

I saw Mrs. Hayes lying in her hospital bed. I saw the pain in her eyes when she asked me to protect her son. I remembered what she didn't say. I felt the lightness of her hands as she clasped mine.

"I think she already knows."

Chapter
17

Professor Fell folded his hands over his belly again, sat back in his chair, and raised an eyebrow. "What, exactly, does Mrs. Hayes know?" he asked.

"She asked me to protect her son."

"She used those words?"

"Yes."

"From what?"

"From the police. In regards to his sister's disappearance."

"Why should they?"

"She wouldn't say."

"I see," he murmured.

"Obviously, you're not going to tell me anything I haven't been thinking of already," I added.

"So it would seem." He leaned forward, picked up a pen, and jotted something down on the yellow pad in front of him. Then he put the pen down and made a clicking sound with his tongue.

I waited. Finally he cleared his throat and began to speak.

"What I want to emphasize," he said. "Is that what I'm about to tell you is nothing more than a gut feeling. And that it might not have anything to do with Melissa's disappearance. In fact, it probably doesn't."

"So you said."

"Have you talked to Melissa's brother?" Fell asked.

I nodded. "He's the one who hired me."

"What did you think of him?"

I answered without considering. "He's got a quick temper."

"What else?"

"He's been in trouble in the past."

Fell nodded. "Go on."

"He became very upset when his sister was only an hour late."

"Perhaps overly so?"

"What are you implying?"

"I'm just asking, why the overreaction? Did he know something? Was he overcompensating?"

"Are you saying Bryan killed his sister, hid the body, and sounded the alarm?"

Fell looked at me impassively.

"That doesn't make sense. If that were true, then why go to the trouble to hire me? A little over four months have passed since his sister has disappeared. For all intents and purposes, he's free and clear."

"Guilt is a powerful emotion. It makes people do strange things."

I thought about what Fell had just said to me about Bryan as I leafed through the pages of the Melissa Hayes file. According to Duffy Warner, the rent-a-cop who'd caught Bryan's call, Bryan had appeared frantic, pacing back and forth, when Duffy had arrived at Melissa Hayes's room. He'd then shown himself to be extremely unwilling to take Duffy's advice, yelling, "We have to look now" over and over until Melissa's roommate, Beth, had calmed him down.

Was Bryan just scared for his sister? Was his reaction a case of nerves? Had he known something? Or was this, as Fell had said, a case of guilt made manifest? It would be interesting to hear what he had to say, I decided as I was about to turn to the next page. Then I heard footsteps in the hallway outside and stopped thinking about Bryan and started thinking about me. Even though Morrell's secretary had assured me Morrell wouldn't be back for a few hours, there was always the chance that his meeting had run short or that he'd come back for something he'd forgotten.

And if he did and found me here, he'd be very unhappy. And so would I.

Because if he walked through the door, here I'd be, big as the Statue of Liberty. Only instead of holding a lamp, I'd be holding a file, a file I had no business having. My eyes darted around the room as the footsteps got closer. I told myself the person outside was just another secretary on her way to somewhere else, but judging from the way my heart was hammering away in my chest, I didn't believe me. There was no furniture I could hide behind. No back door to go through. But there was the window. I might be able to squeeze through that.

I'd started toward it, when the footsteps passed. My heart rate slowed back down. I let out the breath I didn't know I'd been holding and glanced at the clock on the wall. I had ten more minutes before Morrell's secretary came back from lunch. I planned to be out of the office in five.

"I'm going down to Didi's," she'd told me. "Today I'm going to have a hamburger. They cook them to order, you know. It usually takes about twenty minutes since I order it well done. I used to eat them rare, but not anymore. Not with that botulism thing going around. No, don't say anything," she'd said when I'd opened my mouth to speak. "Us ex- and soon-to-be-ex-secretaries have to stick together. Revolt of the working women. And anyway, I think the university should have done more. They should have tried harder. Instead of just covering their asses. Which is really, in my estimation, the only thing they care about. Besides money.

"You know, I used to care about education. I used to think it meant something. I used to think these people knew something I didn't. But that was before I started working at the university." And she got up, slipped her coat on, and patted her pockets. Then she opened the door to the outside hall. "Now, when was your appointment with Mr. Morrell?" she asked in a voice designed to carry down the corridor.

I glanced at my watch and gave her the present time.

"Well, I'm sure he'll be here soon. I'll be right back. I'm just going to run out and pick up my lunch. He's usually very prompt," she added as she walked out the door, leaving me alone in the empty office.

"I'll just sit down and wait," I called after her retreating back.

Two seconds later I was in Morrell's office, searching for Melissa Hayes's file. Unfortunately, it wasn't on Morrell's desk. I'd been hoping it would be, but given the pristine appearance of his office, it didn't surprise me that it wasn't. Morrell had probably refiled it in one of the two cabinets decorating the place. I started with the closer one and moved on to the one on the left when I didn't get any results. My fingers felt as if they'd been dipped in slurry, and I developed a bad case of the dropsies, something that always happens to me when I'm nervous.

It took five minutes before I located Melissa's folder, five minutes that felt more like twenty.

I flipped through the pages.

There weren't any surprises.

Not that I'd expected there would be.

But I was hoping. Otherwise I wouldn't have been in Morrell's office.

The truth is, I'm a closet optimist. To do the kind of work I do, you have to be. And anyway, I was due for some luck.

Only it didn't seem as if I was going to get any.

Nevertheless, when I reached the last page, I turned back to the first and started in again.

It turned out to be a good thing that I did.

Not that I understood the importance of what I was reading at first.

According to the page I had in front of me, security had logged two more incoming calls from Bryan Hayes that evening. One at ten at night, the second at two-thirty in the morning. In both, he had demanded that the campus cops conduct a full-scale search for his sister. He had also, according to the record, told them he'd called the city police. All three calls had led to the same advice: wait. Advice that Bryan Hayes had evidently found impossible to follow, since other security personnel reported seeing him and an unidentified female in places as diverse as Oakwood Cemetery, Tyler Park, and M Street. A fact that dovetailed with what Beth had told me about her and Bryan searching for Melissa throughout the night. Finally, at one o'clock the next day, following yet a third call from Bryan Hayes, security had begun canvassing the area.

After calling the local hospitals and checking with the university health center, the rent-a-cops had proceeded to question Melissa's roommate, her two suitemates, the students on her floor, her boyfriend, and the guys in his fraternity. I read their statements. Tommy West said that he and Melissa had spoken the night before she'd disappeared. They were supposed to meet at the house the next day, but she hadn't called or shown up. He, in the meantime, had been shopping and at the movies, a statement the report said the police had corroborated.

As for the time between two and four, he'd been in an American history and a sociology course. These classes, the report dryly noted, held over three hundred people and attendance was taken by sign-in sheet. However, several classmates remembered seeing Tommy, although the report also leveled a certain amount of doubt at their veracity.

I moved on to Beth. When questioned, she noted that Melissa had gone out the night before—she didn't know where, she hadn't asked, it wasn't her business, thank you very much—and come in at ten-forty. Asked how she could be so certain, she explained that her watch was broken and she'd been looking at her clock radio to see how long she'd stayed at the Shake, a bar on the west side of town, when Melissa had walked in. They'd both done some studying and at one o'clock they'd ordered a small pizza from Pete's on M Street, a fact the report confirmed. After eating it, both girls had gone to bed.

Beth further stated, as she'd done with me, that Melissa had had a nine o'clock class and was gone by the time Beth got up and that she, Beth, had spent the day in classes, in the library, and hanging out with her friends, movements the campus police had confirmed.

Brandy Weinstein saw Melissa walking down the dorm hall on her way to the stairs at around eight-thirty that morning, and Melissa's second suitemate had seen her in her ten o'clock English class on the postmodern implications of science-fiction. Whatever that was.

God, I was glad I'd gone to school when I had, I decided as I turned to the next page. I'd had enough problems with American lit.

Another girl on the floor, a Hayley Holliday, if you can believe it—what had her parents been thinking about, I wondered—had also seen Melissa in her next class, Soc. 206. Even though they hadn't sat next to each other— Hayley was reserving that honor for her boyfriend—they'd exchanged a few words. Hayley had asked Melissa if she could borrow the notes from the psych course they were taking together—evidently she missed the last two classes— and Melissa had told her to come by her room that evening to get them.

Hayley had knocked on the door around ten but left when she didn't get an answer. Beth and Bryan must have been out searching for her.

"I figured, she'd forgotten," Hayley said. "Or something else had come up. No biggie. I went and got them from a friend in another dorm."

And that, aside from lunch with her brother, Bryan, was the last time anyone could be found who had talked to Melissa. The lunch had taken place at Green's, a new health food place that had opened up six months earlier on M Street. The girl behind the counter remembered serving Melissa and her brother because she was in Bryan Hayes's stat one course and thought he was kind of cute. She'd been happy when she'd overheard Bryan calling Melissa "sis" as she'd taken their order.

"Maybe I'll invite him for some coffee," she'd told the security guard. "He must need cheering up." A sentiment that would have been dear to my grandmother's heart.

As far as the girl knew, lunch between Melissa and Bryan had been uneventful. They'd eaten and talked, but she didn't know about what. "Of course," she allowed. "They would have had to be screaming at each other for me to have heard anything. At that time of the day we're totally swamped."

As I turned the page, I felt a sharp pain and brought my finger up to my mouth. When I took it away, I watched a tiny droplet of blood from near one of my cuticles. Why are paper cuts so painful, I wondered as I went back to reading about where Bryan had gone after lunch. According to him, he'd gone to the library to study. The police were questioning selected witnesses to confirm that statement.

Obviously they'd succeeded, because otherwise Bryan would have been under arrest by now. I sucked my finger. One thing was certain. The library sure was a hell of a lot busier than when I'd gone to school. Maybe people were more studious now.

I turned to the next page. The sheet was taken up with a description of the physical search of the university and adjacent sites. Basically, security had retraced the path Bryan and Beth had taken, and they'd had just as little luck. The first thing they'd done was go through Melissa's dorm, taking care to check both the basement and the roof. Nothing was found to be amiss.

Next, they'd driven through the main campus, pausing at each dormitory to query students and to check basements and rooftops. Then they'd made a careful circle through Tyler Park, stopping to question a number of joggers and Frisbee players about any unusual activity they'd noted the day before. The results had been negative. Finally, they had driven through Oakwood Cemetery, a place designed at a time when people thought visiting with the dead was the proper way to spend Sunday afternoons, and now used by dog walkers, frats for their initiations, and by groups of junior high and high school kids for spontaneous beer parties and other less savory adventures.

According to the report written by campus security officer Mike Chapman, he'd paid particular attention to both the areas around the old, ruined mortuary chapel and the caretaker's house, and to the area where the older graves and mausoleums are located, going so far as to get out and try the doors on the mausoleums. All proved to be locked, a circumstance that had not always been the case several years before.

And that was that.

Seven hours later, the university finally conceded the truth of what Bryan Hayes had been saying all along by deed if not by word, and notified the Syracuse Police Department, who, although I didn't have their report, I was willing to guess had gone through the same steps the campus cops did and came up with the same results.

Nothing. Zip. *Nada.*

I closed the file.

I was just about to put it away, when I heard a sound that set my heart racing.

Chapter
18

What I had heard was a thud as the door to the outer office slammed shut.

That was bad. What followed was worse.

"Betsy," Morrell yelled out. "Where are you? I forgot. I need our department's projected expenses for next year for my meeting with Andrews."

I was moving toward the window, when I noticed what I should have noticed before but hadn't, because the joining had been obscured by the curtains. There was a Plexiglas sheet fastened over the bottom half of the glass, put there, no doubt, to keep people like me out. Simple but effective.

Given the circumstances, there was only one thing left to do.

So I did it.

Taking a deep breath, I walked over to the door, opened it, and stepped into the outer office.

Morrell's jaw dropped.

I gave him my biggest smile. "Your secretary will be right back," I told him. "She said to wait out here, but I was sure you wouldn't mind my sitting in the chair in your office. The ones out here are bad for my back."

"Is that right?" By then Morrell had gotten control of his face back. He put his hands on his hips. "What the hell were you doing in there?"

I looked him in the eye and lied like a trooper. "I told you. Waiting for you. I have a question I forgot to ask you."

"There's going to be hell to pay," Morrell managed to get out through clenched teeth as he pushed his way past me.

"Well, if you feel that way, I guess I'll speak to you another time." And I hurried out the door and into the hallway. It seemed like a good time to leave.

I was almost at the front door, when a hand grabbed my shoulder. I lifted it off and spun around.

Morrell was holding a file, the Melissa Hayes file I was willing to wager even though I couldn't see the label, in his other hand. "You got this out of my cabinet, didn't you?" he demanded, brandishing it under my nose.

I lied again. "No."

Morrell's eyes narrowed, his mouth thinned, he pushed his chin forward. The guy was really pissed. No doubt about that.

"I'm going to have your license revoked," he growled.

"Go ahead." I don't think this was the time to tell him I didn't have one.

A woman opened the door of the office we were standing next to and poked her head out. "Is everything okay?" she asked Morrell.

"It's fine." He waved her away. "Go back to work. Everything's under control. I'm going to arrest you," he continued in a lower voice.

"On what charge?"

"Breaking and entering, for a start."

I laughed. "I doubt it."

He waved the file in my face again. "This was misplaced. That means that someone—and that means you—put it back in a different place."

"Maybe you misfiled it."

"I never misfile things." Then Morrell opened the manila folder and pointed to a page. "I suppose I did this too?"

"What?"

"This." He pointed to a small spot of blood. A souvenir of my paper cut.

Terrific. I shrugged. "You cut yourself?"

Small drops of spittle formed at the corners of his mouth. "I can have this analyzed. I can prove you were here."

I laughed. "A DNA screening for a B and E. The D.A.'s not going to underwrite something like that for something like this. And anyway, do you really want it to get out that the head of security's files get broken into? How is that going to sound? Think about it." I half turned to go.

Morrell's fingers burrowed into my shoulder. He wrenched me around.

"This is the last time I'm going to tell you to get off me."

He brought his face to within an inch of mine. "I find you on campus again, and you're going to be very sorry."

"I'll bear that in mind." I slammed my elbow into his ribs as hard as I could.

Morrell let out a stifled gasp. His grip loosened.

I walked off without looking back.

I didn't take Morrell's threat too seriously—what was he going to do, print up a poster with my face on it and distribute it to all the secuirty guards?

It was a little after one-thirty in the afternoon and I was sitting on one of those blue chairs in the lobby of Schaefer, watching the students walk in and out, and waiting for Beth to return. According to the girl in the room across the hall, she should be coming by any minute, but any minute had proved to be over twenty minutes ago. I checked the clock on the wall, and then I tried calling Bryan Hayes again, but he wasn't in either. I went back to the *Times* crossword puzzle.

At one-forty Beth came through the doors. Even though it was a little over thirty degrees and the wind was blowing, she was wearing a light cotton jacket. She'd been seduced by the sun, just as I had, into thinking it was warmer than it was. Her backpack was half hanging off her left shoulder, and she was carrying a white take-out bag, held out in front of her. She noticed me as I got up to greet her, and smiled.

I pointed to the bag. "Anything good in there?"

"Just my lunch. Have you made any progress with the Melissa thing?" she asked.

I told her I hadn't.

She told me that was too bad, but then she really hadn't expected any.

I nodded and said that there was just one little detail I wasn't clear on.

Beth wanted to know what it was.

"Why don't we go up to your room so you can eat that while we talk?" What I had to ask her was best asked in private.

She nodded her head in agreement. As we walked to the stairs, I filled Beth in on what I'd been doing in regard to Melissa. Even though I'd put in a fair number of hours— it's amazing how many hours trying to get information from people takes—it didn't sound as if I'd been doing much of anything when I laid it out.

"Your new roommate never seems to be in," I observed as Beth placed her key in the lock.

"That's because she's living with this guy off campus."

"Then why is her family paying for a room in the dorm?"

"They don't know."

We stepped inside. "Seems like a leitmotif."

The sugar glider was running around in excitement. Beth dropped her backpack and jacket on the floor, then went over and took the little animal out of his cage.

"Did you miss me?" she crooned to him as he ran up her arm and perched on her shoulder. He chittered a reply. She reached into the white paper bag and brought out a carrot stick and gave it to him. "Besides oranges, that's his favorite food," Beth explained to me. "Only you can't give him too many because they upset his stomach." Then she sat down on the bed, took her sandwich out, and began to eat. "Sorry," she said through a mouth full of food. "I'm starving."

I was too, but eating would have to wait till later.

The wind was rattling the windows as I sat down next to Beth. It sounded colder out than it was.

"I just have one question."

Beth took another bite. "What's that?"

"Did you meet anyone interesting at the Shake?"

"Oh, my God," Beth cried. Then she started to cough.

Chapter
19

Beth continued to cough. Alarmed, the sugar glider leaped off Beth's shoulder and onto the nightstand.

"Are you okay?" I inquired, thoughts of the Heimlich maneuver dancing in my head, when Beth didn't stop. Her face was getting red. Her eyes were beginning to tear.

She nodded and pointed to her throat. "Down the wrong way," she managed to gasp out before another fit of coughing overtook her.

I ran into the bathroom, got a glass of water, and handed it to her.

"Sorry," she said when she could speak again. "I took too big a bite. My mother is always telling me to eat slower." She wiped the tears away from under her eyes with the back of her hand, and began coaxing the sugar glider back onto her arm with low clucking sounds. A moment later he skittered up her sweater sleeve and settled himself on her shoulder.

"That's not why you choked," I said gently.

Beth raised her chin slightly and straightened her spine. "I don't understand what you mean," she insisted.

"If you didn't want anyone to know you went to the Shake, why did you tell the security guard the name?"

Beth took another bite of her sandwich. This time she seemed to be directing all her energy into chewing. The sugar glider gurked, and she tore off a tiny piece of bread and gave it to him. It occurred to me as I watched her that it was fortunate she hadn't asked how I knew, because I wouldn't have had a good answer to give her.

"Why didn't you just say you were someplace else?" I persisted. "No one would have known."

"What's wrong with the Shake?" she inquired defiantly after she swallowed.

"Nothing." I studied Beth. Resolution had strengthened her features. "Nothing at all." She was staring straight ahead at the wall across the way. Suddenly the answer to the question I'd just asked dawned on me. "You didn't think anyone would know what the Shake was, did you?"

Beth finished the rest of her sandwich and carefully wiped her hands with the paper napkin that had come in the bag.

"You know, no one really cares anymore," I said into the deepening silence. "I certainly don't." And it was true. I didn't.

"Cares about what?" she asked, playing dumb.

Hoping to get a reaction, I replied, "Cares that you're a lesbian. Excuse me, bisexual."

Beth opened and closed her mouth, then opened it again, like a fish gasping for air. She was trying for outrage and ended up with silly. I'd seen high school kids give better performances in school plays. "Just because I went to—"

I interrupted, pointing out that most women would have picked another place.

"There was a group I wanted to hear, not that it's any of your business."

"In this case, I think it is."

"Anyway, did you forget? I have a boyfriend."

"No. I didn't forget." Years after the fact I'd found out my college roommate had been sleeping with my boyfriend and her girlfriend at the same time.

Beth crushed the white bag into a ball and tossed it into the direction of the trash can. It arched, hit the rim, and bounced off. She cursed under her breath and started to get up. The sugar glider let out an alarmed gurk, and she turned to quiet it.

I told her not to bother. "I'll get it." I scooped up the paper, tossed it in the trash, and sat back down. "It's very fashionable these days. Magazine covers. Sitcoms." When I'd been in school we'd never mentioned lesbianism, but then we hadn't talked much about heterosexual sex either.

Beth tugged the neck of her turtleneck up and gave me a blank look. "So I hear."

I tried the direct approach. "Were you having an affair with Melissa?"

"Don't be ridiculous," she retorted after a pause of a second or two had gone by. We were back at indignation. She wasn't too successful doing it the second time around either.

I tried again. "Was Melissa having an affair with Jill? Is that why she was so upset when she died?"

Beth laughed shrilly. "Where do you get this stuff? That's the stupidest thing I ever heard. What makes you think Melissa was doing anything like that?"

"Someone told me." I didn't think it was necessary to tell her the someone was Marks.

Beth gnawed on her bottom lip.

"You know," I continued as I studied the top of the dresser that had once housed Melissa's clothes. Now it was covered with pictures of Beth's roommate's boyfriend. I wondered what Melissa had decorated it with when she had lived here, but it was an idle thought and I didn't pursue it. "You're not talking to a Christian fundamentalist. I couldn't care less what you or Melissa did. The only reason I'm asking is that it could give me another line to explore in searching for her."

Beth didn't reply. I put one of my fingers under her chin and gently turned her face around until we were looking into each other's eyes. She looked very young. If I'd had to have put an age to her then, I would have said thirteen. I lowered my hand. "You do want me to find her, don't you?"

"Of course I do," she cried. "Why do you think I told you to talk to Professor Fell? Did you?"

"I just came from there."

"And?" Beth demanded, her voice high and hard.

I thought about what he'd said about Bryan. "He gave me some ideas. Now I'd like to hear yours."

The corners of her mouth turned down. "What do you mean?"

"Exactly that. You seem to be the person she confided in the most."

"But I thought . . ."

"I know. Evidently, though, he and Melissa talked mostly about psychology. You're the one Melissa seems to have talked to the most." I reached inside my backpack and got out a stick of gum. I would have killed for a cigarette, but that would have to wait till I got outside. "Want one?" I asked, offering the rest of the pack. Beth nodded. She reached over and took a stick. "I don't think Melissa really confided in anyone," I observed after a moment had gone by.

Beth smoothed out a wrinkle on the comforter in an automatic gesture, after which she lifted the sugar glider off her shoulder. He was so small, he fit into the palm of her cupped hand. "He reminds me of a stuffed animal I used to have when I was six years old," she said. "I carried him around everywhere. His name was Leon."

"What happened to him?"

Beth shrugged. "My mother threw him out. She said I was too old for toys like that."

Mine had thrown out my blanket. "Were you?"

She shrugged again. "Probably. Anyway, how can I remember how I felt about something that happened that long ago?" She lightly petted the top of the tiny animal's head. "I wonder if that's why I've always liked small things?" she mused.

"Is that why you kept him?"

Beth nodded. "No one else wanted him. It was the least I could do."

"Why did you feel you had to do anything?"

Beth turned to face me. Her expression was fierce. "Because I was her roommate. I should have known something was wrong."

"The same could be said about her brother and her boyfriend," I pointed out.

"That's different. They're guys. The only way they'd notice anything was wrong is if you bled all over them."

"A lot."

Beth gave me a ghost of a smile and went back to fiddling with her comforter.

"So Bryan didn't know about his sister?" I asked.

"He knew she was upset."

"I'm not talking about that."

Beth's chin went up again. She wasn't going to give it up. "There's nothing to know," she insisted, but this time her tone was a little weaker.

"But if there was," I went on, determined to get something, anything, out of her. "Hypothetically speaking, would he be upset?"

Beth shook her head ever so slightly as the sugar glider chittered and climbed back on her shoulder. I wondered if the little animal thought she was a tree.

"I haven't the vaguest idea what he would think," she said. "We never talked about that kind of stuff."

"How about Tommy?"

She shook her head again. But this time there was an almost imperceptible pause.

"Did you tell him?"

"No." Beth studied her sneakers.

"Who did?"

"My boyfriend," she whispered.

"Why did he do that?"

"Because he was his friend. He thought he should know."

"What did Tommy say?"

"He had a fit."

"When did Chris tell him?"

"Right before Thanksgiving."

"You mean right before Melissa disappeared?"

Beth grabbed one of my hands in hers. "Tommy would never do anything to hurt her. You have to believe that."

"How can you be so sure?"

"Because I just am." And she started to cry.

"Who the fuck are you to come into my place and start talking trash to me?" Tommy demanded. His face was suffused with anger, so was his voice, but he was keeping the volume low. He didn't want any of his fraternity brothers popping their heads out of their rooms again to see what was happening.

He'd been in the middle of studying when I'd walked in on him unannounced. Other than his books being scattered all over his bed, the place looked the same as it had when I'd been there a couple of days before—messy.

"I can't believe you're saying something like that," he continued.

"Believe it." At first I'd tried being tactful, but that hadn't worked. I'd intimated and he'd ignored. Finally I'd just come straight out and asked and Tommy had gone ballistic. His fraternity brothers rushing out had quieted him down though.

"Why don't you drop the act," I'd told him after they'd left. "I know you know. According to Beth, her boyfriend already told you about Melissa."

"Yeah?" Tommy hurled the book he'd been holding down on the floor. It landed on a shriveled-up piece of pizza that had been sitting in an open box. "Well, she's a goddamned liar, because Chris didn't tell me anything. And I wouldn't believe him if he did. Which he wouldn't."

I caught his gaze and held it. After a few seconds he glanced away. "Why should Beth lie?" I asked.

"How the fuck should I know?" His voice was truculent. He was glowering, all contained energy ready to charge. "Maybe because she's jealous of Melissa."

"Why should she be?"

He poked himself in his chest with one of his fingers. "Because she was going out with me and I ditched her for Missy."

"This is just a regular little Peyton Place, isn't it?"

"What the hell is Peyton Place?"

"Nothing." Suddenly I felt incredibly old.

I folded my arms across my chest and leaned against the door to his room while I wondered if what Tommy had just told me was true. By now it was almost four o'clock and I was tired and irritable. Maybe having a Snickers and a Coke for lunch had something to do with my mood. Or maybe it was getting another parking ticket, my third this month. Or it could have been finding out from Tim when I'd called that the crickets we'd ordered hadn't come in, and that two of our baby boas had mouth rot. Or maybe it was the information that George had dropped by Noah's Ark wearing a scowl that would have scoured the paint off a wall. Or maybe I was just tired of smart-assed fraternity boys swaggering around as if they owned the world.

But by any measure I was having a crappy day. Maybe it was time I shared the wealth.

"Tommy," I said, "I'm told a lot of guys consider that kind of thing a turn-on, but I guess you're not one of them. Or are you?"

Tommy's jaw clenched. So did his fists. He jumped off his bed and started toward me. In the mood I was in, I was half hoping he'd take a swing at me.

"My father was right," he growled as he approached. "He's spoken to people about you. They said you were scum. And you are."

"I'm glad to live up to my reputation," I told him in the kind of smarmy voice guaranteed to set someone's teeth on edge. "I wouldn't want to disappoint you. Or him."

"Get out," he screamed, doing a good imitation of a train barreling down the track as he came toward me. "I won't have you talking about Melissa that way."

So much for not making a scene in front of his fraternity brothers. I could hear doors opening around me. Guys were out in the hall, demanding to know what the hell was going on. Not that I could answer them. All my attention was focused on Tommy.

By now he was a little less than six feet away from me.

He was still coming.

I didn't budge. I didn't even flinch. Six years ago I would have run for cover. But not now. The kid was just a punk. After some of the guys I've handled, he didn't faze me at all. I continued talking.

"You're going to get hurt," I told him.

Tommy grunted and took a swing at me with his right hand. He put his weight into it, but he was too slow. I had time to move out of the way. He hit the door frame, knuckles first. I heard a thunk.

He turned white and grabbed his hand.

"I think I broke it," he gasped, doubling over in pain.

Chapter
20

I hung my jacket on one of the pegs in George's closet and shut the door. It was nine-thirty at night, and given the last couple of days, I should have been home in bed, but George had called me at the store around seven and insisted I come over. "I have a surprise for you," he'd told me.

"It better be good," I said, thinking of our last conversation.

"It'll make up for the other night," he'd promised.

How could I have said no?

"Where's your dear nephew?" I inquired, stifling a yawn. The house smelled of spaghetti sauce and garlic bread. I wondered if George had any left.

"Gone for the evening." George grinned. "That's my surprise. Quiet, isn't it?"

"Very." The TV was off. So was Raymond's boom box. "Are you sure you didn't tie the kid up in his room and duct-tape his mouth shut?"

"Now, that's a tempting thought." George bent down and scratched Zsa Zsa's rump. She leaned against him and let out little woofs of pleasure. The dog was shameless. "Alas, no. He's at a Junior Crunch playoff game."

I raised an eyebrow. "You reneged and let him out of the house to go to a hockey game? What did he do to earn time off for good behavior? Scrub your bathroom floor with a toothbrush?"

"Don't get smart. He's with a teacher I know."

"That was nice of him."

George straightened up. "Don thinks he and Raymond can connect." He made the quote sign with his fingers around the word *connect,* leaving no doubt about what he thought of the sentiment.

"What gives him that idea?"

"Because he was raised in the suburbs and doesn't know any better."

"I'm sure Raymond will teach him. It will probably be an educational evening all around." I got down to the important question. "When will this teacher friend of yours bring him back?"

George's grin grew wider. "Not for a while."

"A while, a while?"

George nodded.

"Works for me." At this point I would have taken a five-minute quickie—not, of course, that I would ever have said that to George. I wouldn't want his ego to get even larger than it is.

The wind was rattling the glass in the storm door as I walked toward the hall closet. The wooden floor was cold under my feet. A draft eddied around my ankles. Zsa Zsa looked up from George's sofa, woofed a hello, and went back to sleep again. She looked elegant with her blond curly fur framed against the leather, although I was sure George wouldn't think so. The wind shook the windowpanes and prowled around the house's corners, looking for a way in. I repressed a shiver as I reached for my jacket and started looking through my pockets. Maybe it was the middle of March, but it sounded like February outside. According to the Weather Channel, it was going to be twenty degrees with a windchill factor of three tonight. I hurried back up the stairs, wishing I were wearing something besides George's shirt.

George opened one eye as I came in the room. "Where'd you go?" he asked, his voice heavy with the sleep I'd disturbed.

"To get this." I handed him the restraining order against me that had been taken out by Tommy's father. I'd been carrying it around in my jacket pocket ever since I'd been served earlier that day.

He turned over on his back. "What is it?" he asked, holding up the paper so he could read it by the bathroom light.

"You'll see." I pointed toward the ceiling. "You want me to turn on the overhead?"

George shuddered. "God, no," he said, and kept on reading. "Too bright. Nice," he commented when he was done.

"Not to mention fast," I observed, getting back under the beckoning warmth of the covers.

George stifled a yawn. "Less than twenty-four hours. That guy definitely lit a fire under someone's ass."

"And I didn't even do anything."

"If I'm reading right, it says here his son broke two knuckles on his right hand."

"It's not my fault if he was trying to punch me and missed."

George grunted. "MacVaney obviously didn't see things the same way you did."

"That man would sign anything someone put in front of him. Okay, I admit I may have upset the kid a little, but that's it." I turned on my side and supported my head with my hand. "It just goes to show what high-priced legal talent and contacts can do. I couldn't have gotten something like this rammed through."

"One thing I'll say about you," George began to say.

"That I'm good in bed?"

"No. I was going to say that you certainly have a flair for making enemies."

"Well, my grandma always said . . ."

"Let me guess. If it's worth doing, it's worth doing right," George finished for me. "Do me a favor. If you're going to go back and talk to Tommy again let me know, so I can have some bail money set aside."

"You don't think they'd release me on my own recognizance?"

"Not with these people involved."

"Maybe," I mused, "I should go talk to Tommy's father instead. He seems to be the man calling the shots."

George chuckled dryly and handed the restraining order back to me. "Good luck," he told me after I'd put it on the nightstand.

"Why not? What could he do to me?"

"That's not the issue. The issue is why bother? If he knew anything, and I doubt he does—what kid confides in his father?—why would he talk to you anyway?"

I shrugged. "You never know."

"In this case, I do." The planes of George's face composed

themselves into a serious expression. "Robin, don't annoy this guy. You're like a mosquito to him."

"Mosquitoes draw blood."

"They also get squashed."

"Not if they're fast."

"There's always Raid," George pointed out. "You can't run from that."

"I can mutate."

"Puhleeze."

"All right. But I'm beginning to wonder if there isn't something seriously wrong here."

"With the kid or the father?"

"Take your pick."

"I disagree." George made the kind of soft popping sounds with his mouth that he did when he was interested in something.

"Okay," I said after turning everything over in my mind for a minute. "I'll grant you the kid going off was in the normal range. I come in; I make some sexual insinuations about his missing girlfriend."

"And him," George reminded me.

"Right. I could see where he wouldn't take it well." I stretched and tugged the blanket up. "I concede I shouldn't have pushed so hard, but until I did, I couldn't get anything out of old Tommy-boy."

"Well, you did get a reaction."

"True." The wind keening outside interrupted my thoughts. "God, I wish it were spring."

"It will be soon."

"I don't want soon. I want now."

"You know that's your besetting sin. Impatience."

Personally, I thought anger and arrogance were, but I wasn't going to argue the subject.

"Do you think Tommy knew about Melissa?" George asked after a couple of seconds had gone by.

"Definitely. Why should Beth lie?"

"Because if he did know, it would give him a motive for killing Melissa."

"I've been thinking about that, but it seems a little excessive."

George turned toward me. "Never underestimate male vanity. It's a powerful force. Maybe Melissa said something like 'You think you're so good.' And laughed in his face. Told him that all the time she'd been pretending and had really been getting it off with Beth. Don't forget. Women kill men in the kitchen, but men kill women in the bedroom."

"I'm trembling already." I fluffed my pillow up. George's sheets were Egyptian cotton. Mine were from J.C. Penney. On sale. Sometimes you really do get what you pay for. "You just wouldn't think that kind of thing would be such a big deal these days," I reflected.

"No matter what the media says, it still is to some people," George said quietly.

"How do you mean?"

"My aunt kicked one of her sons out of her house when she found out he was gay. Her pastor told her it was the right thing to do."

"What happened to him?"

George shrugged. "I don't know. He disappeared."

"I wonder if Mrs. Hayes knew?"

"You could always ask her."

I considered the suggestion for a moment. I couldn't imagine doing it. "Only if I absolutely have to," I concluded. "Even then, I'd think about it."

George yawned.

"What about Tommy's father?" I said.

"You mean, did he know about Melissa?"

"I was thinking about the restraining order."

"He already told his son not to talk to anyone else. This is just one step up."

"Having it issued makes the kid look guilty."

"I'm sure Michael West doesn't see it that way. Look at it from his perspective. If you had a kid, would you want someone coming around and asking him all sorts of sensitive stuff at any time of the day or night? I certainly wouldn't."

"I've talked to the kid only twice," I protested.

"But you're the third person that we know of. Don't forget, he's already been spoken to by the police and campus security and most likely more than once. Then you come along and get his son all hot and bothered. Another problem to deal with. Maybe he can't get his son to listen to him—which must put a hair up his ass—but he sure as hell can get you to back off. Most likely he's got a lawyer on retainer. So it doesn't cost him anything to get a restraining order written up."

"Having a father like that would certainly give you a sense of invulnerability," I mused. "I can do whatever. Daddy will take care of it."

"Or it could make you feel like you don't have any balls."

"Maybe," I agreed, remembering the tentative expression on Tommy's face when he'd come out to greet me the first time.

George reached over and put his arm around me. I snuggled into him. We lay that way for a few minutes, listening to the sighing of the wind. He kissed the tips of my fingers and then he kissed me. I kissed him back.

He wrapped his arms around me. I moved closer.

A car stopped in front of the house.

Zsa Zsa began barking in the high-pitched yappy way small dogs do.

"Jesus, your dog is a pain in the ass," George grumbled in my ear. "She barks at everything."

That wasn't true, but I wasn't going to argue the issue now.

Instead, I yelled at her to shut up and we went back to doing what we had been doing before.

I heard the front door opening.

The word "yo" floated upstairs.

George glanced at the clock and cursed. I followed the arc of his look. It was almost eleven. Somehow we'd both lost track of time.

Then we heard footsteps running up the stairs.

"I didn't know it was so late," George muttered.

I think we both realized at the same time that the bedroom door was opened. What had we been thinking, I wondered as I pulled the sheet up under my chin. George leaped out of bed and raced across the room. He tripped over his shoes, stumbled then righted himself, and continued on.

The stumble cost him no more than a second or two, but that second or two was enough.

George had his hand on the doorknob when he and Raymond met.

Raymond's eyes slowly traveled the length of George's body. He grinned.

"Damn," he said. "There goes another myth."

Chapter
21

The next few minutes were frenetic. George grabbed Raymond by the shoulders and jacked him up against the door. I heard a thud as the kid's body made contact with the wood. He hung there, his arms flattened against the door, his feet dangling a couple of inches off the ground. His mouth was open, his eyes were wide with surprise. He looked like a scarecrow on a pole. Too bad he didn't have a field to guard.

"Listen, you little shit . . ." George was saying in a tone of voice that would have frozen Lake Erie solid when I yelled from the bed for him to put Raymond down.

The sound distracted George, and he turned his head toward me. He must have loosened his grip slightly at the same time, because suddenly Raymond's feet were planted on the floor while his jacket was still being pinned to the door by George. As he took a step back, a tight, smug little smile flitted across Raymond's lips for a few seconds before vanishing. Seeing the expression on Raymond's face jolted me. It made me realize that maybe Raymond had gotten what he wanted: George out of control. Except I don't think he was aware of the possible ramifications. This was someone who'd never heard the saying about reaping the whirlwind, or if he had, he hadn't paid close attention to the message.

Raymond took a couple of steps back. His movements were jerky with nervous energy. George let the jacket go. It dropped at his feet in a heap. He didn't even look at it. He was too busy glaring at his nephew. I hadn't realized how skinny Raymond was until that point. If he weighed in at one hundred forty pounds I'd have been surprised. George had about eighty pounds on him, and all of it muscle. It was like watching a cairn terrier and a rottweiler.

"I was joking, man," Raymond whined as he rubbed his shoulders. His voice cracked when he spoke. For the space of a heartbeat he sounded like the fourteen-year-old boy he was. "Don't you do snaps?"

George didn't answer immediately. He was too busy taking deep breaths, trying to get himself under control.

"Get out of here. I'll talk to you later," he finally ordered when he had.

"I bet you don't even know what snaps is," Raymond persisted.

But George didn't reply. If he had, if he hadn't ignored him, if he'd even said something like good night, I think things might have ended there. Instead, he turned around, walked inside the bedroom, and began closing the door.

Raymond took a step forward. "I'm talking to you, man."

"Well, I'm not talking to you," George told him, flinging the words over his shoulder as he shut the door.

But that wasn't acceptable to Raymond.

Maybe he just had to have the last word.

Maybe his ego insisted.

Maybe he'd always started stuff, watched the show, and slipped away when things got out of hand.

Or maybe he had a death wish.

"You know what your problem is?" Raymond yelled at George from the safety of the hall.

I could see George's hand tightening on the doorknob. "Let it go," I begged.

He didn't listen. Instead, he yanked the door open and stuck his head out of the bedroom. "I know what your problem is going to be if you don't get in your room," George growled.

"Your problem," Raymond countinued, ignoring the warning in his uncle's voice, "is you're tagging so much white pussy, you forgot what it's like to be a nigger."

George let out a roar and ran out into the hall. The next thing I heard was the door to Raymond's room slamming shut, followed by a *kerthunk,* which I took to be the sound of George hitting it. I wound the bed sheet around myself and ran down the hall. George was using his shoulder as a battering ram when I got there.

"Don't," I said.

George didn't answer. He just kept methodically working on the wood. *Thwack. Thwack. Thwack.* The door was trembling. I had an idea that Raymond was too.

"George!" I screamed.

He kept on going. I don't think he even heard me.

"Leave it alone," I told him, and grabbed his left arm.

He spun around and threw a punch with his right hand. I jumped back. But I wasn't quite fast enough, and his knuckles grazed my shoulder. I groaned and staggered back. It felt as if I'd been clipped by a truck.

George's eyes widened in remorse when he realized what

he'd done. His hand went to his lips. He took a step toward me. "Jesus, I'm sorry."

"Forget it." I grabbed his forearm and led him back to his bedroom. His skin was lathered with a fine coat of sweat.

"I could have killed him," he whispered as he sat down on the edge of the bed. I couldn't believe the sheets were still warm. It seemed as if hours had passed since I left it. "I wanted to."

George's shoulders sagged. His mouth crumpled. He looked as if he were going to cry as the implications of what he'd nearly done sunk in.

"It's okay." I stroked his arm. He pulled away. I put my hand down.

"No, it isn't." His voice was anguished. "I've never been out of control like that in my life." He leaned his elbows on his thighs and dropped his head into his hands. "I don't know what I'm going to say to him."

"Think of it this way. Tonight Raymond has definitely learned about the power of words," I said, trying to make a joke. But even to my ears, it sounded lame.

George lifted his head. "I can't believe I just did what I did. Jesus, the kid's only fourteen. How could I have let him get to me like that?"

George didn't expect an answer, and I didn't give him one.

"Family," George moaned, and dropped his head back in his hands. "Now I remember why I'm living up here."

The sound of his breathing filled the room. I watched the muscles in his back bunch and release by the thin light streaming through the bedroom blinds from the streetlamp outside. I wanted to comfort him, but I didn't know how.

We sat separated by six inches of crumpled-up comforter for the next half hour as I watched the minutes on George's digital clock come up and listened to the house's creaks and groans. Finally I got up and started getting dressed. There didn't seem to be much point in staying. George didn't ask what I was doing as I hunted around the room for my clothes, and I didn't tell him.

He was still sitting on the edge of his bed, staring off into space, as I left. When I said good-bye, he nodded his head to indicate he'd heard me.

I paused in front of Raymond's room on my way out and asked if he needed anything. But he didn't reply either—like uncle, like nephew, I suppose—and after repeating my question I walked down the stairs and whistled for Zsa Zsa. She came trotting out from the kitchen, where she'd probably been cowering under the table. She wasn't big on loud noises and angry words.

"Let's go." I fished a dog biscuit out of my jacket pocket and gave it to her. She wagged her tail and gobbled it down. This is why I like dogs, I decided as I fed her another biscuit. They always respond.

The wind stung my face. I watched the upper half of a skinny cedar across the street bend from side to side and automatically calculated the path it would take if it fell. It was an exercise I and a number of other people tended to indulge in since the previous year. Late last March we'd had a storm that had tipped over a fair number of tall, shallow-rooted evergreens. They had caused a great deal of damage as they crashed into roofs, through windows, and onto cars. The one across the street looked like a good candidate to behave the same way if we had another spell of bad weather. I wondered why the owner hadn't taken the tree down already, but maybe he was like me—always giving things the benefit of the doubt well past the point when I should.

I turned on the radio as I drove through the streets on

my way home and lit a cigarette, drawing the smoke deep into my lungs. I was surprised to find my hands were a little shaky. I tried not to think about what could have happened in George's house, but I couldn't help it. One good, solid punch from George and his entire life and Raymond's could have been changed forever, but then, I suppose you could say that about crossing the street and getting hit by a car.

I turned up the volume on the radio. The news was on. That was always good for a laugh. The announcer was saying something about the state funding a new marina on Onondaga Lake, which was pretty funny if you considered that it was one of the most polluted bodies of water in America and that in the summer, if an algae bloom started, it stank so bad that you could smell it five miles away.

However, I thought as I switched to another station, who was I to argue with economic progress. Especially since there'd been so little of it recently in Syracuse. Or maybe I was just jealous. After all, a lot of people were going to get rich from this project. Only I wasn't going to be one of them. Which was too bad. It would be nice to stop having to worry about money for a change.

The streetlights reflected off the bare tree branches and the cars parked in the driveways and the lawns and the houses. Here and there people had left out old furniture or washing machines for the DPW to collect. A few people were out walking their dogs, but most everyone else was inside, either asleep or watching TV or getting ready for the next day. At night Syracuse seemed tidy and quiet, removed from the problems of places like New York City. That's why Raymond's mother had sent him here.

But Syracuse wasn't problem-free. It wasn't the quaint small city, Cecilia thought it was. We had our murders, shootings, and robberies just like anyone else. Recently guns and drugs had become more visible as gang members had moved upstate. I shook my head as I pulled into my driveway and killed the cab's engine. Suddenly I felt completely drained. The evening had taken more out of me than I thought. I watched my cat jump up on the hood and walk to and fro in front of the windshield, meowing for me to come out and let him in the house and feed him. Patience isn't James's forte.

But then, as George had pointed out, it's not mine either.

After I opened up a tin of tuna for him—white meat packed in oil to make up for my not having come home sooner—I listened to my answering machine.

There were four phone calls. One was from Professor Fell, one from Melissa's mother, one from Beth, and one was from Bryan Hayes. I didn't care.

Whatever they had to say would keep until morning. I was too tired to talk.

Chapter
22

Bryan hovered behind me as I stood in the doorway of his sister's room. "You didn't have to come over," he told me again.

He hadn't been happy to see me when he'd answered the bell and seen me standing on his porch. Sporting a three-day stubble, bloodshot eyes, hair that needed a shampooing, and a stained flannel shirt and khakis, he looked as if he'd been on a bender.

"Had a late night?" I'd asked.

He'd run his hand over his chin. "Late enough. What are you doing here anyway?"

"You called, remember?"

He squinted. "Yeah. Right. Last night. I was just calling to find out how things were going."

"The same as before. Which is why I decided I wanted to take another look at Melissa's room."

"You already went through it."

"I wasn't very thorough though. I'm hoping I missed something the first time around." Coming here had been a spur-of-the-moment decision made with the help of a doughnut, a second cup of coffee, and the sinking feeling I wasn't getting anywhere.

"Like what?" Bryan demanded.

"If I knew, I would tell you."

"I see." Bryan had stepped aside and let me in the house reluctantly. Then he'd followed me up the steps to his sister's room.

"I don't like people pawing through her things," he'd announced when we'd reached the doorway.

"Really." I'd half turned. "You didn't seem to mind the first time."

"I didn't like it then either. I just didn't say anything." Bryan pushed his glasses up the bridge of his nose with his index finger. They stayed there for a minute before sliding back down. "Melissa is a very private person. She'd be angry if she knew people were going over her belongings."

"Given the circumstances, I'm sure she won't mind."

"Yes, she would," he insisted. "You don't know her like I do."

"And therein lies the problem." I took a couple of steps into her room.

Bryan followed me. "What do you mean by that?"

"I mean I don't know her. I don't have a sense of her. Now if you don't mind, I'd like to do this alone."

"Why?" Unconsciously he ran the tips of his fingers over a small stuffed lion sitting on top of one of Melissa's dressers. "I can help."

"I'm sure you can, but I really would prefer to go through her things by myself." Everything else being equal, I couldn't concentrate with Bryan crowding me.

He scowled, reminding me of nothing so much as a Dober-
man who'd been told to stand down. "All right." He took
a hesitant step back. "But if you need me, I'll be in the
kitchen."

"Don't worry, I'll call you if I do," I assured him.

He walked to the door and stayed there, anxiously watching me in what I was willing to bet had become for him a
shrine. Either that or he was afraid that this time I was going
to find something I shouldn't.

"Go," I ordered, and waved him away.

Finally, when it became clear I wasn't going to do anything
until he left, Bryan turned and walked down the stairs. A
moment later, after I heard the opening of a cabinet door,
the clink of cutlery, and the scrape of a chair being dragged
across the floor, I went and sat down on Melissa's bed. The
mattress was surprisingly soft and I sank down into it. I
sighed, reached in my backpack for a cigarette, and studied
Melissa's room. Nothing had changed. It still looked the
same way it had the first time I was here. Her desk was still
piled high with books, notebooks, miscellaneous sheets of
paper, and a variety of pens and pencils. The duffel-sized
laundry bags still lay on their sides on the beige carpeting,
next to the four cartons crammed with stuff from her dorm
room.

I sighed again, took another two puffs of my Camel, and
flicked the ash into a glass that was sitting by the nightstand.
I tried to block everything I'd been told about Melissa out
of my mind, and just think about what her room was telling
me.

But I guess it wasn't feeling conversationally inclined.

Because it wasn't telling me a thing.

Of course, if the room had spoken to me, I would have
headed straight for the hospital. Which shows you what

happens when you get old. In the days when I was dropping acid on a regular basis, the room could not only have said "hi" but metamorphosed into the frigging Australian outback, and the only thing I would have said was "cool."

Now I'd be dialing 911.

That's progress for you.

Oh, well. I stubbed my cigarette out, stood up, and got to work. I skipped the cartons—I'd already inventoried their contents pretty thoroughly—and began with the laundry bags. I dumped the first one out. A musty odor filled the room as Melissa's sheets and towels fell onto the carpet. The only thing they told me was that she liked purple and green. The second bag contained variously colored T-shirts, shorts, jeans, cotton sweaters, sweats, men's shirts from the Gap, and a variety of underwear from Victoria's Secret.

I put everything back and started on the closet. I went through her blouses, mostly man-tailored, and skirts, mostly straight. I looked in the pockets of her jeans and slacks and jackets, but outside of the odd movie ticket stub, I didn't find anything of interest, after which I eyeballed a couple of pairs of inexpensive jogging pants and jackets. Those, along with the sweats I'd found in her laundry bag, made me remember that Chris had told me that Melissa jogged.

The three pairs of old running shoes I found on her top shelf confirmed his statement. I wondered why no one other than Chris had mentioned it to me as I dragged a chair over so I could get a better look at the other shoes sitting on the shelf. But maybe Melissa had been just a casual runner, someone who jogged once or twice a week, when the mood took her. I sighed. So far I hadn't turned up anything surprising. Melissa's clothes, sober, middle-of-the-road, confirmed the picture I'd built of her. If she was leading a double life, it had nothing to do with her wardrobe.

Ditto that for her shoes. They were boring, functional pumps, sandals, loafers, and boots, all in black and brown. No high-heeled red slingbacks, purple suede clogs, or black stilettos for her. Somehow, Melissa seemed awfully old for her age, I decided as I started in on her pocketbooks. There were four of them altogether, also in black and brown. The only things they contained were loose change, pens, more ticket stubs—the kid had been a moviegoer—and crumpled-up tissue.

I checked the back of the shelf. I found two empty shoe boxes, a sewing kit, eight wadded-up pairs of paint-stained sweat pants and shirts, some old socks, a couple of stained blouses, and a black plastic bag. The smell of mildew hit me when I opened it. Well, that was better than some of the other things I could be smelling, I reflected as I stepped off the chair and dumped the contents onto the carpet. A pair of jeans, a once-white T-shirt, a pair of socks, and sneakers tumbled out.

Everything was splotched with gray and lavender patches of mold. Melissa must have been out for a quick run and gotten caught in the rain, changed, thrown the stuff in a bag, and then forgotten about it. I'd done that kind of thing myself. Several times. I put the clothes back in the bag and set it where I'd remember to bring it down to Bryan. He could throw them out. Next I looked through Melissa's drawers again. The same wadded-up T-shirts, the same sweaters, the same nightgowns were still in there. I took out the collection of birthday cards tied up in a neat blue ribbon and went through them again.

All of them were from her mother and brother. Evidently, Melissa had saved everything they'd sent her since she was six years old. The thought that they might never see her again depressed me, and I tried to shove it out of my mind as I took the drawers out of the dresser and checked along the sides and the bottoms. I found three old sales slips, a jogging bra, and a pair of earrings. Not exactly earth-shattering finds.

I put everything back where it belonged, sat down on Melissa's bed, and began going through her nightstands. The last time I'd done that, I hadn't paid much attention, just opened and closed the drawers. This time I did more. The nightstand drawer on the left yielded a box of tissues, a bag of cough drops, and a tweezers. I moved on to the one on the right. I turned on the clock radio. It was still set to the campus station. I paged through the stack of *Glamour* magazines piled next to the radio.

Then I opened the nightstand drawer. I wasn't hoping for much, but in the back, underneath the paperback copy of *Carrie,* another box of tissues, and the bottle of prescription antihistamines, I found a manila envelope. I opened it. Inside was the first article on Jill Evans's death. On the border, above the headline, someone, Melissa, I assumed, had written, "Our responsibility to the dead informs our lives." At the bottom, in the same handwriting, were three lines of poetry.

> *She fell,*
>   *a butterfly,*
> *wings plucked, unable to fly.*

I reread the poem.

It reminded me of the one written in Melissa's philosophy textbook on moral responsibility.

I spread the sides of the envelope and shook it.

A laminated rose petal fell out.

I picked it up and held it to the light.

Chapter
23

I took in the Hayes kitchen as I walked toward Bryan.
Because the room was in the back, I hadn't seen it the first
time I'd been in the house. It had been done colonial style
with knotty-pine wooden cabinets, wrought iron hinges, and
curved moldings. Given the look of the appliances and the
style of the cabinets, I'd say the kitchen had been remodeled
about twenty years earlier. Aside from a few burn marks on
the white Formica counter and some areas near the door
where the linoleum was curling around the edges, the place
showed evidence of having been lovingly cared for up until
recently.

Several healthy-looking spider and ivy plants hung from
hooks positioned in front of the window over the sink. The
lettering on a set of blue ceramic jars clearly proclaimed
they housed sugar, flour, and salt. A variety of kitchen imple-
ments sat in a matching blue and white splatterware pitcher.

The salt and pepper shakers were also blue and white. So were the wall clock and the potholders.

Of course, the blue and white motif didn't quite go with the dozen or so Corona bottles sitting on the counter. Or maybe it did. After all, Corona's label was blue, wasn't it? A guy who color-coordinates his beer with the decor can't be all bad—although I had a feeling Mrs. Hayes wouldn't have seen her son's interior decorating style that way. I also had no doubt she wouldn't have been pleased to see the condition her son had reduced her kitchen to. I'd be willing to bet the room had been immaculate when Melissa and Mrs. Hayes had been here. But not now.

Now the white Formica counter was spotted with food stains, the sink was overflowing with dishes, the garbage can smelled as if it needed to be emptied, and the white linoleum floor had sticky black patches on it. Evidently housework wasn't Bryan's forte. But then, it appeared several other things weren't either: like coming up with answers to the questions I was asking him.

For the second time in as many minutes, Bryan eyes shifted to the newspaper article I'd laid out on the kitchen table and then back up at me.

"What's your point?" he finally said.

As I moved my chair a little closer to the table, Bryan's scent washed over me. He smelled as if he needed a bath. I pointed to the poem. "My point is what these lines indicate."

"They don't indicate anything. Jill was her friend. She felt lousy when she died."

"Her wings were plucked? Who plucked them?"

"Jill was a girl with a lot of problems." Bryan ran his fingers through his hair. "Missy felt responsible for her, but then, she felt responsible for everyone."

"Including you?"

"Yes. Including me."

"So what kind of problems did Jill have?"

Bryan shrugged and scratched his side. "The usual college-coed kind."

"And what are those?"

"In a word—guys."

"Guys in general or one guy in particular?"

"One guy in particular. She was having a relationship. The guy dumped her and she got all depressed."

"Depressed enough to throw herself out the window?"

Bryan shrugged again. "I guess."

"You don't seem that upset."

"What do you want me to say?" he demanded.

"You could pretend to be concerned."

"I could, but I'm not going to. What she did was stupid. Wasteful. Thoughtless. She wasn't sick. There was nothing wrong that couldn't have been fixed. You don't take the gift of life and just toss it away."

"You're thinking of your mother, aren't you?" I asked softly.

Bryan picked up the lacquered rose petal I'd found lying on top of the article and gently stroked it was his thumb. "My mom used to make these before she got really sick." He took his wallet out of his pants pocket and opened it. "See," he said, showing me his petal. "Every year she'd give Missy and me new ones. It's a good-luck charm. It means that Christ will protect you." He reverently lay both petals on the table. "Although in this case it doesn't seem as if He's doing a very good job, does it?" He ran his hand through his hair again, then pushed his glasses back up the bridge of his nose. "God, I hate this not knowing. It's making me crazy."

"I can imagine."

"I can't concentrate on anything anymore. I go to the store and I forget what I went in for."

The morning sun streaming though the window highlighted the circles under Bryan's eyes, the ashy undertone of his skin, and the stubble on his chin. Constantly moving his hands and shifting his weight around in his chair, he seemed unable to find a comfortable place to sit.

"What's that?" he asked, pointing to the bag I'd found in Melissa's closet.

I pushed it across the table.

Bryan wrinkled his nose when he opened it. "Running stuff. I think I can throw this stuff in the trash," he told me, hastily closing the bag back up.

"It was in the back of her closet."

Bryan's laugh ended in a choked little sob. He moved the petals around with the tip of his finger. "I remember once she forgot to put my clothes in the dryer. My mother discovered them in the washing machine a week later. She was furious. No matter how many times we washed them after that, we could never get the smell of mildew out. We finally had to throw them away."

Bryan reached for the petals. "Do you mind?" he asked, picking them up. When I told him I didn't, he put both petals in his wallet and put the wallet back in his pants pocket. "Did you find anything else up there?"

"What I showed you is it."

He grunted and took a sip out of the can of Coke in front of him. "What now?"

"I think we have to talk."

"We are talking."

"No. I mean really talk. If you want me to find your sister, you have to start being honest with me."

"I have been."

"Are you sure?"

"Yes." Bryan picked up his pen and doodled a tulip in the margin of the paper he'd been editing.

I watched the dust motes dancing in the air around Bryan and listened to his breathing. He had a slight wheeze I hadn't heard before. I wondered if it was stress-induced.

"I don't think you have been."

Bryan kept drawing. His eyes were fastened on his paper. "Why do you say that?"

"For openers, you didn't tell me you'd been arrested for threatening someone with a gun."

Bryan's hand froze. Then he put down the pencil. "That was a long time ago. And I wasn't threatening, I was waving the gun around."

"I like the distinction."

"I don't see what that has to do with my sister going missing."

"Why'd you have a gun in the first place?"

He leaned back in his chair and ran his finger along the edge of the table. "I needed it for protection."

"Who were you protecting yourself from?"

"I owed some guys some money."

"For what?"

"What difference does it make?" Bryan raised his voice.

"Was it for drugs?"

"It was a gambling debt, if you have to know."

"That's not the story your mother told me."

Bryan bowed his head. "I didn't want to upset her. She had enough on her plate."

"How charitable. What happened to it?"

"The gun? The cops confiscated it." Bryan picked up his pencil, drew a top hat, and began carefully coloring it in.

"You never got another one?" I asked. I was curious. Most

people I know who have had a gun continue to want to have one.

"No." Bryan laid the pencil back down. He blinked his eyes and looked down at the floor. "No, I didn't."

He was lying. "Are you sure?"

"Of course I'm sure."

I didn't say anything. The refrigerator began to hum. The condenser had turned on.

"Why? Who told you different?" he demanded after a couple of moments.

I still didn't say anything.

"It was Tommy, wasn't it?"

I hoped this kid never got it into his head to play serious poker. "As a matter of fact, it wasn't."

"I don't believe you."

"You don't have to."

We glared at each other. Two crows sitting on the branch of the oak tree outside the house cawed. Recently Syracuse had become inundated with them. They seemed to be everywhere.

Bryan swallowed. "What are you implying?" he finally said.

"I'm not implying anything. I was just asking if you'd ever gotten another gun."

"What if I did?"

"Can I see it?"

"It was stolen."

I raised an eyebrow.

"Someone broke into our house and took off with some stuff."

"Stuff?"

"Yeah. Stuff." Bryan's tone was truculent. "Some of Melis-

sa's jewelry. My gun. The cash we used to keep by the refrigerator in the kitchen.''

''When did this happen?''

''The middle of October.''

''I don't suppose you happened to report the break-in to
the police?''

''Melissa did.''

''If I checked, would I find the report?''

''Go ahead.''

''Would I find the gun mentioned in it?''

Bryan didn't answer.

I answered for him. ''I wouldn't, would I? Because it wasn't
registered.''

''So what! Big deal! Lots of people have unregistered
guns.''

''True. But their sisters aren't missing.''

Bryan got up, strode over to the sink, turned on the tap,
filled a glass with water, and took a long swallow. As he
drank, I noticed his hand was trembling slightly.

''See, this is why I didn't tell you about the gun in the
first place.'' He drained the glass, put it in the sink, and
wiped his mouth with the back of his hand. ''You do a couple
of bad things and they follow you around for-fucking-ever.''

''I take it that's also the reason you didn't tell me you
were sent away when you were younger.''

''That has nothing to do with now.''

''I understand that among other things you had problems
with your sister. I understand that's why you were sent away.''

Bryan's jaw muscles tightened. ''Is that what my mother
said?''

I moved a bread crumb away from the edge of table with
my finger. ''Not directly. But she certainly implied it.''

Bryan crossed his arms over his chest and planted his feet

about six inches apart from each other. "The reason I was sent away was because my mother was never here to look after me. That's the reason I was sent away."

"Then you never hurt Melissa?"

"No."

"Are you sure?"

"I was a kid. Kids do dumb things. We got into a fight. I don't do that kind of stuff anymore. Period. End of story."

I thought about Bryan's run-in with Tommy. Somehow I didn't think it was. "Your mother is worried that you have."

"Is she now?" Bryan's eyelids dropped slightly, giving his eyes a hooded appearance. He jiggled his left foot up and down.

"She loves you."

"She sure has a funny way of showing it." The jiggling got faster.

"She asked me to make sure nothing happens to you."

Bryan twisted his mouth in an imitation of a smile. "It's a little late now to be so concerned. You can tell her to relax. I've got everything covered."

"She's worried."

Bryan laughed bitterly. "I just bet she is. Don't look at me like that."

"Like what?"

"You were staring at me."

"Sorry, I didn't realize I was."

He hit the edge of the sink with the flat of his hand. "How would you feel if your mother suspected you of killing your own sister?"

"I don't think *suspect* is the right word."

"It seems right enough to me." Bryan began pacing back and forth in front of the sink. "No matter what I do, it's never good enough. No matter what I do, she's never going to trust me."

I didn't say anything.

"The fact that my own mother—" He lifted his hands in the air and dropped them back down. "That she . . . do you know what that makes me feel like?" he demanded.

"Not good, I imagine." I lit a cigarette. "What kind of gun was it anyway?"

Bryan poured Rice Krispies and milk into a white bowl. "Just a cheapo Saturday night special. No big deal. The gun was a mistake. I admit it. But I like having one around. It makes me feel safe," he told me as he fished a spoon out of the sink and rinsed it off. Then he sat back down next to me.

I put my lighter away. "Did you get another one?"

"No. I didn't. You know the old saying, three strikes and you're out. I figured two were enough in my case."

What Bryan was telling me might be the truth—although I doubted it—but I let it go. I wanted to hear what else he had to say.

"Anyway, you shouldn't be talking to me, you should be talking to Tommy," he informed me, going back to his old song.

"I've spoken to him."

"And?"

"And I don't have anything to link him to Melissa's disappearance."

"Speak to him some more." He ate a spoonful of cereal.

"Why are you so set against him?"

"Because the guy's a schmuck."

"That covers a lot of territory. Could you be a little more specific?"

"I bet he didn't tell you how upset Melissa was when he told her they weren't going to get married."

"No, he didn't, but you didn't tell me either," I pointed out. "In fact, you didn't even tell me they were planning a wedding. I wasn't sure that you knew."

"Oh, I knew all right!" Bryan pushed his cereal bowl away. "I spent all night trying to get Missy to calm down."

"Why didn't you tell me?"

"I had my reasons."

"Which were?"

He lifted the spoon up and brought it back down with more force than he should have used. Little droplets of milk splattered onto the table. "I was afraid you'd tell my mother," Bryan said, mopping up the spots with a paper napkin. "She doesn't need to deal with that on top of everything else."

I leaned forward. "Why is that so horrible?" I inquired, thinking of Melissa's relation with Beth. Mrs. Hayes would probably have liked that a lot less. "Did Tommy calling it off have anything to do with her relationship with her roommate?"

"No," he snapped.

"Because Beth—"

"Beth is an idiot. And a liar. She looks nice but she's one of those people who likes causing trouble for the pleasure of it. You can't believe a thing she says."

"Then what did it have to do with?"

Instead of answering, Bryan looked away from me, twisting his head toward the doorway that led to the hall, as if he were expecting someone to appear there, and mumbled something I couldn't understand.

"What did you say?"

He turned back and looked at me. "I didn't say anything."

"Yes you did."

He glared at me. Mr. Defiant.

I don't know, maybe he expected me to beg him. I pushed my chair back and got up instead. Suddenly I was tired of Bryan, tired of his games, tired of trying to root out snippets of information from him. I wanted to get back to my store and my dog. I'd been leaving her alone too much lately. And I wanted to call George.

"Where are you going?" Bryan demanded.

"Back to work." And I told him why.

"You can't."

"Why? There's no point in staying if you won't talk to me."

Bryan's expression turned sulky. Maybe he didn't like having his fun interrupted. "All I said was that Tommy's father is a putz."

I put my backpack down and perched on the edge of the chair, ready to get up if Bryan stopped talking. "Tommy told me his father was responsible for the marriage being called off."

"Just because he's got all this money now he thinks he's better than everyone else."

That's America for you. The Land of Upward Mobility. "It sounds to me as if you knew Mr. West before your sister became involved with his son."

Bryan frowned. "I did."

"And," I prodded, making a come-on motion with my hands.

"My mom used to work for him when he first started out. She did the bookkeeping for him."

"I thought you told me she sold dresses."

"That was later."

"Why did she switch?"

''Because the bastard had her blackballed,'' Bryan confided in a burst of bitterness.

''Was she stealing money?''

He scowled, indignant at the suggestion. ''My mother would never do anything like that. She was fired because she wouldn't sleep with him.''

Chapter
24

It just goes to show, you learn something new every day, I thought as I left Bryan's house and drove over to the campus to keep my appointment with Dr. Fell.

Mrs. Hayes and Mr. West.

Who woulda thunk it? Bryan's fixation on Tommy was beginning to make more sense. Bryan's mother had gotten involved with Tommy's father, Bryan's sister with the son. We were talking soap opera–land here. I wondered if that was the reason Mr. West hadn't wanted his son seeing Melissa.

Could be.

Did this connect with Melissa's disappearance in some way? Had she not known and just found out about it and decided to run away? Had she provoked a fight with Tommy? Or, despite what Bryan had said, had he found out about the wedding and tried to stop Melissa? Had the disagreement escalated the way family matters often do?

Or had the bluebird of happiness come and taken Melissa away?

Tune in next week, folks, and find out.

I paused in front of Fell's office and looked at what was to become the new computer center. Sheets of blue tarping were draped over the girders of the building like fabric on a mannequin, shrouding the workers inside from view. Every once in a while a gust of wind would pull the tarps aside and I'd catch a glimpse of a man scurrying around on the newly laid floor. The building was definitely coming along.

Too bad I wasn't progressing as well.

I felt a twinge of guilt, thinking about how Mrs. Hayes had sounded on the phone. Her voice had been a faint whisper, an echo of herself, when I'd spoken to her earlier that morning. I wasn't looking forward to having to tell her, when I saw her that evening that I hadn't made any progress, and I especially wasn't looking forward to asking her about her relationship with Tommy Hayes's father. But I put those concerns aside for the moment and concentrated all my energy on thinking about my upcoming interview with Professor Fell. I was curious to hear what he had to tell me. Hopefully it would be worth my time.

Fell glanced up from the journal he was reading and put his pencil down as I came in. He had bags under his eyes. Tufts of hair were sticking out from his head at odd angles. He laughed self-consciously and smoothed them back down with the palm of his right hand.

"I had trouble sleeping last night," he said, alluding to his appearance. "I'm told that happens when you get older."

"So I've noticed." I took the seat in front of his desk. The chair really was uncomfortable. He needed to requisition a new one.

Fell fiddled with his pen, then put it down. "I've been

thinking about our last conversation," he began. Then he stopped talking and picked up his pen again.

I made encouraging noises. I seemed to be doing that a lot this morning.

"The last time we spoke, you asked me about Jill Evans. About whether her death could have affected Melissa?"

"Yes?" I thought back to the clipping about Jill I'd found in Melissa's nightstand.

"And about how I said it probably hadn't." Fell combed his mustache with his fingers. "I think I was wrong."

I told him about the poem I'd just found.

"Plucked wings," he murmured, his face composing itself into a thoughtful expression. "Evocative phrase. I didn't know Melissa wrote poetry, but then, everyone does when they're young, don't they? I wonder when we all give it up?" He picked up his pen once more, put it down, and leaned back in his chair.

"I think the question is: Who plucked her wings?"

"I'm inclined to think of that phrase as metaphorical myself."

"Why do you say that?"

"Jill had a drinking problem. I think the plucked wings refer to alcohol or the demon rum," said Fell, making quote marks in the air with his fingers around the words *demon rum,* "as we liked to say in the old days."

"I take it Jill Evans was a student of yours?"

"In a manner of speaking. She was in my introductory psych lecture, but that's a large class. The T.A.'s take—"

"I know how it works," I told him.

He gave an apologetic smile. "I'm sure you do. No. The reason I know is that Melissa and I had a number of conversations about alcoholism and the courses of action open to people who are dealing with friends or significant others who are grappling with that type of issue."

"I take it these weren't hypothetical discussions."

"I thought they were in the beginning, but then she broke down and told me the truth."

"What did you say?"

"I suggested she inform her R.A. and talk to the psychologist at the health center."

"Did she?"

Dr. Fell chewed on the ends of his mustache for a few seconds before replying. "She said she was going to, but I don't think she ever did. Actually, I'm sure she didn't." He sighed and pushed himself away from his desk. "It's a hard thing for someone her age to do that kind of thing. At that point in your life you see it as ratting out your friend. Then, of course, when something happens, you feel all that guilt, all those if-onlys."

"Actually it's hard for someone of any age to do," I said, thinking back to my dead husband. "You don't want to lose a friend or a lover. You're afraid if you say anything, they'll get mad and stop talking to you. It takes a lot of courage."

"Exactly." Fell shook his head enthusiastically, seemingly genuinely pleased that I'd gotten the correct answer. I could see where he would be a good teacher. He seemed to have what the best ones do—a generosity of spirit.

"Can I ask why you didn't?"

"Speak to her? Oh, I did. No. That's not true. What I did was tell her if she ever had a problem, she should come speak to me." A regretful expression flitted across his face. "I should have done more. Made more of an effort to reach out." He constructed a steeple with his fingers and touched the tip of his nose with it. "If I had known what was going to happen, I definitely would have, but at the time I felt it wasn't my place. After all, I didn't really know the girl. We'd never really spoken. For all practical purposes, as far as I was concerned, she was just a name on a class list.'' He combed his mustache with his fingers again.

"I did pursue the subject a little further anyway, or at least I tried to, but as soon as Melissa found out I'd talked to Jill, she began backtracking. Telling me maybe she'd made a mistake, maybe she was overreacting. It's a common form of behavior when people are afraid to act. If I don't see it, then I don't have to do anything about it.''

"I'm not unfamiliar with the process. I know what denial is.'' In fact, I could have said I was the queen of it.

Fell gave a dry little laugh. "I'm sure you do. Everyone does.'' He shook his head. "Forgive me. I didn't mean that the way it sounded. I know I tend to become incredibly pedantic.'' He picked up the pen, began gnawing on the tip, then put it back down. "I stopped smoking two weeks ago,'' he told me. "I don't know what to do with my hands anymore.''

"That's one of the reasons I went back.'' I watched two trucks roar their way up the access road toward the construction site, blue exhaust fumes trailing behind them.

Fell swiveled in his chair to the left and followed my gaze out the side window. "They say they're going to be done in another month, but they said that two months ago. I really can't stand this anymore. I've complained. Everyone has. For all the good it's done.'' He snorted and swiveled his chair back in my direction. "Sorry, go on.''

"Thanks. Bryan told me Jill was having guy problems.''

Fell rested his hands on his belly. "Melissa mentioned something about that, but she didn't go into much detail. Mostly we talked about Jill's drinking problem.''

"What did she say?''

"About the boy?"

"Yes."

Fell scratched his cheek reflectively while he thought. "As near as I can remember, it was your classic unrequited-love story. Jill was involved with some kid on campus. Then the kid decided he'd rather be involved with someone else, and she couldn't accept that. I thought her drinking was her attempt at self-medication."

"Do you know who the kid was?" I asked.

"No, I don't, but I can try to find out if you think it's important."

"It isn't really."

Fell sat up and planted his elbows on his desk. "As I said, most of the conversations Melissa and I had were hypothetical." He made a clucking noise. "Tell me, by any chance, have you talked to Bryan recently?"

"I just came from his house. Why?"

"I wondered how he was doing."

"Not well." Suddenly without meaning to I found myself telling Fell about the conversation I'd had with him.

Fell leaned forward when I got to the part about the gun. He shook his head sadly. "I should be shocked. Ten years ago I would have been. It's frightening how many people today choose to carry weapons," he continued. "Frightening. The NRA has a lot to answer for. I will never understand why someone would want to own a gun. Never."

I don't think it said a lot about me that I did.

Chapter
25

The sun had finally come out. The clouds had thinned and the gray sky was laced with bands of blue. As I got into my car I watched a gray and a black squirrel chase each other up and down the branches of the maple across the street. At twelve o'clock we were probably at the high for the day. Forty-five degrees. People were walking around with their jackets open. As I drove over to where Jill Evans had died, I spotted groups of students decked out in shorts, T-shirts, and Dock Siders. Two black Labs trotted beside their Frisbee-toting master. Everyone was waiting for spring.

I should have been at the store filling out order forms and figuring out where to put the new bird toys I'd ordered instead of pondering the house Jill Evans had taken a header off. I didn't know what I was hoping to find. Over a year had gone by since the accident. And although in the cosmic scheme of things a year is nothing, it's a lot if you're looking for evidence. Not that I was. I just wanted to be able to picture what had happened.

Besides, the house was close by. Ten blocks away at most. Smack-dab in the middle of student-apartment heaven. Or hell. Depending on your roommates. And your landlord.

Two hundred seven turned out to be a large, dilapidated yellow and brown colonial with green trim. Gingerbreading festooned the two attic dormers. A porch that would be good for sitting out on in the summer faced the street.

Two old cars were parked in the driveway, and a third one sat, ticket affixed to its windshield, half on, half off what had once been grass in the small patch of lawn that constituted the front yard. Typical absentee-landlord property, the paint was peeling off the wood, the garbage cans were still standing out by the curb, and the foundation plantings, five scraggly arborvitae, looked as if they might not make it through to enjoy the coming spring.

I walked up the steps and pressed the bell. It gave out two anemic rings and stopped, as if it were too tired to continue. I tried again. A minute later a tall, skinny guy in his mid-twenties answered. The sounds of flamenco guitar spilled out through the open door. The guy was wearing jeans and a ripped black T-shirt. His hair was in a ponytail, he had three rings through his eyebrow and his hands were stained with ink. He had a pen tucked behind one ear and an annoyed expression on his face. I'd obviously interrupted him in the middle of something.

When I told him why I was there, his expression softened a little. Yes, he said, he had heard about what had happened here, his mother had told him, but he hadn't been in Syracuse then so he really couldn't help me. For that matter, everyone else in the house was new too. They were all at class anyway. I was welcome to come back and talk to them later if I wanted, but he was in the middle of a project and had to go.

As he began shutting the door, I asked him if I could see the room Jill Evans had fallen out of and he said that was up to the guy who was living there and that he'd be home around six tonight. Now, if I'd excuse him. He had work to do.

He touched one of his eyebrow rings pensively. "You know," he said to me as an afterthought, "it feels kinda funny living in a place where you know someone has died." And he finished closing the door.

He was right. It did. After I'd found Murphy dead in the garage, I hadn't gone in there for months and I'd given the car he'd died in away. I hadn't wanted it around. Come to think of it, I still parked the cab in the driveway, and it had been how many years now? Interesting. I stood on the sidewalk, lit a cigarette, and drew the smoke into my lungs while I stared up at the attic dormer and thought about the night Jill Evans had died.

She'd gone to the party. According to the article in the *Post Standard,* she'd had way too many beers. Too much vodka. Then she'd gone up to the third floor. A student said she'd told him she'd wanted to lie down. Why the third floor? Because the other bedrooms were occupied? Because it was quiet? Because she was looking for someone? And she'd done what? I walked around the house.

The fire escape leading up to the third floor looked as if it had been constructed from a child's Erector set, but I was sure it was up to code. If it wasn't, that would have been reported in the papers. Had Jill stepped out on it for a breath of fresh air because she was feeling dizzy, then felt even worse, put out a hand to steady herself, and gone over instead. It would be easy enough to do. The fire-escape railings weren't very high. What was certain was that it had been her bad luck to land wrong. Instead of breaking a leg, she'd broken her neck and, according to the M.E., died instantly. Which was just as well.

Because she'd landed in the back of the house, no one had seen her. She'd lain outside for a couple of hours before anyone had realized she was gone. By then everyone had assumed she'd gone back to the dorm. It wasn't until the person who was living next door had come home that she'd been found.

I thought about the quote Melissa had written in the margin of the newsapaper article detailing Jill Evans's death, the one about "our responsibility to the dead."

What did she mean by *responsibility?*

Responsibility for what?

Keeping her memory alive?

Why should she feel that way?

Guilt.

Why? For what? Not getting her to stop drinking?

I stubbed out my cigarette and lit another one. As I watched the flame catch the paper, I thought of something else. Could Melissa have felt guilty for another reason? A more specific one. Where had Melissa been the night Jill Evans died? I always assumed she hadn't been at the party. No one said she was. But then, no one said she wasn't.

Maybe she'd felt guilty because she was there when her best friend died.

I studied my gold cigarette lighter for a minute, felt its satisfying weight in the palm of my hand.

I had about ninety-seven hundred things to do. I went to find Beth.

I found Holland Adams instead.

Chapter
26

Holland was sitting cross-legged on her bed, applying metallic green polish to her nails, when I walked into her dorm room to ask her where Beth was.

"She's in class," she informed me, pushing a strand of blond hair off her forehead with the back of her right hand. "She won't be back until five."

"Maybe you can help me."

Holland carefully coated her pinky, then leaned over and put the applicator back in the bottle before answering. "I already told you everything I know about Melissa."

She didn't ask me to come in, so I stayed leaning against the door. "This is a little different."

"How so?" She blew on her nails. I wondered if she ever used them in place of a knife in case of an emergency.

"You were suitemates with Jill and Melissa, right?"

"I already said I was," she replied, tilting her head slightly to the left and opening her eyes wide.

Funny, I could have sworn they were brown, not green. I

was about to ask her when the girl from the room across the hall came over and asked Holland if she had a Diet Coke.

"Sure," Holland replied, indicating the mini refrigerator sitting next to the desk. "In there."

As the girl got the soda, I marveled once again about how much stuff Holland and her roommate had managed to fit into their room. When I'd gone off to college, I'd brought my clothes, my typewriter, bedding, and towels. Period. We didn't even have a phone in our room. We'd had to use the one in the hall. Things were sure different now. This room had more stuff in it than a closeout sale at Macy's.

Aside from the phone and the refrigerator, Holland's room contained a microwave, a TV, a VCR, a stereo, and a computer, not to mention color-coordinated bedspreads, drapes, rugs, posters, and tons of stuffed animals. The only thing I could see missing were the books, but then, college had never been about studying anyway.

"So," Holland said, waving her left hand in the air to help the polish dry after the girl left, "what do you want to ask?"

I explained.

"Duh. Of course she was there." Her tone indicated what she thought of my question. She waved her hand around again. "So was Beth. Everyone knows that."

"Including the police?"

Holland shrugged. "I assume they know. It wasn't like it was any secret. It was a big party. Lots and lots of kids were there."

"Are you sure about Melissa?"

Holland blew on her nails. "Of course I'm sure. She came to my room about four o'clock in the morning wanting to borrow some Advil. She said she had a really bad headache. She said she'd been at the party and had too much to drink."

"How do you know it was the party Jill Evans died at? Did she say it was?"

"Not specifically."

"Then how do you know?"

"I assumed."

"Why?"

"Because it was the one everyone was going to," Holland said impatiently. "I already told you that."

"Did she say anything else?"

"Yeah. She was weirding out."

"How do you mean?"

Holland indicated her night table with a nod of her head. "Open the drawer. I would, but my nails are still wet."

I did what I was told.

"Good. Now, all the way on the bottom you'll find a kind of bracelet made of brown cloth."

I began looking. "I don't see it," I told her as I pawed through a multitude of lipsticks, bottles of nail polish, emery boards, cotton puffs, jewelry, packets of tissues, and bags of hard candy.

"It's there," Holland insisted. "I kept it because I felt funny about throwing it out."

When I finally found it, I could see why she'd said that.

"She said I should take it," Holland told me. "She said she didn't believe anymore, that maybe it would protect me. I didn't know what to say. I don't believe in all that religious crap. But I didn't want to upset her any more. She looked upset enough as it was. And anyway, I'd never wear anything like that. Would you? Look at the color."

Mrs. Hayes took the scapular in her hand and looked at it sadly. I hadn't known what it was called until I'd showed the brown cloth bracelet to Tim.

"Melissa gave this away?"

I nodded. "To her suitemate."

"She told me the clasp broke and she lost it."

"She gave it away the night Jill Evans died."

"It's very bad luck giving it away." We studied the pictures on the scapular together. "I made this for her. I made one for her and one for Bryan every year. Like the rose petals." Mrs. Hayes turned her face toward the window. "To keep them safe. If Melissa had worn it, maybe she'd be here now."

I doubted it, but then, I've never believed in magic of the conjuring kind. I didn't say that though. It wouldn't have been right. Instead, I watched people walking to and from their cars in the parking lot outside the hospital, and when I got bored with that I studied the red and white blinking lights of a plane flying through the night sky until I couldn't see them any longer.

"Why didn't she tell me?" Mrs. Hayes whispered, her face still turned away. "Maybe I could have helped."

The classic question. Why doesn't anyone ever tell the people that matter the important stuff, the stuff that counts? I didn't know. No one does.

"I could have helped," Mrs. Hayes repeated.

What was that line about wishing making it so? A hospital cart clattered by outside. Someone down the hall laughed. Someone else moaned.

"She probably didn't want to worry you," I said, trying to console her.

Mrs. Hayes turned her head toward me, but her eyes weren't on me. She was staring off, looking, I suspected, at a scene from an earlier, happier time.

"When she was little and she lost something, we used to pray together." Mrs. Hayes's voice became higher, quavered, and cracked. "Please St. Anthony, come around. Something lost must be found."

I reached over and took her hand. It was as pale as the bed sheet, as fragile as a luna moth's wing.

"Tell me about Tommy West's father," I urged.

I was sitting in front of Tommy West's fraternity house, watching the ends of the orange streamers wound around the pillars on the front porch blow in the wind, while I waited for him to turn up, thinking about the story Mrs. Hayes had told me. It was an old one, a classic. Flaubert or Stendhal would have elevated it to art. Proust would have dwelled on it for four volumes. It went like this.

A woman works for a man for a while. He's married, has a kid, a business that's expanding. She's widowed with two children, happy to have something that pays the bills, dreaming of more, seeing her position growing as the firm does. She and her boss have what the woman considers to be a good working relationship, which is the way she wants to keep it.

Then he starts putting the move on her. At first it's just hints, jokes. She thinks he's kidding. He steps it up a notch. Finally she gets "it." But she pretends she doesn't and ignores the hints, hoping if she plays dumb, maybe her boss will get bored and stop. He doesn't. He gets more persistent, figuring, no doubt, that she'll change her mind. After all, he's gotten where he is today by never taking no for an answer. Only she doesn't change her mind. Instead, she spells it out. Now it's his turn to pretend he doesn't understand. At this point she could have packed up her pencils and left, but she doesn't want to. She needs the work. And she has her eye on the promotion he's promised her.

Which is when she makes her mistake. She threatens to tell his wife, figuring that'll end things. But she's miscalculated with whom she's dealing. He promptly fires her, and then, when she goes looking for a job, proceeds to tell everyone who calls up for a recommendation he canned her for stealing. Only she doesn't know this at first and she can't figure out why she can't get hired.

"Today you have agencies you can go to about that kind of thing, but we didn't back then. I used to lie awake at night, wondering how I was going to feed my children and planning my revenge. But then one of my friends offered me a job in her store, selling dresses. I thought I'd take it for a little while. But I stayed."

"Did you still think about revenge?" I asked. I know *I* would have.

"At first." Mrs. Hayes gave a little smile. "But then I forgot about it. Between the kids and my jobs and the house I was too tired when I got into bed at night to do anything but sleep. Later, I decided that maybe things had happened the way they had for the best."

I leaned forward slightly. "Why?"

Mrs. Hayes squeezed my hand with hers and let go. "Because that was when I found my faith again, that's when I began to pray. If everything had been going the way I'd planned, I don't think I would have." She closed her eyes and opened them again. I noticed her eyelids seemed as thin as rice paper.

She was fading. I asked my last question. "How did Bryan know?"

"He overheard me on the phone when I was talking to one of my friends." She made a disapproving sound, moving her tongue against the roof of her mouth. "There was a little alcove off the hall. I found out later he'd sit under the table I'd put there and listen to my conversations."

Her eyelids fluttered and dropped for the second time. Her lower jaw fell, bringing even more prominence to the hollows under her cheekbones. A gentle snore escaped from between her lips.

I got up from my chair, leaving her there, all alone in her bed. People should have someone with them when they die, I thought as I walked to my cab. The lights in the parking lot leached the color out of my hands, making them look ghostly, making me wonder if loneliness wasn't contagious. I shook my head to clear it, lit a cigarette, and drove over to Tommy West's fraternity house, but he wasn't there. I could have gone home, but I decided to kill a couple of hours waiting to see if he'd show up. Fifty minutes later he did.

Tommy West stared at me in amazement when I tapped him on the shoulder. I'd caught him as he was about to go into the fraternity house. He was holding a pizza box in one hand and a six-pack of soda in the other.

"Pineapple?" I asked.

He wrinkled his forehead in befuddlement. "What are you talking about?"

I pointed to the box. "Does your pizza have pineapple?"

"You're not supposed to come near me," he sputtered. "I have an order of protection out on you."

"True," I replied, taking advantage of his confusion to take the pizza and the soda out of his hands and lay them on the porch floor. I didn't feel like getting belted in the face with six full cans of root beer. "Now you know why no one pays attention to the judicial system. It doesn't work."

He reached for the pizza. I put my hand on his shoulder to stop him. "After you answer two questions."

"I can have you arrested."

"So you said." I grinned.

Tommy West turned toward the door. "I'm calling the police."

"Go ahead, but then I'll tell them."

"Tell them whatever you like."

"Do you really want them to know you were at the party the night Jill Evans died," I said, making a logical extrapolation.

He whirled back around. "Who told you that?"

"It doesn't matter."

"Well, they're full of shit because I wasn't there." His voice rose. Anyone driving by could have heard him.

"Beth was. Melissa was. From what I heard, for all practical purposes the entire undergraduate body was."

"But I wasn't," he insisted. "Even if I were, so what? Since when is going to a party a crime?" His voice was high with fear.

"It's not. I just want to know why my mentioning it upsets you so much?"

"It doesn't. You do." He went inside the fraternity house where, I had no doubt, he was at that very minute calling the police.

Gee, I thought, kicking an empty beer can lying on the sidewalk as I walked back to the cab. And I hadn't even gotten around to asking him my second question. I paused to light another cigarette, all my attention momentarily diverted to shielding my lighter flame from the wind.

I accomplished it on the second try.

Maybe I should have started with the question about his father.

Oh, well.

I guess I'd have to talk to Builder Man tomorrow.

I took another puff and blew smoke rings out into the night air.

Call it intuition, I thought as I watched the white vapor vanish, but somehow I didn't expect him to be much more cooperative than his son had been.

Chapter
27

Con Tex's parking lot had been emptying out for the last half hour or so. At six at night the only items remaining were a dozen cars and a flock of sea gulls squabbling over the day's litter left behind on the macadam. I was parked off toward the edge of the lot, partially shielded from full sight by a scrim of arborvitae, which gave me a good view of both Onondaga Lake and the entrance to Michael West's office building. The lake was a sullen dark gray in the early evening dusk, while the white stone ultramodern office building, lit by spotlights placed every thirty feet or so, seemed garish and ill at ease among its evergreen plantings, like a girl who'd overdressed for a party.

I took a sip of my root beer, another bite of my corned beef sandwich, and wiped off the drop of Russian dressing that had fallen onto my black leather jacket with the tip of my finger. Luckily, I thought as I watched Michael West head out of his office building, the man didn't believe in strict security procedures. I hadn't seen one guard come by since I'd been parked there. But for all practical purposes Con Tex's office was a ten-minute ride away from the city. This wasn't the sort of place you'd drop in on. If you didn't have a reason to be there, you probably wouldn't be. Anyway, it wasn't as if they were manufacturing weapons. I took a last bite of my sandwich, put it down on the brown paper bag resting on the seat next to me, started my cab up, and drove toward West.

He was a fast walker. He looked neither to the right nor the left, just took one small, rapid step after another, swinging his briefcase in time with his stride. He walked, I decided, like a man who was preoccupied with the day's events, a man eager to get back home. I put my foot down on the gas. Lost in thought, he didn't look up. Which was fine with me because I wanted to waylay him before he got to the protection of his car. Since I'd been sure he wouldn't see me if I called his office to make an appointment, I'd chosen this route instead, hoping that the element of surprise would work for me.

For once it looked as if I'd made the right decision.

West had his hand on the door handle of his black Infiniti when I rolled alongside of him and called his name.

He turned toward me. "Do I know you?" he asked, puzzled. Given the circumstances, some men would have been alarmed, but not him. Part of it, I suspect, was that I was a woman, and part of it was his assurance in himself, an assurance he wore like a well-tailored suit.

"I doubt it," I said as I stopped my car and got out.

"You look familiar."

"It's possible." By then I was standing next to him. I was surprised to realize that he was only five feet six and on the slender side. Somehow he'd looked bigger when I'd seen him in the fraternity house.

He studied my face. Then he frowned. His expression hardened. Enlightment had struck. "I'm going to have you arrested," he informed me, using the same words his son had the night before.

Only Tommy hadn't made the call. Or if he had, the police hadn't shown up at my house.

"On what grounds?"

"Trespassing."

Maybe Tommy hadn't told him after all.

West reached in his briefcase, took out his cell phone, and pressed the power button.

As he did, I noticed something that wasn't apparent in any of the pictures I'd seen of him in the local papers. A faint scar zigzagged its way from the corner of his mouth to just below his eye. It was hard to see unless the light was right. Whoever had done the sewing had been good.

"Mrs. Hayes doesn't have long to go," I informed him as I wondered how he'd gotten hurt.

"I'm sorry to hear that, but that doesn't have anything to do with me." He began to depress the phone's buttons.

"Given the circumstances, don't you think you owe her," I said quietly.

He puckered his lips in an expression of distaste. "She told you 'the story,' didn't she?"

"Yes, she did."

Under the streetlights I could see anger warring with irritation on his face. Then the irritation was replaced by an expression of martyrdom. He sighed and pressed the phone's off button. Nearby, a couple of gulls squabbled over a McDonald's wrapper. "I don't know why I still care about this, but I do. Maybe it's because I went out of my way to help that woman, and all she's been doing ever since then is bad-mouth me to everyone she meets and blame me for all her troubles.'' He sighed again. He was put upon, misunderstood.

"So you're saying what she told me about you harassing her isn't true?"

West flashed me a forbearing smile. "Ask anyone. In fact, I'll give you a list of people to call. I tried to help her, I kept her on for as long as I could, but then I had to fire her."

As I crossed my arms over my chest and waited for the rest of his explanation, I pondered the wonders of self-justification. It wasn't long in coming. In the gloom, West's blue eyes looked gray.

"She wasn't showing up for work, she was making mistakes, she was taking money. Nothing big. Little stuff. But nevertheless, you don't like to see that." He turned up the collar of his coat against the wind that had begun to blow, bringing with it the sound of the waves lapping against the lake's shore.

"Why was she doing that?"

He leaned forward slightly. "Because she'd developed a drinking problem," he confided, one friend telling another an unfortunate piece of news. "In those days we didn't do interventions. I tried to overlook the absences, the petty thievery, for as long as I could. I felt sorry for the woman, but when they got to be flagrant I had to fire her. Naturally, when anyone called for a reference, I had to tell them the truth."

"Naturally."

He looked pained. "You don't believe me, do you?"

"Not at all."

He frowned. This was not someone who was accustomed

to having his word doubted. "That's the way it was. For God's sake," he added, "when her son got in trouble, who do you think she turned to?"

"You?"

"Damn right." He made a fist and punched his leg. "Damn right. Why do you think I paid for those years at that fancy school?"

"Guilty conscience?"

He glared at me. "That's insulting."

"Maybe." Obviously, he'd expected a different answer, but from what I'd heard, this was a man who'd never contributed anything to charity until he'd decided to get involved in politics. "Then why is she going around saying those bad things about you?"

"Because it's easier than admitting she screwed up her life herself. If she hadn't found religion, she'd probably be dead from cirrhosis."

I thought about what Bryan had told me and about how Mrs. Hayes had said he had found out.

"It's simple," West snapped when I asked him for an explanation. "They're both lying, just like they always have. It's a family habit." He poked me twice in the shoulder with one of his fingers for emphasis. It felt as if I were being jabbed with the blunt end of a butter knife. This was someone who had done manual labor for a living, that was for sure.

"Ask anyone. Anyone at all. Now you see why I don't want to have anything to do with her? Now you see why I didn't want my son to have anything to do with her daughter? The whole family is crazy. Who needs that kind of aggravation in your life?" He bit his lip. "You want to know what happened to Melissa, ask her brother why he was sent away."

"I already have."

"Did he tell you he punched Melissa in the face?"

"Lots of brothers punch out their sisters."

"He shattered her jaw."

"That was a long time ago."

"People don't change. Not fundamentally." West got into his car and peeled off, leaving me standing in the parking lot nursing a growing headache.

Everywhere I looked, Bryan's name kept coming up.

I could see why Mrs. Hayes was concerned.

Chapter
28

"Jilly was such a nice girl," Ms. Cascoff told me.

We were sitting in her kitchen, sipping tea and talking about her niece, Jill Evans.

I'd called Ms. Cascoff on impulse at eight-thirty the previous night when I'd gotten back to the store after my conversation with Michael West, telling myself as I dialed the number that since Melissa's problems seem to have started with Jill's death, perhaps Ms. Cascoff could provide me with a lead. But the truth was, I was making the call because my other option, the thing I should have been doing, trotting over to the hospital to talk to Mrs. Hayes about her son and her past, was something I wanted to delay as long as possible. I was hoping by some miracle I'd find something that would render the conversation unnecessary.

Which was why I was drinking caffeine-free Lemon Lift from a mug at three-thirty in the afternoon and paging through copies of the *Post Standard* that contained the articles on Jill's death, hoping to get something that would point me in the right direction. So far, though, I hadn't learned anything except that Ms. Cascoff's niece was the perfect child, and that she herself was thankful, after seeing what this had done to her sister, that she'd never married and had children, a sentiment I was interested to note also put forth by Professor Fell and George.

Ms. Cascoff was one of those small, thin, birdlike women who always seemed to be in perpetual motion. She'd brought the copies of the newspaper out unasked, and under her urging I'd been dutifully plowing through the articles on her niece's death again because I didn't want to tell her that I'd found her by doing what I as doing now: reading Jill Evans's obituary.

"She was so nice," Helen Cascoff was saying as she laid a plate of Oreo cookies on the table in front of me. She'd been talking nonstop in a quick staccato manner since the moment I'd walked through the door ten minutes before. "So quiet. She always came in when she was supposed to. She aways got good grades. My sister never had a minute's trouble with her. I don't understand it. I don't suppose I ever will." She sat down across from me, then jumped back up to get something else.

"My sister and her husband moved away right after the accident," Ms. Cascoff said, throwing the words over her shoulder. "They're in Arizona now. In Phoenix. They just couldn't bear being here anymore. Who can blame them?" She handed me a napkin and pointed to where I was sitting. "That used to be her seat. She used to come here when my sister couldn't watch her."

I helped myself to three cookies. As I ate them, I realized I felt so hungry because I hadn't had lunch yet.

Ms. Cascoff began pleating the napkin in front of her

into tiny little folds. Her fingers were long and thin and I couldn't help thinking that they suited the job she did: lab technician at one of the local hospitals. "I don't know what I can tell you," she said for the second time. "There's nothing really to tell. One moment she was here. The next moment she wasn't."

I took a sip of my tea and remembered why I preferred coffee, but Ms. Cascoff hadn't offered any and I hadn't asked. As I put my mug down, I studied her face. She had deep lines running from her nose down to her mouth, and more lines radiating from her eyes. If she hadn't told me she was in her forties, I would have made her for fifty at least. Her hair didn't help. A deadening shade of black, it leached the color out of her skin, giving it a sickly pallor.

"She wasn't used to drinking," she continued. "She really wasn't. I don't know what could have possessed her to do what she did."

I didn't tell her that wasn't what I'd heard about Jill. Her memories were all she had left. I wasn't going to spoil them. Instead, I asked her if the police had hinted at anything peculiar occurring.

She cocked her head to one side and looked at me as if she were a sparrow and I was a bug she'd never seen before. "What do you mean?"

"Was there anything peculiar regarding Jill's death?"

"Are you saying there was?"

"No."

"Then why did you ask that question?" Ms. Cascoff's voice was sharp with suspicion.

I absentmindedly ran my finger around the rim of my mug. "I guess I'm looking for something that would help me understand Melissa's disappearance."

"Well, you shouldn't make statements like that," she exclaimed. "Especially if you don't know anything."

I conceded that was true, which seemed to mollify Ms. Cascoff, because a few seconds later she started talking again. "Those two were good friends. The best of friends. Melissa was always at Jill's house. I think she just couldn't stand the idea of her death. She could never accept it. She didn't go to the funeral, you know. Her suitemates said she couldn't stand the idea of seeing Jill in a coffin."

Ms. Cascoff sniffed and began pleating the napkin again into smaller and smaller folds. "It was an accident. Just one of those stupid things that happen." She gestured at the newspapers. "Why don't you take them with you. I've kept them too long. Now, if you don't mind, I have things to do." She stood up abruptly.

I thanked her and left, which was just as well, because I couldn't think of anything else to ask. I'd gone fishing and come back with nothing.

My failure and the absolute pointlessness of Jill Evans's death combined to depress me, and I was glad to get back to the store. At least I could do something productive there. For the next three hours I cleaned cages in the bird room, rehoused a couple of boas, and rearranged the terrarium in the front of the store. But no matter what I did, I still couldn't stop thinking about Jill Evans and Melissa and the connection between them. It seemed fairly obvious.

Best friend dies in a drunken accident. You feel doubly guilty because you think you should have done something about the problem that killed her and didn't. You show your distress by giving your religious keepsake away to a friend. The guilt doesn't go away. It gets worse, till it colors everything you do. Finally you can't stand it anymore and you take off, planning to kill yourself somewhere where no one can find you.

Maybe what happened to Melissa was as simple as that.

Or maybe not.

I stretched, then refastened the loose strands of my hair in the clip that was holding it off my neck.

Because even if she had offed herself, one question remained.

Where was her body?

If she had shot or stabbed herself, her remains would have been found by now.

Because for them not to be found, for Melissa to get to a deserted enough area for no one to come across her body, for a dog not to have dragged part of her home to his master, Melissa would have needed a car.

Melissa didn't have one.

And she hadn't gotten on a bus or train or plane because the police had canvassed them all and come up empty-handed.

Which left me back where I started.

I sighed and began taking the newspapers Jill's aunt had given me off the front counter, when an article down on the bottom of the first page caught my eye. I hadn't noticed it at Helen Cascoff's house because I'd been concentrating all my attention on her. A column and a half long, the piece described a hit-and-run that had taken place on the night Jill Evans had died. The police were estimating the time of the accident somewhere between two and four in the morning. The accident had taken place on East Genesee Street. The victim was a male in his late sixties. No identification of the body had yet been made. The article urged anyone with any information to contact the police. A number to call was given.

I closed my eyes and thought.

I thought about Melissa coming into Holland's room around four-thirty in the morning.

I thought about Tommy West's reaction when I asked him if he'd been at the party with Melissa.

Just for the hell of it, I thumbed through the paper till I came to the weather forecast. Rain had been predicted for later on in the evening.

Interesting.

I thought about the bundle of clothes I'd found shoved in the back of Melissa's closet, the ones that had been rotten with mildew.

Zsa Zsa nudged my calf with her nose. I gave her a rub as I stared at the rain cloud pictured in the weather forecast section.

Was everything connected, or was this just chance?

I wondered if the police had ever made an arrest in this guy's death.

I clicked my tongue against the roof of my mouth, then I picked up the phone and dialed Calli's number. She should know. And if she didn't, she could find out.

Unfortunately, she wasn't there.

I left a message on her voice mail, telling her what I needed, and hung up.

I called George next. I wanted to bounce my idea off him, but he wasn't around either. Who knew? Given the other night, maybe he was out making Raymond disappear. I left a message on his answering machine and hung up.

Where was everyone anyway? I bit a cuticle and told myself to get back to work.

But I couldn't concentrate.

As my grandmother used to say, I had ants in my pants. Only she'd have said it in Yiddish.

I wanted confirmation and I wanted it now. So even though I knew I should wait until I had more info—asking questions is like investing money: You get more if you have some to begin with—I called Tommy West. But he wasn't in either.

Great. I was the only person left on the planet.

On a whim I tried Con Tex. Which was when I got lucky. West Sr. was still there.

I launched into my spiel before he could hang up on me. He heard me out. I think he was afraid not to. Then he told me I was mistaken, his son was at home that night.

"I thought he was at a party." I didn't say which one.

"No. He was home with me." The voice of total confidence.

"Why am I not surprised?" I shifted the phone from my right ear to my left one and began filling in the two As on one of the Noah's Ark flyers that was lying on the desk.

"You think I'm lying to protect my son?" Factual. No emotion.

"I think most parents would lie to protect their children." I moved on to the O.

"Well, I wouldn't," West insisted.

I couldn't argue with that, so I came at it from a different angle. "How can you remember back to that night? That was over a year ago."

"Because I remember reading about the Evans girl's death in the paper the next morning and thinking how horrible it was and asking Tommy if he knew her."

"What did he say?"

"What do you think?"

"Of course he knew her." Irritation at my denseness? My clumsiness? "She was Melissa's roommate. But I'm sure you knew that."

I told him I did. "What else did he say?"

"That she had been upset. That she had been going out with someone. That he had broken it off."

"Did he say who this someone was?"

"No. He told me he didn't know. Melissa knew. But she never told him."

"Isn't that odd?"

"Everything about that girl was odd," West replied. This time there was heartfelt emotion in his voice. "Is that enough, or do you still want to talk to my son?"

"Wouldn't you if you were me?" I started filling in the H and the N.

West's sigh traveled along the wire. "I suppose."

"Why are you afraid to let me speak to Tommy directly?"

"I'm not afraid." A touch of asperity. "It's not that at all."

"Then, what is it?"

"I know, given the way he acts, you''ll find this hard to believe, but Tommy is more sensitive than he looks. Even though it might not seem that way, this thing with Melissa has really affected him. It bothers him when he talks about it. He ends up going out with his buddies and drinking, which is what happened the last time you visited him. Frankly, I'd rather have him finishing up his papers. Actually, he's on academic probation. He can't afford not to."

"But this isn't about Melissa, this is about Jill Evans," I objected.

"Don't insult my intelligence," West rapped out. "I'm trying to help you."

"I thought you were trying to keep me from talking to your son."

"I'm trying to do both." There was a short pause. "The way I see this is we can both get what we want or I can have a son who could fail out of college and you can be arrested for ignoring the order of protection."

"How can we both get what we want?"

"Tomorrow I'll arrange to have Tommy talk to you."

"I want to talk to him tonight."

"Why?"

"Because I'm tired of being jerked around."

"All right," West said. "If you insist."

"I do."

There was another pause on the oher side of the line, then West said, "Tonight, then. I have to pick someone up at the airport, but Tommy and I could meet you on the way."

"That sounds good."

"But I'll be there," West warned. "And if I don't like what you're saying, I'll step in."

"Does your son ask permission to piss too?"

"My relationship with my child is none of your business," West snapped. "I'm giving you an opportunity to talk to my son. Take it or leave it."

I took it.

It wasn't great, but it was better than nothing.

Or so I thought at the time.

Which shows you that I wasn't thinking at all.

Chapter
29

The house where I was supposed to meet West was located somewhere near Mattydale. Even though the area was called suburban, some of the houses around there were spaced fairly far apart from each other. The homes tended toward the modest and the working-class and it wasn't uncommon in the summer to see flower borders made of triangles of black rubber and lawns decorated with wooden deer.

What this area didn't have was streetlights, and given the moonlessness of the night, the numbers on the mailboxes were impossible to read. I'd gone up and down the road several times before I'd spotted the place I'd been looking for. As I negotiated the long, narrow driveway that led from the main road to the house, I remember being worried I'd missed West. He didn't strike me as a man who would wait if I were late.

I felt a momentary qualm when I saw the Camry parked by the garage. West's Infiniti was nowhere in sight, but I told myself maybe the Camry was West's second car. Given his financial position, he could have afforded a fleet of vehicles. Or, best of all, maybe the car belonged to the people who lived there and West hadn't arrived yet. I pulled up in back of it and cut the engine. When I jumped out, I was struck by how dark it was. If the snow was still on the ground, the lights coming from the house would have reflected off it, but since, except for a few patches here and there, it had melted, the lights served only to accentuate the surrounding blackness.

As I moved toward the house, I automatically began buttoning my jacket. The wind was blowing, making it feel colder than it had back in the city, and I could hear the rustle of the branches on the cedar trees surrounding the house as they tossed this way and that.

Maybe that's why I began to feel nervous. Because I should have heard more noise. People talking. Voices from the television. A radio. Dogs barking. Something. Anything. But all I heard was the susurration of the trees. The word setup flashed through my mind, but being eager to talk to Tommy, I ignored that little warning voice and continued toward the house. So I guess you could say I deserved what I got. Because by now I should know better.

I was about about fifteen feet from the front porch when I sensed rather than saw someone coming up from behind me on my left side.

"I have a message to deliver," the person said.

And then, before I could turn or answer, I felt pain roaring through my body, inhabiting every cell of my being, taking everything else away. I heard a strangled high, keening noise. What an awful sound, a corner of my brain thought before it rolled itself up into a ball. Later, of course, I realized I was the person who'd been making it. The next thing I knew I was rolling around on the ground, gasping for breath. Everything was spinning. Tears were pouring out of my eyes.

I heard a voice speaking. It seemed to be coming from somewhere above me. I knew it was telling me something I needed to know, but the words were garbled. I couldn't understand them, and then somehow the noise arranged itself into syllables.

"Let me repeat myself," it told me. "That was a Taser. Think of it as an aide-memoire, to help you remember what I am about to tell you. Now, my employer is a busy man. He doesn't appreciate being bothered by you. He doesn't appreciate having his son bothered by you. Nod your head if you understand what I said."

I did, surprised that I could.

"Good. You'll be all right in about twenty minutes."

"Who's your employer?" I heard myself croak, even though I knew. For some reason, I just wanted to hear West's name.

"Guess," the man said.

Or at least I think that's what he said, because at that moment, overcome by a wave of nausea, I turned my head and threw up. Just as my stomach stopped heaving, I heard a car door close. Then I heard an engine start and tires going over gravel. The man was leaving. I didn't have the strength to try to see the license plate on the car. I didn't even care. I was just profoundly grateful he was gone. The cold rising up from the ground was seeping into my back. A rock was poking into my shoulder. I didn't care about that either. Instead, I closed my eyes again, listened to the cedar branches talking, and waited for my heartbeat to return to normal.

When I could finally muster the strength to get up, I found I'd peed in my pants. My legs were wobbling. Little red clusters of light were still dancing before my eyes. I had trouble opening my car door. For some reason, my fingers weren't doing what they were supposed to and the palms of my hands were slick with sweat. Later, when I came back the next day, I saw the For Sale sign leaning against the maple tree. But I didn't see it then. I wasn't looking to see anything. The only thing I wanted to do was get the hell out of there and go home.

Michael West's secretary gave me a blank look. "You're not in the appointment book," she informed me, checking it again. "I don't see you down for this morning."

Damned right she didn't, since I wasn't supposed to be there, but I smiled and fiddled with the collar of my brown cashmere coat, having dressed for the occasion. "Maybe you made a mistake," I suggested.

"I doubt that." She emphasized the word *doubt* while she frowned and touched her blond hair. Clearly she, unlike lesser mortals, did not make errors.

I wanted to tell her her hair wasn't going anywhere. Lacquered to within an inch of its life, it was piled on top of her head in a style that had been resurrected from an earlier era and should have been left to die.

"Why didn't the receptionist call and announce you?" she demanded, asking me the question she should have asked me first.

"How should I know? Don't blame me for her incompetence."

The fact is, she couldn't have seen me because I'd come in through the side entrance, but I saw no reason to share that information.

The secretary, one Beth Ann Widner according to the

nameplate on her desk, narrowed her eyes. The lines radiating from their corners looked like a road map on her leathery skin, making me thankful that my grandmother had made me stay out of the sun when I was younger. "What's your name again?"

I told her to go back to reading her magazine. "I'll tell your boss I'm here myself." And I brushed passed her and headed for his office.

I could hear her squawking in the background. I ignored it. No doubt she was now paging West to tell him I was on my way. Too bad. It would have been more fun to take him by surprise, but I didn't have the patience setting something like that up would entail. I was too angry. I'd had the whole night to stew about what had happened to me and think of something to do about it.

So far, though, I hadn't been able to come up with anything to do, at least nothing that wouldn't land me five to twenty in jail. Of course, I could have gone to the police, but what would have been the point? I couldn't ID the guy who'd zapped me, I didn't have the Camry's license plate number, I didn't have any marks on my body, and no one I knew of had heard West setting up the appointment, so what could the cops have done? Nothing. It was my word against Michael West's, and I'd need a lot more than my word to get them to act, especially considering who he was and who I was.

So why was I at Con Tex at nine in the morning? Maybe because I'd wanted to see the look on West's face when I came through the door. Or maybe I just wanted to show that low-life son of a fish dropping that he'd picked the wrong person to try and intimidate.

"It's all right," he was saying into the intercom as I barged through the door. I noticed he was already standing. "I'll handle this." He looked at me with expressionless eyes. If he felt surprise at seeing me there, he didn't show it. "How dare you walk in here like this?" he demanded, puffing himself up. His voice boomed across the room.

But the anger in West's voice lacked conviction. I had the feeling he was displaying it more for the benefit of his secretary than for me. I wondered if this guy had taken voice lessons, because he could certainly project. I shut the door behind me. "Too bad you couldn't make our meeting. I hope you didn't stand up the guy at the airport too."

"Is that what this is about?" The corners of West's mouth turned up. "I left a message on your machine. Did you get it?"

"I know." I'd listened to it when I'd gotten home. So sorry can't keep our appointment. Family emergency. Blah. Blah. Blah. Hope you weren't inconvenienced.

Inconvenienced! If I'd had the energy, I would have thrown the answering machine across my kitchen. The sheer chutzpah of the message, the confidence behind it that there was nothing I could do to him, had taken me from numb to livid. I would have gone out to his house—never mind that I was still feeling as if someone had turned me inside out—then and there if I'd had his home address. But I didn't. And it wasn't listed in the phone book. No big surprise there.

"You'd better tell me what you want. The only reason I haven't had my secretary call security . . ." West began.

"Is because you have a lingering curiosity about what I'm going to tell you, and you figure you might as well give me a minute or two since you don't think I can do anything to you." I walked over to his desk and dropped my backpack on it. It landed with a thud. "Ever think that you're wrong?"

He glanced at the backpack nervously.

I smiled. "What's the matter? Scared that I have a present for you?" I reached inside my bag.

He took a couple of quick steps back as I brought out my cigarettes and lighter.

"Expecting something else?" I asked as I thumped the pack and extracted a Camel.

"I don't know what you're talking about."

"Really?" I took out my gold lighter, lit my cigarette, and blew a stream of smoke in West's direction. "Silly me. I figured maybe you thought I had a Taser in here. Or a gun."

He snorted derisively. "I heard you were crazy."

"I am." I flashed him my crazy-woman grin, the one I'd perfected when I'd been riding the New York City subways alone at night. "You think you can do whatever you want, don't you?"

"You really need help. I can recommend a few people if you want."

"You're too kind." I blew a smoke ring. "So what you're telling me is I imagined you sent one of your goons to warn me off last night?"

"Don't be ridiculous." He snorted and dismissed the idea with a wave of his hand. "I don't employ people like that. I am a respectable businessman. A good, solid citizen. Someone who has brought money and jobs to this community. The only reason I've put up with you so far is because of the lingering regard and affection I have for Mary Margaret Hayes. When will you get it through your head that Melissa's disappearance has nothing to do with my family, nothing at all."

"Are you so sure?"

"Of course I am."

"If you're so sure, then why did you have me attacked?"

"I didn't."

"You know what I think?"

"I don't care."

"I think your son may have been involved in a hit-and-run the night Jill Evans died. I think Melissa either witnessed it or your son told her. I think that may be why she disappeared."

West kept his face devoid of expression. "Can you support these allegations with proof?"

I lied and said yes.

"Let's hear it."

I didn't reply.

"That's what I thought," West told me. He shook his finger in front of my face. "You be very careful about what you're saying. Very careful. You're opening yourself up to libel charges here. I didn't spend years building up this business for my son to take over so you could slander him. He's going to be someone big, someone important, and I'm damned if I'll see him brought down by some crazy female who can't get her priorities straight."

"Crazy female? Is that what you think I am?"

"Frankly, I don't know and I don't care." West straightened his tie and reined in his emotions. "Now, I've been patient with you, much more patient than I should have been, but I've had enough. If you're smart, you'll quit now."

"And if I don't?"

He shrugged. "You may be nuts, but I don't think you're stupid."

Chapter
30

On the way out of Con Tex's parking lot I spotted West's Infiniti. Crazy, hunh? I thought about me last night rolling around in the dirt. I thought about West in his nice little office with his nice little secretary. I looked at the car again, all nice and new and shiny. When I got done with it, all it would be good for would be scrap metal. I started to whistle. Maybe West was right. Maybe I was a crazy female. I laughed. If I got caught, that's what I'd tell the judge.

Instead of going back to work, I drove around the area until I found a Mini Mart. There I bought three one-pound boxes of granulated sugar, a Snickers bar, a cup of coffee, *The New York Times,* and gas for the cab. On the way back to Con Tex I ate the candy bar and drank the coffee. The paper would have to wait until I got to work.

West's Infiniti was parked around the corner from the entranceway to the office building in the space reserved for him. A Taurus sat on one side and a Blazer on the other, effectively shielding the Infiniti from sight. The view from inside the office was obstructed by evergreen foundation plantings. Since it was a little after nine-thirty, the lot was full of cars but devoid of people. Everyone was inside, working. I parked on the periphery and waited for thirty minutes to see if security drove by, but they didn't. Just like the other day. They didn't seem to patrol. Something told me, though, that that was about to change. I waited another five minutes just to be sure, but the only living thing in the lot were the sea gulls and a couple of crows.

As I was waiting I asked myself if I wanted to do this. I told myself yes. Now, if I'd asked myself if I *should* do it, the answer might have been different. But I didn't. Which proves how important the right question can be. I was thinking about that as I pulled my cab up behind the Infiniti, killed the motor, and got out. It took me less than a minute to pry open the spring lock to the Infiniti's gas tank top with a nail file (the manufacturer should really redesign the lock) ten seconds to screw off the gas cap, and another twenty seconds to pour the two boxes of sugar in the tank. (I was taking the third one back to the office.) Then I screwed the cap back on and closed the lid to the gas tank. There were a few scratches in the paint where I'd pried the top open, but none, I decided, that would be apparent if you weren't looking for them.

I smiled.

Too bad I couldn't be there when West heard why his car wouldn't start, but it was a pleasure that I'd have to forgo for obvious reasons.

I hummed as I pulled out of the parking lot.

Suddenly I was feeling better about last night.

Today was going to be a good day after all.

Maybe revenge isn't good for your soul, but it certainly does wonders for your disposition.

Even the rain couldn't change my mood. It had begun coming down when I was halfway to Noah's Ark. The leaden sky had turned even darker, and large drops splattered on the windshield and drummed on the roof of the cab. The gray of the sky accentuated the gray of the city's streets, the brown of the grass, the peeling paint on the houses, and piles of litter dumped on the curbs. The people huddled inside the bus kiosks waiting for their rides to arrive looked damp and uncomfortable. It was a good day to be inside, and I felt guilty about the fact that I was glad I was going to spend it working inside the store instead of running around looking for leads to Melissa's disappearance. Which I couldn't have done even if I'd wanted to, since Tim had taken the day off. But it was just as well that he had, because I needed time to think.

Also I needed to hear from Calli.

I was getting increasingly impatient, when she finally phoned me at five-thirty that afternoon.

"It's about time," I told her as I moved the mail out from underneath my cat Pickles's stomach. Her reply was eclipsed by static. "What?" I yelled.

She came back on a few seconds later. "Can you hear me now?"

"Yes. Just." She sounded as if she were talking from Afghanistan. "Where are you?"

"In my car. Right outside Morrisville."

"What the hell are you doing there?"

"I'm on my way to cover an accident at Colgate." There

was another short burst of static, and then she said, "You want to hear what I have or not?"

"What do you think?" I put the mail on top of the cash register and gave Pickles a catnip mouse. She looked at it disdainfully, jumped off the counter, and sauntered away.

"Here goes." She told me what she'd been able to glean from the paper's files. It wasn't much. The hit-and-run I'd asked her to research had never been ID'd. The guy had been in his fifties. A Caucasian. Probably a street person, from the look of him.

"Malnourished. Rags for clothes. Also no teeth."

"That doesn't help," I observed. Somehow dentures weren't the same as dental records.

"No, it doesn't," Calli agreed. Her voice faded out and came back in.

"How about fingerprints?"

"They ran them but nothing came up. Nothing came up through the feds' NCIC list either."

I sighed and reached for a cigarette. So far this was not going well.

"The guy's probably not a local, because the cops showed his picture around. None of our bums could put a name to him."

"Ah. A tourist. He was pretty far from the highway and the bus station to just be passing through, don't you think?"

"Maybe he was going to visit someone. Maybe he was looking for the Salvation Army and got lost. Who knows?"

"Who indeed." Which got me thinking about Melissa and wondering if this guy had a family out there somewhere, wondering what had happened to him.

"Anything else?" I inquired.

"They're still holding the body, hoping something will break and they can ID him. But no one downtown is real

hopeful about that or catching the person who hit him,"
Calli replied. "They don't have anything. No one saw anything. They checked the repair shops. Nothing came out of
that either."

"So that's it?"

"That's it. I'll talk to you later." She said good-bye and
hung up.

Somehow I'd expected more. Oh, well. I stood behind
the counter and looked at the angelfish and smoked my
cigarette and thought.

George handed me his beer as Zsa Zsa and I walked
through the door of his house.

"Don't you want it?" I asked.

"I'll get another." Even though it was only nine-thirty at
night, George looked as if he should have been in bed hours
before. He had rings under his eyes and stubble on his
cheeks. I'd never seen him so tired and preoccupied. Come
to think of it, I'd never seen his house look so messy. Messy
for him, that is; for me it would have been neat. A ticket
stub was lying on the hall carpet. Two pairs of large black
sneakers and a pair of sweat pants were heaped alongside
one wall, while a parka was draped over the hall table. From
where I was standing, I could see there were still dishes and
Chinese takeout containers sitting on the kitchen table.

"It's been a long day," George offered by way of explanation.

"Ditto. Where's your nephew?"

George scowled. It seemed to be his predominant expression these days. "I don't want to discuss him," he told me.

Since we couldn't talk about him without arguing, that
was fine with me.

"I found out what you asked me to," he continued. "You were right. Tommy did get himself arrested."

I'd called George early that morning to see if he could confirm a hunch of mine. "When?"

"Fifteen months ago. In April of last year."

The timing fit. I waited for George to go on, but he didn't. Instead, he went into the kitchen to get himself another beer. I couldn't help notice that his stride was jerky. As I hung my jacket in the closet, I realized I could hear the dull thud of the refrigerator door opening and closing in the kitchen. What I didn't hear was any rap music, any pounding bass. In fact, I didn't hear any music at all. Which meant wherever Raymond was, he wasn't here.

George was back a moment later with a Saranac for himself and a saucer for Zsa Zsa. We went into the living room, and I sat down on the sofa and poured a little of my beer into the saucer and set it on the floor for Zsa Zsa. She wagged her tail and started drinking.

"You're turning that animal into an alcoholic," George said.

"Don't start," I warned. "I'm not in a good mood."

"Me either."

"No kidding," I observed as he plopped himself down next to me and began cracking his knuckles. When he was done with one hand, he started on the other. A moment later he got up and began pacing around the living room. I picked up a pillow that had fallen on the floor and put it back on the sofa. "Are you going to tell me what you found out about Tommy West or not?"

Raymond was turning out to be the elephant in the middle of the living room, but I was damned if I was going to be the one to mention him first.

George brushed aside the curtain and peered through the blind covering the front window. "Mailbox bingo."

"What?"

George kept looking out the window. "Mailbox bingo," he repeated. "Tommy West and his friends got arrested for mailbox bingo. You ride along a country road and whack at the mailboxes with a baseball bat. You get one point for hitting one, two for knocking it off. Whoever gets the most points wins."

Somehow, the way Tommy's father had been acting, I'd expected something more than a high school prank.

George cracked his knuckles. "They also ran their Jeep over a golf course and caused about ten thousand dollars worth of damage."

"What happened?"

"To young Thomas Claudius West? He got fifty hours community service and adjournment in contemplation of dismissal. I assume the same was true of the other two."

"Did he stay out of trouble?"

If he hadn't, if Tommy had been arrested for anything again within six months of his arrest, he would have gone back to court, the case would go to trial, and the proceedings would go on his record.

"As far as I know, the kid's been a model citizen ever since." George let go of the two slats he'd been holding apart, walked over to the sofa, and sat down next to me. The cushion sighed under his weight. "I heard Tommy's little prank, between court costs, replacing the mailboxes, and fixing the golf course, cost his dad fifteen grand."

I whistled.

"Does what I told you help?"

"Maybe." The time frame was right. I told George what I suspected.

George cracked his knuckles while I talked. I wondered if that really did lead to arthritis like my grandmother had said. "So you're saying Tommy was at this party that he wasn't supposed to be at because he's underage?"

I nodded. "And if he got caught drinking, he would have been arrested, which, given the circumstances, would have been disastrous for him."

"So what?"

"All right." I made a frame with my hands. "Now, just imagine this. Tommy and Melissa are at the party. It's late. They've had more than a few too many beers. Suddenly the next-door neighbor comes running in, yelling that they found a girl lying out in the back. Naturally Tommy and Melissa go take a look, along with everyone else. It's Jill. Melissa is distraught. She's standing there in the pouring rain, crying.

"But Tommy's afraid to. He's scared if he does, he's going to get busted when the police come. And anyway, there's nothing they can do because Jill is dead. So he drags Melissa away. He's taking her back to her dorm. She's crying, they're fighting, when he hears a bump, feels something against the car. He doesn't stop. He figures he's hit a garbage can or something. The next day Tommy sees the report on the hit-and-run in the paper. Doesn't think anything of it. Then he goes out to go somewhere. He notices the fender of the car. There's stuff on it, stuff that shouldn't be there. He remembers the report. He panics and runs to his dad. Tells him everything.

"His father says, 'Don't worry, I'll take care of everything.' That would explain his father's reaction to me."

"So would a lot of other things." George tilted his bottle of Saranac and took a sip of beer. "I bet you got good marks for story writing when you were in elementary school," he said after he'd swallowed.

"It's a possibility," I insisted.

"So is the end of the world. You have nothing substantive with this," he pointed out when I was through. "Melissa's clothes, Jill Evans's death, the hit-and-run. All coincidences."

"But . . ."

George held up his hand. "Let me finish. I can think of lots of other explanations, but let's say you're right. Maybe Tommy West was involved. It doesn't matter, because you can't prove it."

"But the police could."

"Do yourself a favor and don't go there."

"They could test Tommy's car."

"For what?" He drummed his fingers on the table impatiently. "Believe me, if what you say is true, by this time that car has been repaired and repainted."

I knew George was right. I just didn't want to admit it.

"Anyway," he continued. "Even if you could prove that Melissa knew that her boyfriend had hit that guy—which you can't—so what? What do any of those factors have to do with Melissa's disappearance?"

"It offers a motive for her disappearance. Maybe she told Tommy she couldn't stand it anymore and was going to the police."

"After a year? Why?"

"Guilty conscience?"

"Anything is possible, but if it were me, I'd go back and talk to Beth and her boyfriend again."

"Why's that?"

George smiled for the first time since I'd walked through the door. "Do the math."

I gave him a blank look.

"Three is an inherently unstable number."

I was about to reply, when the doorbell rang. George sprang off the sofa and ran to get it.

I followed.

George flung the door open.

A cop was standing on the porch. He had his hand on Raymond's collar. Blood was running down the kid's forehead.

Chapter
31

The cop was a square-faced burly guy. He filled the door frame with his presence. His complexion looked yellow under the streetlights. Beside him, Raymond looked small and fragile, a frightened, skinny fourteen-year-old wearing clothes two sizes too big for him, who'd finally met reality and didn't like what he found.

The cop pointed to Raymond with his free hand. "He says he lives here."

"What did he do?" George asked, enunciating each word. I couldn't read his voice. It was tight and controlled and devoid of emotion.

"I was with you all night, tell him I was with you," Raymond pleaded.

"I'm talking." And the cop yanked on Raymond's collar, using a little more force than necessary.

It was, I noted, the kind of maneuver dog trainers use

on dobes and shepherds when they needed to get their attention.

"He and his friends stole a car earlier this evening."

George pointed to the gash on Raymond's forehead. "How'd he get that?"

The cop looked George square in the eye. "He probably hit his head on the steering wheel," he replied without missing a beat.

George stared back at him. "I see."

I wondered who was going to blink first.

Raymond's hand went out to his uncle. "He whacked me, man. He whacked me hard."

The cop gave George's nephew another shake. "I told you to shut up." He handled the kid as if he were a rag doll.

"What happened?" George demanded, his eyes still on the cop.

The cop shifted his weight from one leg to another before replying. "He and a couple of his buddies took a Dodge up around the university, isn't that right?" he asked Raymond. When Raymond didn't answer, he continued. "Guess what else they had? A forty-five."

"The trunk was opened," Raymond whined. "Don't you be trying to pin something like that on me."

"The owner says it's not his. Now, why do I believe him and not you?"

"How would I know?" Raymond retorted. He was beginning to get his confidence back.

George interrupted. "Anyone hurt?"

The cop shook his head. "Not this time. They crashed the car into a tombstone at Oakwood. Next time, who knows?"

"What time was the car reported missing?"

"The owner called it in around nine o'clock.

Raymond bit his lip. I reflected that if his forehead was hurting, he didn't show it. "I was with you, George. Tell him I was with you then. Tell him I just went out 'cause I wanted to get a slice."

The cop looked down at Raymond. "Then how come you ran when I asked you about the car, hunh? Answer me that?"

"Because I was scared. 'Cause you don't look like no Officer Friendly."

Raymond was a little like me. He couldn't keep his mouth shut even when he knew he should.

"Why were you scared if you didn't do anything?" the cop demanded.

"Because I'm black, that's why. Something goes wrong, pick up the black kid. What you guys got, a quota or something? So many A-f-r-o-Americans a week or they dock your ass?"

"That's enough," George snapped at Raymond.

"It's—"

"Be quiet," he thundered.

Raymond stopped talking. For a moment, all I heard was the cackle of the radio from the patrol car parked by the curb.

"You get the other ones?" George asked.

"Just him." The cop glanced at Raymond the way you would an unappetizing piece of meat. "I'm hoping he'll tell me who his friends are."

"We was just getting something to eat," Raymond said to his uncle. "Honest."

I was surprised he didn't choke on the word. The kid was lying. That much was obvious. But I couldn't help feeling sorry for him anyway. Maybe because the cop was so big and he was so small. I sure didn't expect George to see it that way, though, so I was surprised at what he said next.

He started to say something, changed his mind, stared at Raymond for a second, ran his hand over the top of his head and replied, "My nephew was here with me."

Raymond grinned. Christmas had arrived.

The cop blinked. He obviously was having trouble believing what he was hearing. For that matter, so was I. "Excuse me?"

"You heard what I said."

"You're making a mistake."

George pointed to the gash on Raymond's forehead. "That looks as if it's going to need stitches."

"I told you, he probably cut himself on the car steering wheel."

George began rocking back and forth on his feet. "So you said."

"What's the matter?" the cop demanded. "Don't you believe me?"

"I was out there. I know how these things go."

"I know you do. That's why I was doing you a favor bringing him here. I could have brought him downtown instead."

"He's fourteen."

"Fourteen going on twenty-five. And I could have still brought him downtown."

"Well, thank you for bringing him here instead, Officer." George gave the word *officer* a slight inflection. "I'll take care of it now."

The cop shook his head in disgust and took his hand off Raymond's collar. "You people are all the same," he muttered. "That's why things are the way they are."

George's eyes flashed. "What did you say?" His voice had grown dangerously soft.

"I didn't say anything at all." The cop turned and walked back to his patrol car.

"See. See. I told you the guy was a racist pig," Raymond said after the car had pulled out. He was practically dancing with glee.

"Shut up," George snarled. "Just shut the hell up."

For once Raymond did.

Because it was a Thursday night, I'd expected the ER to be almost empty. Otherwise I would have brought a book. But it wasn't. The hard dark blue plastic chairs in the waiting room were filled to capacity. A few of the men were watching the TV anchored overhead, but most sat their faces pinched with fatigue and pain, resigned to their wait, while the women alternately comforted and yelled at their crying, fidgeting children, and the guard stationed by the door answered questions in bored monosyllables.

I picked up one of the magazines lying on the table next to me. It was over a year old. I started to read it anyway.

"I should have brought my work," George said.

"Me too." I flipped the page. It was ragged from use like the beige paint on the wall, a too-gray brown that was marred with nicks and pits.

So far Raymond, George, and I had been sitting there for the past three hours and we'd been told we had at least another half hour to go. Unless there was a real emergency, of course. In which case, we'd be here even longer.

At this point, if I had a needle and thread I would have been tempted to stitch Raymond up myself.

"You don't have to be here," George said to me for the hundredth time.

I looked up from reading about last year's ten hot new trends, none of which had materialized. "I know I don't. I guess I just miss the place."

George didn't even smile. Instead, he buried his head in his hands. It was, I noted, becoming his standard position. "Why did I say that?" he asked again. "What the hell is wrong with me?" he moaned. "This evening I just did something that goes against everything I believe in."

I closed the magazine and finished off the chocolate bar I'd gotten from the vending machine. "A gut reaction. A display of family feeling?"

George grunted.

"I'm throwing out words here, trying to help you. At least let me know if I'm on the right track."

"Maybe if he hadn't hit him."

"You never hit anyone?"

George lifted his head up and studied the backs of his hands. "Yeah, I have. I lost it a couple of times. I can even understand why he did it. Look at what I almost did to Raymond the other night."

"I remember."

George sighed. "You know there's a ninety-nine-percent probablity that that little shit and his low-life friends took the car."

I'd put it at a hundred. "What about the gun?"

"That wouldn't surprise me either." George straightened up. "Where is he anyway?"

I pointed to the vending machine around the corner. "Over there. He was hungry. I gave him a dollar to get a candy bar. Tell me something," I asked after a few seconds had passed. "I'm curious. If the cop had been black, would you have given Raymond up?"

George scuffed the floor with the edge of his heel. "You know what I came away with from my seven years out there?"

"What?"

"That the system stinks. That nobody gives a shit. They say they do, but they don't. They just make it worse."

"That doesn't answer my question. I wanted to know. I had a feeling it was important to our relationship."

"I realize that." George closed his eyes and leaned his head back. "God, do I hate children."

A moment later Raymond returned. He nodded toward George. "Is he all right?"

"I'm fine," George said, opening his eyes and sitting up.

"You can go back to your house if you want. I'll do this by myself."

"No you can't. You're not eighteen."

Raymond sat down next to George and unwrapped the candy bar he'd just bought. "So," he asked. "Are you going to send me home?"

"No," George said. "I'm not."

Chapter
32

The sun was shining. The sky was blue. The snow was gone. God was taking callers. If you looked very closely and used a little wishful thinking, you could see buds beginning to swell on the branches of the willow trees. It was the kind of day that made you believe spring was finally on its way, I thought as I watched Chris Furst do a couple of laps around the outside track at the university athletic center. Beth's boyfriend moved with an easy, confident stride, giving the impression that he was running for the sheer pleasure of the activity and that he would be happy to keep on doing it for miles.

I cupped my hands and yelled out to him as he passed me by for the third time. He turned and trotted over, approaching me reluctantly, obviously unwilling to abandon his run.

"Yes, ma'am," he said as he got within speaking distance. His voice was steady and strong. The back and sides of his gray T-shirt were streaked with sweat, as was the waistband of his sweat pants, but he wasn't winded.

"I have a question for you," I told him, having decided to follow up on George's observation about three being an unstable number. Perhaps George had been right. Perhaps I had taken a series of random events and turned them into something they weren't.

"And what would that be?" Chris asked, jogging in place.

"It's about Melissa and Beth."

"What about them?" He kept jogging.

Watching him bobbing up and down was making me seasick. I asked him to stop and take a walk with me instead.

"Sorry. I still have two miles to go," he protested.

"You can finish your run after we're done."

"I can't. I have a class soon."

"So cut it."

"I have a quiz."

"Make it up."

"What if that's not possible?"

"Then you can give your answers to the police downtown."

"Fine," Chris growled, and he put his head down and strode toward the athletic building, pushing by the chattering groups of T-shirt-and-jean-clad students dotting the lawn. "Have it your way."

It was all I could do to keep up with him.

"Aren't you going to ask me your question?" he flung over his shoulder after a few seconds had gone by.

"I want to know how Tommy reacted when you told him about Melissa and Beth."

The kid halted abruptly and swiveled around so he was facing me. I almost crashed into him.

He folded his arms across his chest. "I don't know what you're talking about."

"Beth told me."

"Told you what?"

"That you told Tommy about her and Beth."

"Really?" He gave a snarl of a smile. "That's an old trick telling someone somebody said something when they haven't."

"True, but in this case, she did. And why would I be trying to trick you?"

He remained silent. The enemy wasn't going to get any information out of him, by God.

"I need to know."

"There's nothing to know. You've been misinformed."

"So you're telling me your girlfriend lied?"

Chris shrugged. His eyes followed a coed walking by. "I'm not telling you anything at all."

I realized I was tapping my foot on the ground, and stopped. "I thought you were sworn to uphold the ideals of your country."

"I am."

"Does that include lying to protect a murderer if he is your friend?"

"You don't know Melissa was murdered. You don't know what happened to her."

"You're right. I don't."

"Even if she was, Tommy would never do anything like that."

"Then you shouldn't mind answering my question."

"What does what you're asking have to do with the other thing?"

"Simple. If Tommy was jealous, it might help to explain Melissa's disappearance."

"Tommy wouldn't be jealous of something like that."

"Maybe not. But he was sure upset when I asked him."

"He was upset because you were saying things that you shouldn't have been saying."

"So you two talked about this?"

"What are you saying? That we shouldn't have?"

"No. Not at all." Chris looked cold standing there. The skin on his arms had developed goose bumps.

"Why don't we keep walking," I suggested. "I know you're supposed to cool down after a run, but I don't think that means standing around in forty-degree weather when you're sweaty."

Chris nodded and started off again. "Tommy would never hurt Melissa. He's one of those guys who's all noise." This time he spoke without prompting.

I lengthened my stride to keep up with him. "How can you be so sure about the way Tommy would react."

Chris stopped again. This time I did bang into him. All this stopping and starting was making me feel as if I were on the Long Island Expressway during the Fourth of July weekend.

"I can be so sure because Tommy is my fraternity brother," Chris told me. "We pledged together. You don't go through three to four months of pledging and not know someone."

"I wasn't aware of that."

Chris gave a half-shrug, indicating there were a lot of things I didn't know.

I gnawed on my fingernail. "Is that why you told him?"

"I thought he should know."

"Why?"

"Wouldn't you want to know if you were him?"

"Not if I were happy with the way things were."

"But then you'd be living a lie," Chris protested.

"There are worse things."

"I don't agree."

"I didn't think you would. You're too young to." Out of

the corner of my eye I watched a black Lab running after a Frisbee. He leaped and made the catch in midair. For a moment he was freeze-framed against the blue sky.

"What could be worse than lying?"

"What if you told somebody something that upset them so much, that made them so angry, they went out and killed someone? What then?"

"Okay. Then maybe the truth isn't the best thing," Chris conceded after he'd considered my question for a couple of seconds. "But this wasn't like that."

"What was it like?"

Chris didn't answer.

"You know, by not answering, you're making Tommy sound guilty."

Chris gave me a pleading look. "He's not. I just don't like talking about another person's private life. I don't think it's right."

"I can understand that. And in the normal course of events I wouldn't be asking, but this isn't the normal course of events."

He looked down at the ground, then back up at me. "I guess you're right."

I waited.

"He laughed."

"He laughed?" This wasn't the answer I'd been anticipating.

"Yeah." Chris gave me a sheepish look. "If it had been a guy, that would have been one thing. But another girl. He thought . . ." Chris searched for the right word. "He thought it was interesting. It raised . . . you know . . . possibilities."

I raised an eyebrow. Possibilities? Things really had

changed. When I was in college, woman on top was considered daring. "What did you think when you found out?"

Chris turned beet red. "That is none of your business." He looked away, avoiding my eyes. "Tommy didn't have anything to do with Missy's disappearance."

Since I was getting nowhere fast with George's theory, I decided to try out mine instead. "Maybe not, but he seems to have gotten himself into a fair amount of trouble on another front," I said to Chris.

"Meaning?"

"Being arrested."

"Are you talking about that mailbox thing?"

I nodded.

Chris snickered. "Big deal."

"How about hit-and-run?"

He furrowed his brow. "What are you talking about?"

"I'm talking about a guy who was killed a little over a year ago."

"What does that have to do with Chris?"

"I think he hit him and left the scene of the accident. I think Missy was either there or surmised what had happened, and I think Tommy killed her because of it."

Chris stared at me for a few seconds. "You really are crazy," he finally said. "Where do you get stuff like this from, the *National Enquirer?*"

"I'm willing to listen to a better explanation."

Chris pointed a finger at me. "You want to know what happened to Missy, you ask her brother."

"Why should I do that?"

"Ask him about the gun."

"The one that was stolen?"

"Stolen?" Chris laughed. "If it was stolen, what the hell was Melissa doing with it?"

I drove around the university for a little over two hours before I finally tracked Bryan down. I found him at the Yellow Rhino. He was sitting at a corner table, wolfing down pizza and leafing through a magazine. At one-thirty the lunch crowd was gone, and I noted that a good half of the tables were empty as I threaded my way through them.

Bryan must have been engrossed in what he was reading, because he didn't hear me come up. "This must be our place," I said when I reached him.

He looked up. "Oh, it's you."

Judging from the expression on his face, he wasn't happy to see me, but then, lots of people aren't. I took his jacket off the seat next to him, put it on the table, and sat down.

"I'm not staying," he informed me. "I have to go to the library. I have a paper due."

"Everyone is so busy these days. So eager to achieve."

He gave me a blank look.

"Forget it." I wasn't even going to bother to explain. "You can go. After you tell me about your sister and the gun."

Bryan froze for a fraction of a second. Then he recovered, took another bite of pizza, and chewed. "I don't know what you're talking about," he told me after he swallowed, but the slight tremor in his hand belied his nonchalant manner.

"Really?"

"Really."

"That's not what Beth's boyfriend said. He told me to ask you about it, so I'm asking."

Bryan put what was left of the slice back on the plate. "Chris is a liar. I wouldn't believe anything that moron tells you."

"I could say the same of you."

"Hey." Bryan began to get up.

I grabbed his arm and pulled him back down. "Maybe we should settle this at the Public Safety Building."

Bryan glowered at me. "What was all that bullshit you were giving me a while ago about how you were going to protect me? Now you're accusing me of popping my sister."

I corrected him. "I didn't say that, you did."

"Having a gun isn't a crime."

"Yes, it is. Now tell me what the hell Melissa was doing with it. This is, by the way, the same one that I assume you swore you didn't have anymore. The one that was stolen. Tell me, was there a robbery?"

"Jesus." Bryan cupped his hands and ran them over his face, momentarily distorting it. "Jesus."

"I don't think he's going to help you now."

Bryan pushed his plate away and gave me a defiant stare. "Okay. I know giving Missy the Glock was wrong. But at the time—"

"You gave your sister your a Glock?"

"She wanted to borrow it for the afternoon."

"Why?"

"She was going to go target-shooting with a friend."

"That strikes me as a rather unusual activity for a girl like her."

Bryan pushed his glasses back up the bridge of his nose. "Which shows you how much you know! Actually, she used to go to the gun room and practice target-shooting from time to time. She said it relaxed her."

"You expect me to believe you?" I said even though I remembered the key chain with the nine-millimeter bullet I'd seen on the top of her dresser.

Bryan grabbed my forearms and pulled me toward him.

"You have to." His voice was fierce. I could smell the peppermint on his breath.

"Why? Because everything you've told me so far has been true?"

Bryan loosened his grip and slumped back in his seat.

"This is why your mother thought you might be arrested, isn't it?"

He nodded his head. "God, I can't seem to do anything right." He covered his face with his hands.

I gave him a minute to get himself back under control before I asked him my next question. "How did your mother find out?"

Bryan chewed on his lower lip. "I told her," he admitted after a few seconds had gone by.

"Why?" I would never, ever have told my mother something like that. Hell, I never told her if I got a C on a test, let alone something like this.

"I've never been able to keep things from her. Never."

I was glad I hadn't been there the day he had. "What did she say?" I massaged my temples with my fingertips. I could feel a headache coming on.

"It wasn't what she said. It was the way she looked at me." Bryan shut his eyes for a few seconds, as if blotting out the memory. "She cried and then she prayed. She said she didn't want to lose us both. She said that maybe with Jesus's help, Melissa would come back to us."

Three chattering coeds sauntered by our table. We sat in silence till they passed.

"So," I asked when the last one was gone, "when did you give your sister the gun?"

"The day before she disappeared."

Which, of course, would explain why Bryan had been so frantic when Melissa hadn't shown up.

"Who was she supposed to go target-shooting with?"

"I don't know. She said someone from school."

"And you didn't ask?"

"No."

"Why?"

"I don't know why, okay? I just didn't. I had other things on my mind." Bryan took his glasses off and wiped them clean on his T-shirt. "I assumed it was Tommy."

"Which is why you're sure that he killed her?"

Bryan nodded his head.

"Why did you assume it was Tommy?"

"Who else could it be?"

"It could be you. You could have taken her out and shot her, dumped her body somewhere, come back, waited for her to show up, and then called the cops."

"Why would I shoot my own sister?"

"You tell me."

"What would it take to convince you that I didn't?" Bryan cried.

"At this point, I'm not sure."

Bryan buried his face in his hands.

"Look at me," I ordered.

He raised his head. His eyes were wet with unshed tears. I wasn't impressed. Anyone can learn to cry.

"Tell me why I should believe what you're saying now?"

"Because it's the truth."

I got up.

"Wait," Bryan said, and he clutched my hand. "Are you going to tell the cops about the gun?"

I shook him off. "I don't know. I haven't decided yet."

When I left the restaurant, Bryan was still sitting there, staring at his half-eaten slice of pizza. I almost felt sorry for him.

Almost being the operative word.

Chapter
33

Beth stared at me defiantly, arms crossed over her chest. The room smelled of an odd but not unpleasant combination of baby powder, shampoo, cherry Twizzlers, and Chanel No. 5. I'd woken her up from an afternoon nap, and she still bore evidence of her sleep in the slight dishevelment of her hair and her blouse.

"Of course I knew her brother had a gun," she told me, sounding exasperated.

"You knew?" I felt like a parrot.

"She told me Bryan had one. She was thinking of buying it off him for three hundred bucks."

Which could explain what Melissa had done with the three hundred dollars. A new Glock pistol retails for five hundred dollars. Maybe her brother was giving her a deal.

"Why?"

"I don't think she had a reason. She just liked having one around."

I blinked. "This didn't strike you as a significant fact?"

"Not really."

Maybe I was living in Oz and I just didn't know it.

"Hey, I can name four girls on these three floors who have handguns hidden in their closets," Beth said.

"Four?"

Beth looked at me coolly. "Times have changed since you were at school."

No kidding. And obviously not for the better. The only thing we would have hidden in our closets would have been a six-pack of beer.

I leaned against her roommate's dresser and studied the view out the window. The trees and the grass were still brown. It was hard to believe that in another three weeks Tyler Park would green up.

Beth picked up a notebook and set it back down. "Once in a while she used to go target-shooting. Big deal."

"Who did she go target-shooting with?"

"Her brother, mostly."

Another significant fact Bryan had omitted.

"Did she ever go with her boyfriend?"

"She talked about it, but I don't know if she and Tommy ever went."

"Bryan told me she was planning on going out with someone the day she disappeared."

"If she was, she didn't tell me."

"She didn't tell you much, did she?"

"That's what I've been telling you. Why would I lie?"

"I don't know. To protect Bryan? Or Tommy?" Another thought occurred to me. "Or Chris?"

"Are you out of your mind?" Beth squeaked.

"If you think about it, Chris was the logical person for her to go shooting with. He's familiar with guns."

Beth put her hands on her hips. "Chris had nothing to do with her. Nothing," she declared angrily.

"How can you be so sure?"

"Because I am, that's why. Don't you try and pin her disappearance on him."

"That's not a very good answer."

Beth shrugged. "Have it your way." She turned and began straightening up her room. She picked the shirts up from the chair, put them on hangers, and placed the hangers in her closet. Then she started on her desk. Absorbed in her task, each of her movements was precise. Maybe she figured I'd get tired of watching her and go away, but she'd figured wrong. I walked over to where she was standing.

"Let me backtrack," I said as Beth continued to line up her pencils in a single row. "You roomed with Melissa for how long?"

"Almost one semester." Done with the pencils, she started on her pens. What was going to come next? The paper clips?

"And she told you that she was going to get married . . ."

"I explained about that." Beth's voice was sharp as she gathered her note cards into a neat pile.

"Did she tell you Tommy had changed his mind?"

"You're worse than the police. How many times do I have to tell you, Melissa wasn't the confiding type." She began looking through her papers, discarding some, putting others in a bright yellow folder.

"I guess I must be having a little trouble believing that. Tell me, given your relationship with Melissa, *were* you, perhaps, jealous of Melissa and Tommy?"

Beth whirled around. "What are you implying?"

"It should be fairly obvious."

"Don't be ridiculous."

"How about Chris? Did he care about you and Melissa?"

Beth slammed the folder she was holding down on her desk. She was breathing heavily. "Why don't you leave me alone?"

"I'd like to."

Her eyes widened. Her nostrils flared. "It doesn't matter what I say, does it? Because you're not going to listen anyway. Well, believe what you want . . . I already told you. Melissa kept to herself. The only people she really confided in were Jill and—"

"What about Jill?"

Beth and I turned.

Holland Adams was standing in the doorway to Beth's room. We'd been so intent on our conversation, neither one of us had heard her appraoch. "I couldn't help overhearing. You guys are getting a little loud."

"We weren't as loud as you are," Beth muttered.

"What's that supposed to mean?"

"Figure it out."

The two girls glared at each other in the manner of long-term antagonists squaring off for another round. One thing was certain. They wouldn't be sharing a suite next year.

"What are you doing here anyway?" Beth demanded. "Aren't you usually over at Jim's this time of the day?"

"I was trying to study."

Beth pursed her lips. "Now, that's a novel idea."

"Cute," Holland said.

I intervened. "That's enough," I said, wanting to bring the topic back to the subject at hand.

Holland shrugged. "Fine with me. I'm leaving anyway."

"No. I want you to stay. I have some questions I need to ask you."

"About her?" Holland tilted her head toward Beth. "She won't mind, will you?"

"Do I have a choice?" Beth snapped.

"Not really." And I told Holland to come in and shut the door behind her. With her green nail polish, black eyeliner, long, blond hair, and dark purple lipstick, she looked like some exotic tropical bird, whereas Beth reminded me of a small brown house wren.

What do you know about Jill?" I asked when Holland had turned back toward me.

"The saint? You already asked me that question."

"I know I did, and now I'm asking it again."

Holland shrugged. "Whatever."

"Why did you call her that?"

"The saint? Because Melissa spoke to her and she spoke to God."

"That really is not nice," Beth commented.

"I'm not nice, or haven't you noticed," Holland told her.

"Oh, I've noticed all right. It would be hard not to."

Holland glowered at her. "At least I don't say one thing and do another."

"Meaning?" I asked, assuming she was talking about Jill.

Holland turned her gaze from Beth to me. "Meaning that I don't go snitching to the R.A. when someone has a few bottles of beer in their room."

"Jill did that?"

"Twice. A third time, and I'd have been kicked out."

"Jill and Melissa sounded like a match," I observed.

"And how," Holland agreed. "A match made in room-mate hell."

"You had a keg," Beth said.

Holland tossed her hair out of her eyes. "So I had a couple of parties. Big deal. It was still none of her business. I never would have ratted her out."

"You were disturbing the whole floor."

"The whole floor was there. It's not my fault that Jill was such a little nerd."

"She couldn't drink then. She explained that to you."

"That's ridiculous. I know lots of people who drink when they're on Prozac. I do."

"She was on Prozac?" I interrupted.

Holland waved her hand and then inspected one of her nails. "Damn. Do you have an emery board?" she asked Beth.

"Could we stick to the point," I said.

"Jeez. I was only asking." Holland put her hand down. "Paxil. Prozac. Wellbutrin. One of those things. I told you that. Why are you taking notes if you don't reread them? What's the point?"

I let the dig go by. "I remember. You said something about her being depressed."

"She was when she stopped taking the stuff," Holland observed. She shuddered. "She was so unpleasant. Really. I was praying she'd go back on. Always moaning about that guy who dumped her. It got so I just went around her whenever I could. So she got dumped? Big deal. Get over it. I offered to introduce her to some of the guys I know. She wasn't interested."

"Given your friends, I can understand that," Beth observed dryly.

Holland bristled. "At least I tried to do something. Which is more than I can say for you."

Beth opened her mouth to reply, but I cut her off before she could. "What guy?"

"I don't know," Holland replied. "She didn't tell me, and frankly, I didn't ask. I told you this before. It would have just been encouraging her to talk about him some more. To listen to her, you would have thought this guy was better than the second coming. He was so smart. So sweet. So sensitive. He had just broken up with her for her own good. The worst thing was that every once in a while he'd call to chat and see how she was doing. And that would send her right over the edge.''

"Over the edge?"

"She'd spend a day or two in bed, crying. If this guy was so nice, why was he acting like such a shit? Personally, I think he hates women, but, hey, that's just my opinion. He was like a drug to her. She couldn't stay away, but he was absolute poison.''

I turned to Beth. "Did Jill tell you who he was?"

"No." Beth chewed on her lower lip. "I didn't want to hear about him either. I actually agree with Holland about that. Listening to her was too painful."

"Okay. What do you know?"

"I know that Missy was beside herself. She didn't know what to do. She tried pleading with Jill. She tried yelling. Nothing worked. She was even talking about going to speak to this guy and telling him to leave Jill alone. Without telling Jill, of course.''

"That would have put a damper on their friendship."

Beth absentmindedly wound a strand of her hair around one of her fingers. "I think she would have if she could have found out who he was."

Holland snorted. "Don't be ridiculous. Of course she knew. She was just telling us that she didn't."

"No. I don't think she did. This was Jill's deep, dark secret. The first love of her life."

"Well I for one still don't believe that."

"Why do you think Missy didn't know?" I asked Beth.

"Because I met her when she was coming out of their room when Jill was in the middle of one of her episodes."

Beth bracketed the word *episode* with her fingers. "And she said to me, 'If I knew who this guy was, I'd wring his neck.' So obviously she didn't."

"She must have had her suspicions."

"Maybe. But she didn't tell me what they were if she did."

I leaned against the wall. "Why wouldn't Jill tell her best friend? What else are they for?"

"I told you Jill was weird," Holland replied.

"Anyone who doesn't spend fifty dollars a week on cosmetics is weird to you," Beth shot back.

"Then how would you describe her?" I inquired.

"She was intense. She took everything very seriously. If you ask me," Beth added, "I really don't think she was ready to be away from home."

"You must have had an idea," I said.

The two girls stopped talking. I could hear the hall phone ringing. Then it stopped. Someone must have picked it up. Rap music began to vibrate through the walls.

"I hate that stuff," Beth announced to no one in particular.

Holland tousled her hair with her hand. "Actually, I always thought she was seeing Melissa's boyfriend or her brother. Why the big secrecy act otherwise?"

"You're crazy," Beth said, but her tone wasn't convincing.

It was clear from the way she sounded that she agreed with Holland. She just wasn't going to admit it, that's all.

Chapter
34

Zsa Zsa was snoring. If I wasn't careful, I was going to join her soon. I rubbed my eyes. They felt as if tiny pieces of grit had lodged themselves under my eyelids. I was falling asleep sitting on the sofa and it was only ten o'clock at night. I looked my coffee table again. Every square inch was strewn with paper. I had the newspaper articles on Jill and Melissa spread out. I had the three sheets of paper detailing everyone's whereabouts during the day Melissa had disappeared lying on top of them. Nearby were my notes, which were lying next to Melissa's book on moral responsibility. I'd even copied the two poems Melissa had written and the quote I'd found in the book on separate pieces of paper.

We are our sisters' keepers
Keepers of ourselves.
Keepers of the flame
Fanning the embers of tenderness.

On the second piece of paper I'd written:

> *She fell,*
> *a butterfly,*
> *wings plucked, unable to fly.*

On the third piece of paper I'd written, "Our responsibility to the dead defines our lives. Without it, our lives are meaningless."

Meaningless. I underlined the word.

I was hoping the answer to what had happened to Melissa was here somewhere.

I poured myself another shot of Black Label and gulped it down.

A lot of the evidence pointed in Bryan's direction. The gun was a big one. All the lies he told. His history of violence. The fact that Bryan was the last person to see Melissa before she disappeared was another biggie. Then there was the fact that there was only Bryan's word that his sister had arrived at the dorm at all. He could just as easily have driven her somewhere else, dumped her body, and driven back. Which would fit in with his overreaction when Melissa was a half hour late for their appointment. His insistence that she wouldn't turn up. As Professor Fell said, guilt is a powerful emotion.

No. Mrs. Hayes was right to be worried.

If I were in her position, I would be too.

I ran my finger around the rim of my glass and let my eyes linger on the TV. I had the cartoon channel on. Tom was chasing Jerry across the screen. I felt a little like Tom. Always chasing my mouse, never catching it. I leaned my head back on the sofa and closed my eyes.

Of course, there *was* Tommy West. There was a history

of fights between him and Melissa. She was supposed to
have been free with her fists around him. Eventually, someone who is hit enough can turn around and hit the other
person. And what about his reaction to Melissa with Beth?
As George had said, male vanity is a powerful force. And
then there was the relationship between Tommy's father
and Mrs. Hayes, not to mention Mr. West's reaction to my
questioning of his son.

Every time I went near the kid, West went nuts. Tasering
me put him over the line. Why was he so protective? Did
he know something about Melissa and Tommy? Or was this
about the hit-and-run? But even if my suspicions about the
hit-and-run were right, even if Michael West's son was
involved in it, did that mean he'd killed Melissa as well to
get rid of the last remaining witness? It was a shaky construct,
and I really didn't believe it myself.

I lifted my hands and began massaging my forehead. I
would have gotten up and taken some Advil for my headache
if I'd had the energy, but somehow it just seemed like too
much trouble.

I tried to focus through the throbbing in my temples. All
right. Taking a different tack. What about Melissa? What
did I know about her?

Not as much as I would have liked. For one thing, Melissa
had felt responsible for her roommate's death, though from
all available evidence she shouldn't have. The two poems
Melissa had written and the quote she'd inscribed in her
textbook had made that clear. But then, Melissa was used
to taking responsibility for things. After all, she'd kept the
house while her mother had gone out and worked ever since
she'd been a young child. And she had a strong religious
upbringing, an upbringing she'd recently become disen-

chanted with, but that still wouldn't have alleviated the sense of responsibility that had been instilled in her.

The problem was Jill Evans's death, like the hit-and-run accident, had occurred almost a year before. How did that tie in with her disappearance? Had she been brooding about it for a year? Even if she had, what did that have to do with anything?

What else did I know about Melissa? She jogged. She wasn't afraid of guns. She had a boyfriend. She wanted to marry him. Yet she was also maintaining a relationship with her roommate. Had she and Jill Evans had something going on as well? Marks seemed to think so. But again, what relevance did that have to her disappearance? I couldn't see any.

I sat back up and opened my eyes. Tom was still chasing Jerry. Only this time they were in a barn.

This is what I did know about Melissa for sure. She didn't confide in people. This was borne out through my conversations with everyone who knew her. She, like her brother, seemed to have trouble controlling her emotions—witness her fights with Tommy West. She didn't let go of things easily—again, witness her reaction when Tommy's father had stopped the wedding. She could have acceded to the delay instead of wanting to call him up and argue about it. Last but not least, she liked to target-shoot, a pastime I found odd in a college coed, but maybe I was just out of date. Or maybe Bryan was lying about that as well, something that wouldn't surprise me, since he'd lied about everything else that he told me.

The bottom line was I still didn't know what happened to Melissa—though I strongly suspected the only way anyone would hear from her again was with the aid of a planchette and a Ouija board.

I reread my notes. Tommy, Bryan, Beth, Chris, Holland, and Brandy all had alibis for the alleged time of Melissa's disappearance. But I could have poured a pot of spaghetti through their alibis. They were all as porous as a strainer with a hole in its mesh.

I took a deep breath and let it out.

All that said, though, as much as I didn't want to come to the conclusion I was rapidly approaching, Bryan still looked like the most likely suspect in Melissa's disappearance. The gun, his history, the fact that he was the last person to have seen her, were hard to overlook.

A fact I did not want to relay to Mrs. Hayes.

Anyway, all I had were suspicions.

Despite what Mrs. Hayes had said about wanting to know, I didn't believe her.

What people say they want and what they really want are usually two different things.

What she had wanted me to do was exonerate her son and tell her her daughter was all right, two things I couldn't do. I poured myself another shot of Black Label, took a sip, and set the glass back on the table. It didn't help much.

I still felt just as shitty.

I was supposed to talk to Mrs. Hayes the following day. I thought of her lying in her hospital bed, and took another drink.

How do you tell someone you think their son has murdered his sister?

I realized I was biting my nails, and stopped. I didn't have proof. Not even a shred.

If I didn't have proof, it was probably better not to say anything at all.

What would be the point?

I could give Mrs. Hayes back the money Bryan had given me and tell her I was sorry I couldn't help.

I rubbed my eyes. God, I didn't know what to do.

Damn George for throwing this case in my lap.

If he were here, I'd kill him.

I clicked off the TV and stood up. I couldn't stand this anymore. It was time to go to sleep.

Only I couldn't. Naturally. I couldn't get comfortable. I was too hot and then I was too cold. The sheet scratched. Finally, about three A.M. I dozed off, only to wake up at four. I lay in bed, staring at the cedars outside my bedroom window, listening to the noises my house was making. No matter how I tried, I couldn't get Melissa Hayes out of my mind.

Maybe I was thinking about this the wrong way. I seemed to be constructing a building out of rumor, conflicting statements, and speculation. I should be able to do better.

Twenty minutes later I put on a flannel shirt and a pair of sweat pants and trudged back down the stairs. Zsa Zsa, eyes heavy with sleep, trailed behind me.

I turned on the TV and settled in with the Smurfs. I watched Papa Smurf and Smurfette picking smurf berries for a few minutes, unaware of the doom that was awaiting them, as I idly leafed through Melissa's book on moral responsibility. The table of contents reminded me of some of the pamphlets we'd gotten in grade school. What we owe ourselves. What we owe our family. What we owe our country. A commerical came on and I reached for the remote and channel-surfed. I zapped through a program on exercise, another on the role of the B-52 bomber, a preacher talking about Jesus, a builder talking about the problems involved in digging a building foundation in limestone.

I put the remote down.

I had another idea. I started to smile as I considered people's tendencies to take advantage of geographical proximity. "You know," I said to Zsa Zsa, "this just might work."

Zsa Zsa kept right on sleeping. A little snore escaped her lips. What I was thinking was a real long shot, but even if it didn't pan out, it was worth a try.

What I wanted to know wouldn't take very long to find out. As an added benefit, that meant I could put off my day of reckoning with Mrs. Hayes just that much longer.

I yawned. Suddenly I was feeling tired. I lay down next to Zsa Zsa and stroked her back. Her hind legs moved in her sleep. The nails on her paws scraped my belly. She growled. I told her it was all right. The rabbit she was chasing was gone. Then I went to sleep too.

My feet kicked up little puffs of dust as I hurried up the path toward the construction site. It was almost four, and from what I could see, everyone was laying down their tools and going home. I'd wanted to get up to the computer center first thing in the morning, but a leak in one of the aquariums had prevented that, so here I was, a minute late and a dollar short—or however that expression goes.

I buttonholed a couple of guys and asked my question, but they both pointed me toward the small trailer off to one side and told me to go inside and talk to the foreman.

He was standing in front of his desk, pondering a blueprint, when I walked in.

"When did we pour the foundation?" he asked in response to my question. He craned his neck and scratched his Adam's apple. "Sure I can check. But why do you want to know?"

I told him.

He clicked his tongue against the roof of his mouth, then gave a disgusted snort. "First the lousy weather, and now something like this. Great. And they'll probably hold me responsible."

"Probably."

"You got that right." He began pawing through the papers on his desk. "I don't know why I took this job in the first place. I was better off when I was a mason. If a tornado touched down and blew the friggin' building away, they'd want to know why I didn't see the friggin' thing coming. Okay. Here we go." He pulled a couple of sheets of paper out from the bottom of the pile and ran one of his fingers down the page as he read. "We started digging the first week in November and we did two pourings. One was the twentieth of November and the second was the twenty-first. It was damp, so the concrete took longer than normal to set up." He looked up. "Is that what you want to know?"

"That's it." I thanked him and left.

When I got back in my cab I used my cell phone to call Marks. He wasn't in. I left a message on his machine asking him to ring me at the store later in the day. I told him I had a thought I wanted to share with him, a thought he might find interesting.

He didn't call though.

He dropped by Noah's Ark instead.

Chapter
35

I was in a good mood when I came home that evening. My talk with Mrs. Hayes had gone well, at least as well as could be expected given the situation. Telling her that Marks was going to follow through on my idea had seemed to offer Mrs. Hayes some solace. Or perhaps she was merely relieved that I hadn't gone there to tell her what I was originally going to: that I thought Bryan was responsible for her daughter's disappearance.

It didn't matter. She was smiling and saying her rosary when I left. I found myself smiling too as I walked down the hospital corridor. Waiting for the elevator, I realized it was the first time I'd moved the edges of my mouth up in over two weeks.

Another thing that was contributing to my good mood was the call I'd gotten from George earlier in the day. He'd phoned to let me know that even though Raymond hadn't thanked him he seemed a little more subdued. He'd even allowed as how a few of the girls around here weren't bad. Maybe things were on an upswing after all.

I was looking forward to an early night by myself. I was going to bake myself a potato and throw a steak in the broiler. Then I'd take a long soak in the tub and finally start in on the book I'd picked up at Barnes & Noble a couple of weeks earlier. Everything was going to be quiet and peaceful. So when the doorbell rang, I wasn't pleased.

I love George, but I just wasn't in the mood to talk to him. Actually, I wasn't really in the mood to talk to anyone. Which is why I'd turned the ringer on both my telephone and my answering machine off. I just wanted a little downtime.

But when I opened the door and saw who it was, I wished it had been George. At least him I could have told to go home.

Fell was standing on the porch. "Why couldn't you have left things alone?" he asked sadly.

I started to close the door, but I was too slow. Before I could, Fell raised the gun he was carrying, the one I hadn't seen, pointed it at me, took a step inside, and kicked the front door shut behind him.

His clothes were rumpled, his hair was sticking out in clownlike tufts, and his glasses were slanting downward, with the left corner being higher than the right one. He looked befuddled, a fatter caricature of Albert Einstein, someone you'd never expect to hold a gun in his hand, until, that is, you noticed the gleam in his eye.

"I don't know what you're talking about," I told him, raising my voice to be heard over the ruckus Zsa Zsa was creating.

"I saw you talking to the foreman at the contruction site today."

"What does that have to do with you? Maybe I had a question about dump trucks I wanted answered."

"Why do I doubt that?"

"All right, you're correct. You should also know that I've already informed the police."

"I don't care."

A chill worked its way down my back.

Fell waved his gun in the direction of the Zsa Zsa. It was a nine-millimeter Glock pistol. I nodded toward it.

"Did you get that from Melissa?"

"Get your dog to stop barking."

"Somehow I can't see you going out to buy one of those on your own."

Fell's voice rose slightly. "I'm the one in charge here, and I'm telling you to keep that animal quiet."

I scooped up Zsa Zsa and told her to hush. Zsa Zsa kept on yapping.

"You'd better control her," Fell said. "The noise is getting on my nerves."

"I'll put her away."

"Fine."

Fell followed along behind me as I deposited Zsa Zsa in the downstairs bathroom and closed the door. At least her barks were muffled.

"What now?" I asked.

"Now we go into the living room."

Fell sat on one end of the sofa, I sat on the other. I noticed his hand was trembling slightly, which, given the circumstances, was not an encouraging sign. Nervousness is not something you want to see in a man holding a gun on you. He pointed to the bottle of Black Label on the coffee table with his chin. "Pour me a shot," he ordered.

"I'll get you a clean glass." I started to get up.

He raised the Glock slightly. "Stay right there. That one will do fine."

"I might have something really bad."

"In the circumstances, I don't think it matters. Pour."

I did as I was told.

"Now push the glass toward me."

I did that too. Fell reached over with his free hand and picked it up without taking his eyes off me.

"You realize you've ruined my life," he said after he'd taken a sip. "You've made it impossible for me to do the only thing I like—teach."

"You mean if you did research you wouldn't be sitting here?"

Fell put the glass down. "I don't think you're in any position to make smart-ass remarks."

"You're right," I said. "I'm not."

"This wasn't my fault," he continued.

"Then whose was it? Melissa's?"

"Yes." Fell shrugged off the tweed overcoat he was wearing, switching the gun from his right to his left hand and back again in the process. "Actually it was. She came at me with this gun."

"I know. She was having a bad day and she said why don't I go attack my psych professor. Sorry," I quickly said as the hand with the Glock came up a little. "I forgot myself."

Fell waved his hand around. I found I couldn't take my eyes off the gun. "See. This is the reason I put her where I did. I knew no one would believe me."

"What wouldn't they believe?" I asked as I wondered if I could make it across the couch and grab the gun before Fell shot me.

"That she attacked me."

I did the math and decided I couldn't chance it. Fell

might be distracted, but he wasn't that distracted, and even if he were, he wasn't close enough and I wasn't fast enough. "She attacked you?" I raised an eyebrow. "Now, why should she do that?"

"She blamed me for her friend's death."

"I take it you were the guy seeing Jill Evans."

Fell wiped his forehead with the palm of his free hand. "It wasn't my fault," he repeated, trying to convince himself more than me. "I didn't know she was a borderline personality."

"It must be nice to have a name for everything."

"I warned you before about being sarcastic," Fell snarled.

"What if I told you I was being sympathetic?"

"I wouldn't believe you." Fell took another sip of Scotch. "She came on to me. I knew I shouldn't get involved with her. I knew it. I kept telling myself I shouldn't. But it didn't help. I kept saying one thing and doing something else. All of a sudden, there I was. And when I realized how many problems she had . . ."

"You tried to break it off."

"I did. Yes." Fell nodded emphatically. "Which was when she told me she was going to kill herself. I didn't know what to do. I wanted to help."

"By giving her Prozac?"

"It was just a couple of months worth. I figured it would get her over the hump."

"Melissa said it made her worse."

"She said that to me too."

"But you didn't listen."

"I did stop giving it to her." Fell swallowed. He wiped his forehead again with the back of his hand. Even though it was cool in my house—the thermostat was set to sixty-five degrees—Fell's face was beaded with sweat. "Then I told

Jill I really wasn't going to see her anymore, that this time I meant it. And I didn't."

"But you kept calling."

"I was concerned. I wanted to make sure she was all right."

"Or maybe it was that you got off seeing this girl fall to pieces every time you got done with her."

Fell's eyes blazed. "You sound like Melissa now. I made a mistake. I admit it. I should never have gotten involved with her. But that doesn't mean I should have to give up my career, something I worked for for twenty years, because some girl is unstable. Jill Evans was a catastrophe waiting to happen. What happened to her could have occurred at any time. I was just the one who was unlucky enough to trigger it."

"Why didn't you try to get her some help?"

"I did!" Fell's tone was anguished. "I pleaded with her to get counseling. She didn't want to. She didn't want to do anything to help herself. That's why I kept calling." Fell took another sip of Scotch. "I was trying to help."

"But Melissa didn't see it that way."

"I tried to explain. At first I thought she understood. She said she did. But she just wouldn't let go of the topic. She wanted me to go to the dean and tell him what had happened. She kept on telling me I had to confess."

"Why didn't she go herself?"

"Because she didn't have any proof. Jill hadn't talked about me to anyone but her."

"Lack of proof hasn't stopped anyone lately."

Fell shrugged. "She didn't think she'd be believed."

"A belief, no doubt, you encouraged her in."

"I just wanted things to go back to the way they were before. Was that so wrong?"

"It turned out that way."

Fell looked confused.

"Three people dead."

"Three? How do you get three?"

"Jill Evans. Melissa. Myself."

"You?" Fell wrinkled his brow. "Why you?"

"Because when you shoot me with that gun, I'll be dead."

"Shoot you?" Fell laughed shrilly. "Is that what you think? That's a good one." He slapped his knee with his hand.

"I didn't think it was that funny."

"Oh, but it is. I thought you'd realized. I came here to kill myself."

"Kill yourself?" I asked stupidly.

"I want you to see what you've done." And Fell put his gun to his head.

He was starting to pull the trigger, when someone knocked on the door.

Chapter
36

"Get it," Fell ordered. His gun was leveled at me. "Tell whoever is there to leave."

"Right." Zsa Zsa was barking again. The knocking had set her off.

As I stood up, I couldn't help thinking that it was too bad whoever was knocking hadn't waited a couple of seconds more.

Fell stood up too. He followed me out of the living room and down the hall.

The knocking got louder.

"I'm coming," I yelled over Zsa Zsa's yapping. Surprisingly, Fell didn't say anything about it. The banging stopped. "Now what?" I asked Fell when we reached the front door.

Fell kept the Glock trained on my back. "I told you. Tell them to go away."

I half turned toward him. "You could always go out the kitchen door."

"Robin," a voice on the other side of the door yelled. The pounding had started again. It was louder now. "Are you there?"

The noise seemed to unnerve Fell. He licked his lips. His gun hand was trembling. "Just do what I say."

I raised my hands. "I was only making a suggestion."

"Robin. Answer the door."

It was Marks. I recognized his voice.

Fell nodded at me. "Go ahead."

I swallowed. Suddenly I realized my mouth was dry. "I'm here," I cried.

"Open the door."

"I can't."

"Why not?"

I looked at Fell.

"Tell him you're not dressed," he whispered. "Tell him you have no clothes on."

"I don't have any clothes on," I repeated.

There was a short pause, then Marks said, "Fell's in there, isn't he?"

I turned back to Fell. "What should I say to him?"

"Tell him . . . tell him . . ." he repeated. He tugged on his beard with his free hand. "Tell him . . . I'll shoot you if he doesn't leave."

Terrific. "What happened to your other plan? I think I liked it better."

"Just do it," Fell shrieked.

"Sorry." I took a deep breath and put my hand on the door to steady myself. "Marks, he says he's going to shoot me if you don't leave."

I heard what I thought was a curse, but I couldn't be sure. Then I heard a "how are you?"

"Things were actually going very well up until five minutes ago."

"Fell," Marks said. "Let her go."

Fell didn't reply. His face was beaded with sweat.

"I know you can hear me."

Fell blinked several times in rapid succession. He pushed his glasses back up the bridge of his nose.

"Walk out the door now, and I'm sure we can arrange something," Marks told him.

Fell motioned to me with the gun. "We're going back to the living room."

"Fell," Marks yelled. "Fell."

But Fell didn't reply.

This time Marks's curse was audible.

"You really should talk to him," I told Fell.

"I have nothing to talk to him about."

"On the contrary."

Fell cupped his free hand and ran it over his face. "God, what a mess."

"What are you going to do now?" I asked.

"Walk," Fell ordered.

I stopped by the coffee table. Fell was about a foot away from me.

"Sit there," he said, indicating the sofa.

"You should give yourself up, because in about twenty minutes this place is going to be crawling with cops," I told him. As I sat down I noticed one of the sofa cushions was tearing along the outer seam.

Fell slowly lowered himself into the armchair across from me. "So what?" His eyes never left me.

I refrained from commenting that it made a big difference to me.

He poured himself a drink with his free hand and finished

it in one gulp. "Go to the window and tell me what you see. Go that way," he said, indicating my route with the barrel of his gun.

I got up and peered through the blinds. "I see Marks's car outside."

"What else?"

I pushed the slats farther apart and looked down the block. Flashing lights were approaching from down the street. "Another cop car is coming."

"That was fast," Fell observed.

"They must have been in the area."

In a little while the whole street would be swarming with patrol cars. My neighbors weren't going to be getting any sleep tonight, I thought as I let go of the slats. They were definitely going to be pissed.

"Sit back down," Fell said.

I did. "You mind if I light a cigarette?" I asked.

"Yes. I do. Keep your hands folded in your lap. And be quiet," he said as I was about to say something. "I need to think."

Fell and I sat in silence for the next five minutes, listening to the crackle of the police radios and the muted mutterings of people talking outside. It was hard sitting there, watching Fell chew on the ends of his mustache, not knowing what was going on. I felt as if ants were crawling on my skin. I wanted to scratch myself, but every time I moved so much as a finger, Fell told me to cut it out.

"I never meant for this to happen," he finally said.

"So you said. Several times."

"Missy showed up at my office. We were supposed to have an appointment the next day, but I had to cancel. She asked me to wait for her, and I said I couldn't, I had to leave in fifteen minutes. I was walking out the door, when she came in with the . . . the gun. She was out of breath. From running." He raised the gun sligntly. "I thought this was a toy, something that she bought at Toys "Я" Us. I don't know . . . I didn't expect . . . She wanted me to go to the dean and tell him what had happened with Jill. She said I had to do that, that it was the right thing to do, that otherwise people wouldn't know why Jill had acted the way she had."

"What did you say?"

"I told her she needed to calm down. I told her she needed to get some counseling. All she did was laugh."

"And then?"

"Then I told her she had to stop this, that I needed to go. That I was going to be late for my appointment. She just laughed some more." A vein under Fell's eye twitched. "I told her if she didn't leave and stop this nonsense, I was going to call security."

"But she didn't."

"No," Fell whispered. "She didn't."

The noise from the voices outside my house was growing. Individual words like . . . hostage . . . situation . . . drifted into the house. I watched the lights from the police cars on the street streaming through the blinds, form patterns on the floor.

Fell swallowed. The noise was making him nervous. I asked him what happened next because I wanted to keep him talking.

"I walked toward the phone. She told me to stop. I didn't listen. She was standing close to me, close enough so I could touch her. She told me if I didn't stop, she'd shoot me, and I told her not be ridiculous and turned around, and I'm not sure, I think I accidentally hit the gun. It fell out of her hand and landed on the floor and went off. Melissa just stood there for a minute. And then she fell to the ground.

It was like she was a balloon and someone had let the air out of her. I didn't believe it. I still don't. I expected people in the other offices to come running, but no one did. The noise from the construction site must have masked the sound."

Fell gnawed on the tip of his mustache again. "I didn't know what to do. It was like being in a dream. I just locked up the office and left. I went home and drove my wife to her doctor's appointment and then I did some errands and came back home, walked the dog, and had my dinner. I don't think I believed what had just happened. I think I thought when I unlocked the office door, Melissa wasn't going to be there, you know? That she'd be gone. Only she wasn't.

"It's really kind of funny when you think about it." He chuckled mirthlessly. "I was terrified I was going to be charged with sexual harassment. Now I'm going to be charged with murder. I must have sat in my office in the dark for two hours, looking out the window and wondering what to do."

"And then you remembered they'd just poured the concrete."

"I rolled her up in my rug and carried her out. My heart was hammering. I was positive security was going to come by. Part of me wanted them to." Fell pushed his glasses up his nose with his free hand. "The funny thing is, I thought I'd feel worse than I did about doing it. The worst part was waiting to be caught. I expected to be," Fell told me. "I did. Every time I saw her face on one of those posters I thought, today is the day. I waited and waited for the police to show up. I even told myself that if they didn't, I'd turn myself in, but they never came."

"And you never turned yourself in."

"Somehow the time never seemed right. I always had papers to grade or the grass to mow. And then an odd thing happened. I began to forget. Forget that she was in the foundation. I erased the idea from my mind. It was as if the whole event had never happened."

"Until I walked through the door."

"Exactly."

I heard the squeal of another car's tires.

"They must have quite a crowd out there by now," Fell noted.

"You should have gone to the police."

"Maybe you're right. Maybe I should have, but it's too late now."

"No, it's not. If you explain what happened, I'm sure you'll be able to work out a deal. Let me call my lawyer. He's very good."

"It doesn't matter anymore," Fell cried. "Don't you get it? My life is over. It can never go back to being what it was. Ever. I'm too old to start again. I don't want to." Tears trickled down his cheeks. "I shouldn't have to." He wiped the tears away with the back of his hand. "Enough of that." He sat up straighter. He laughed. "You're going to enjoy this."

I didn't like the sound of that. "What?"

"Get up."

"Why?"

He gestured with his gun. "Because I say so."

My knees were shaking as I stood.

"Come over to the chair."

I stopped about five feet away.

"Closer."

I took another step.

"Closer still."

I took two more steps. By then I was standing directly in front of Fell.

"Over to the left a little."

I did as told. The side of my thighs brushed against the arm of the chair. I was just thinking that if I were fast enough, I might be able to lean down and grab the gun, when Fell slapped gun into my palm, clamped his hand over mine, and jammed the gun's muzzle against his head.

The whole thing happened so fast, I didn't have time to react.

"I want you to shoot me," he said.

The gun felt heavy in my hand. For some reason, I noticed Fell's hair was thinning on top.

"This is something you should do for yourself." I tried to move my hand, but I couldn't. Fell's fingers enclosed mine like a vise.

"You destroyed my life. Now I want you to finish it." He began to squeeze the trigger.

I made my fingers as stiff as possible, but I wasn't able to resist the pressure from Fell's finger over mine. My finger began to move back anyway. The metal bit into my skin.

"I'm not doing this," I said through gritted teeth.

"You should have thought of that before," Fell said as he pressed the trigger back another millimeter.

I managed to move the gun up a fraction of an inch as it went off.

Chapter
37

"I hear you're going to some of your classes these days," I said to Raymond. The cut on his face seemed to be healing nicely.

"Once in a while," he allowed. He clasped the box with the iguana close to his chest as if he was afraid his uncle would change his mind and make him give it back.

George, Raymond, and I were standing outside Noah's Ark. It was fifty degrees. That morning, in the cemetery at Melissa Hayes's funeral I'd heard a flock of Canada geese flying by. The first of the season. Spring was truly on it's way.

George looked up as he opened the back door of the Taurus. "I thought you liked ceramics?"

Raymond shrugged. "It's not bad."

"I hear *you're* not bad."

The compliment embarrassed Raymond. He ground his

right heel into the pavement. "Miss Goldsmith is just being nice," he mumbled as he studied the cracks in the cement.

"I don't think so. She showed me the bowls you made." George slid the twenty-gallon aquarium he'd been carrying into the backseat of the Taurus. I handed him the bag with the tree branch, artifical grass, and hot rock. He laid in on the seat next to the aquarium. "I can't believe I'm doing this," he muttered.

I pointed out that iguanas don't shed.

George grunted and closed the back door of the car. "This animal does not go out of his cage," he told his nephew when he straightened up.

"I know. Except in my room. And outside. When can I get a collar for it?" Raymond asked me. His excitement made him look younger and softer.

"When he gets bigger." I pointed to the box. "You'd better get in the car before Iggy gets chilled."

Even though the box was lined with newspaper, there was no sense taking chances.

George and I watched him get in the Taurus.

"He seems to be doing better," I said after he closed the door.

"A little," George said. "Last week he went to a quarter of his classes so I guess that's progress. Of course he hasn't done any homework, but I guess that would be too much to expect."

"Is that why you're getting him the iguana?"

"I'm getting him the iguana because my sister thinks it's a good idea."

"And you don't?"

"No. I don't think that doing what you're supposed to do should be grounds for a reward, but I'm not going to argue with her. I'm tired of doing that." George sighed. In truth, he looked exhausted. The weeks with Raymond had taken their toll. "And anyway, he'll be back home soon."

"You're not going to keep him?"

"He needs something all right, but that something isn't me. I told you that."

"Yes, you did."

George changed the subject. "What about you? How are you doing?"

I thought. "Considering what happened, I'm doing okay. I feel sorry for Fell though."

George snorted. "The guy could have stopped anywhere along the line. No one made him do what he did. Talk about a loser. The poor bastard couldn't do anything right, not even kill himself."

"Yeah. Turning yourself into a Gomer has definitely got to suck."

"If you want to do something right, do it yourself."

"Is that one of your mother's sayings?"

"Hey, it applies."

In this case George was right. It did. Miraculously, or not so miraculously, depending on your point of view, the fraction of an inch I'd managed to move my hand had allowed the bullet to graze Fell's frontal cortex before it had exited out the other side of his skull. Basically, he'd managed to give himself a lobotomy.

The *Post Standard* had run a picture of Fell in his hospital bed, bandaged head and all, while he was being charged by the D.A. Calli said she'd heard Fell's lawyer and the D.A.'s staff were chatting and a deal was imminent. Somehow I wasn't surprised. What would be the point of prosecuting someone who kept on asking when he could go to the zoo and see the monkeys?

George leaned up against a parking meter. "They're

charging Bryan too, you know. Illegal possession of a firearm.''

"He told me at the funeral.''

George was about to add something when the cranberry-colored Infiniti that was driving up the street stopped in front of his Taurus.

Michael West hopped out and stood by the door.

"Nice color,'' I said, alluding to the car.

He folded his arms across his chest. "I liked the old one better myself, but, hey, what can you do?''

"I hope you got a good deal.''

"I did. I even got a discount.''

"What brings you around here?'' I asked. "This isn't your area.''

He shrugged. "Things change.'' He pointed to my store. "That yours?''

I nodded.

He grinned unpleasantly and gestured up and down the block. "We're thinking of buying this up.''

I did a double take. "Why?''

"It's a good investment opportunity. How long is your lease?''

"Talk to my landlord and ask him.''

"I intend to.'' He glanced at me meaningfully in case I hadn't gotten it.

"How's Tommy?'' I asked. I'd actually talked to the kid about a week before down at a bar in Armory Square. He'd been so drunk, his friends had had to walk him out the door.

West adjusted the collar on his trench coat. "Tommy's fine. He's transferring to another school next semester.''

"I can understand that. So much has gone on here, he probably has a lot of bad memories.''

"You'll be hearing from me," West said. He got back in his car and drove off.

In retrospect, maybe that business with the car hadn't been such a good idea after all.

"Another charming man," I noted.

"It's amazing what you can do with money," George commented. "How it cushions things for you."

I thought of Tommy crying on my shoulder at the Blue Tusk and telling me how he hadn't known he'd hit the man until the next day and that he was thinking about going into the priesthood and working with the poor to make atonement.

I thought about his father telling me how he'd worked to build up his business for his son.

"Not always," I said to George. "Not always."